Cameos

G000077934

by

Marie Corelli

DEMETRA PUBLISHING

Bulgaria

First published in 1886
Cover Image: Italian Landscape with Trees
Artist: Friedrich Salathé
Date: 1815-1821
License: CC0 1.0 Universal (CC0 1.0)
ISBN: 9781088433294

CONTENTS

THREE WISE MEN
OF GOTHAM

The Three Wise Men sat together in their club smoking-room. They were met there for a purpose — a solemnly resolved purpose — though that fact was not to be discovered in the expression of their faces or their attitudes. The casual observer, glancing at them in that ignorant yet opiniated fashion which casual observers generally affect, would have sternly pronounced them to be idle loafers and loungers without a purpose of any sort, and only fit to be classified with the "drones" or do-nothings of the social hive. Three stalwart bodies reclined at ease in the soft depths of three roomy saddle-bag chairs; and from three cigars of the finest flavour three little spiral wreaths of pale blue smoke mounted steadily towards the ceiling. It was a fine day: the window was open, and outside roared the surging sea of human life in Piccadilly. Rays of sunshine danced round the Wise Men, polishing up the bald spot on head number one, malignly bringing into prominence the grey hairs on head number two, and shining a warm approval on the curly brown locks of head number three. The screech of the wild newsboy echoed up and down the street—" Hextra speshul!

Evening piper! Evening pepper! Piper! Westyminister speshul! Hall the winners!" A spruce dandy alighting from a hansom commenced a lively altercation with the cabby thereof, creating intense excitement in the breasts of four Christian brethren — to wit, a dirty crossing-sweeper, a match-seller, a District Messenger-boy and a man carrying a leaden water-pipe. "Call yerself a masher!" cried cabby vociferously. "Git along with yer, an' hask one of the club blokes to lend yer 'arf a crown!" Here the man carrying the leaden water-pipe became convulsed with mirth, and observed, "Bully, aint it?" confidentially to the messenger-boy, who grinningly agreed, the smartly dressed young dandy growing scarlet with rage and insulted dignity. The dispute was noisy, and some minutes elapsed before it was settled — yet through it all the mystic Three Wise Men never stirred to see what was the matter, but smoked on in tranquil silence with closed eyes.

At last one of them moved, yawned, and broke the spell. He was fair, stoutish and florid; and when he opened his eyes they proved to be of a good clear blue — honest in expression, and evidently meant for fun; so much so, indeed, that though their owner was by no means in a laughing humour at the moment, he was powerless to repress their comic twinkle. His name was George — George Fairfax — and he was a "gentleman at ease," with nothing to do but to look after his estates, which, as he was not addicted to either betting, drinking, or gambling, brought him in a considerably substantial yearly income.

"Fact is," he said, addressing himself to his two companions, whose eyelids were still fast shut, "the world's a mistake. It ought never to have been created. Things go wrong in it from morning till night. Fellows who write books tell you how wrong it is; *they* ought to know." Here he knocked off the end of his cigar into the ash-tray. "Then read the newspapers: by the Lord Harry! *they'll* soon prove to you how wrong everything is everywhere!"

Man number two, in the chair next to Fairfax, happened to be the individual with the hair approved of by the sunshine — a long-limbed, well-built fellow with a rather handsome face. Unclosing his eyes, which were dark and languid, he sighed wearily.

"No world in it!" he murmured in brief sleepy accents, "Social institutions — civilisation — wrong. Man meant for free life — savage — forest; no houses — no clubs — raw meat — suits digestion — no dyspepsia — tear with fingers; polygamy. Read 'Woman Who Did' — female polygamist — live with anybody, noble; marriage, base degradation — white rose in hair — polygamous purity — died."

Exhausted by this speech, he closed his eyes again, and would no doubt have relapsed into an easy slumber, had not Man number three suddenly waked up in earnest, disclosing a pair of very keen bright grey eyes, sparkling under brows that, by their shelving form, would have seemed to denote a fair depth of intelligence.

"Look here, you fellows," he said sharply, "it's no use mincing matters. Things have come to a crisis. We must take the law into our own hands and see what can be done. Life as we live it — married life — has become impossible. You said so yourself, Adair" — this with head reproachfully turned towards the languid being with the shut eyes—" you said no man of sense or spirit would stand it!"

Adair rolled his head feebly to and fro on the saddle-bag chair-pillow.

"Sense — spirit — all up in me!" he replied dolefully. "Pioneers!"

As this word escaped him, more in the way of a groan than an utterance, Man number three, otherwise known as John Dennison, gave a gesture of contempt. Dennison was a particularly lucky individual, who had managed to make a large fortune while he was yet young, through successful land speculations; and now at his present age of forty-eight he bore scarcely any traces of the passing of time, save the small bald spot on the top of his head which the sunlight had discovered, but which few less probing searchers would have perceived. He was of an energetic, determined temperament, and the listless attitude and confessed helplessness of Adair excited him to action. Shaking himself out of his reclining posture, and sitting bolt upright, he said sternly —

"Look here, Adair, you're too lazy to go through with this thing. If you don't show a little more character and firmness, Fairfax and I will have to slope it without you."

At this Adair opened his eyes wide, and also sat up, wearing an extremely astonished and injured expression.

"I say, old man!" he expostulated—" no threats — bad form — sneak out of promise — oh, by Jove!"

"Well then, pay some attention to the question in hand," said Dennison, mollified. "Have we, or have we not, resolved to make a move?"

"We have!" declared Fairfax emphatically.

"*Must* make a move!" groaned Adair.

"I ask you both," went on Dennison, "does it look well, is it creditable to us as *men* — men of position, influence, and sufficient wealth — that we should be known in society as the merest appendages to our wives? Is it decent?"

"Damned indecent, I think!" said Fairfax hotly.

Adair gazed straight before him with the most woebegone expression.

"Awful lot of fellows — same predicament," he remarked. "Wife pretty — drags ugly man round — introduces him casually, 'Oh, my husband!' — and all Society grins at the poor chap. Wife ugly — goes in for football — asks husband to be spectator — kicks ball his way — says 'Excuse me!' — then explains to people standing by, 'My husband!' and the poor devil wishes he were dead. Fact! Lots of 'em, I tell you! We're not the only ones."

"Of course we're not," said Dennison. "I never supposed we were. But we are Three — and three of us can show an example to the others. We will give these women a lesson, my boys! — a lesson they'll never forget. Have you made up your minds?"

"I have!" said Fairfax determinedly. "And I know Adair will be with me — why, he and I were married on the same day, weren't we, Frank?

Frank smiled mournfully.

"Yes, and didn't the girls look pretty then — your Belle and my Laura!"

"Ah! who would have thought it!" sighed Fairfax. "Why, *my* wife was the simplest soul that ever lived then — happy as a bird, full of life and fun, no nonsense of any sort in her head; and as for dogs — well, she liked them, of course, but she didn't worship them; she didn't belong to the Ladies' Kennel Association, or any other association, and she didn't worry herself about prizes and exhibitions. Now it's all dogs — dogs and horses; and as for that little beast Bibi, who has taken more medals than a fighting general, I believe she loves it better than her own boys. It's a horrible craze for a woman to be *doggy*."

"It's not so bad as being Pioneery," said Adair, rousing himself up at this part of the conversation. "Your wife's a very pretty woman, George, and a clever one, but *my* wife — well—" He broke off and waved his hand in a descriptive fashion.

"Yes, I admit it," said Fairfax respectfully. "Your wife is lovely — a really beautiful creature; no one can deny it."

"That being the case," continued Adair, "what do you suppose *she* can want with the Pioneers?"

The other two Wise Men shook their heads desperately.

"Only yesterday," resumed Adair, "I went home quite unexpectedly in time for afternoon tea. She was in the drawing-room, wearing a new tea-gown and looking charming. 'Oh!' said she, with a cool smile, '*you* home! At this hour! How strange! Have some tea?' And nothing more. Presently in came a gaunt woman — short hair, skimped skirt, and man's coat. Up jumps Laura, hugs her, kisses her, cries 'Oh, you *dear* thing! How sweet of you to come!' She was a Pioneer — and she got kissed. *I* had no kiss. *I* was not called a 'dear thing.' I've got short hair and a man's coat, but it doesn't go down somehow, on me. It used to, before we were married; but it doesn't now."

"Stop a bit!" interposed Dennison suddenly and almost fiercely. "Think of *me!* I've been married longer than either of you, and I know a thing or two! Talk of fads! my wife goes in for them all! She's mad on 'em! Wherever there's a faddist, you'll find her. Whether it's the-Anti-Corset League, or the Nourishing Bread Society, or the Social Reformation Body, or anything else you like to think of — she's in it. I've got nothing to say against her intentions; she means well, *too* well, all round; but she is so absorbed in her 'meetings,' and 'councils,' and 'boards,' and what not, that I assure you she forgets *me* entirely — I don't believe she realises my existence! When I go home of an evening she hands me the papers and magazines with an amiably provoking smile, as if she thought the damned news was all I could possibly want; then she goes to her desk and writes letters — scratch, scratch all the time. She never gives me a word; and as for a kiss!" — here he gave an angry laugh—" God bless my soul! she never thinks of it!"

"I expect," said George Fairfax seriously, "we are too old-fashioned in our notions, Dennison. Lots of fellows would go and console themselves with other women."

"Of course they would," retorted Dennison. "There are plenty of dirty cads about who act that way. And I believe, as it is, *we* don't get much credit for keeping clean. *I* daresay our wives think we are as bad as we might be."

"They've no cause to," said Adair quietly. "And if I had any suspicion that Laura entertained a low opinion of me, I should take the liberty of giving her a piece of my mind."

Fairfax and Dennison looked at him, gravely at first, then they laughed.

"A piece of your mind," echoed Dennison. "I think I know what it would amount to; just a 'By Jove! too bad!' and you would go to smoke and think it over. No; we cannot offer 'pieces of our minds' to our spouses on any subject whatsoever, because, you see, we cannot bring any actual cause of complaint against them. They are good women—"

His friends nodded.

"Good-looking women—"

More nods.

"And clever women."

"Yes!" sighed Adair. "That's the worst of it.

If they had only been stupid—"

"They would have been dull!" interposed Fairfax. "And they *might* have grown fat," murmured Adair, with a shudder.

"Well," went on Dennison, "they are *not* stupid, they are *not* dull, and they are *not* fat. We have agreed that they are good, good-looking, and clever. Yet, with these three qualities, something is wrong with them. What is it?"

"I know," said Adair. "It is want of heart."

"Indifference to home and home-affections," said Fairfax sternly.

"All comprised in one glaring fault," declared Dennison; "a fault that entirely spoils the natural sweetness of their original dispositions. It is the want of proper respect and reverence for *Us*; for *Us* as men; for *Us* as husbands!"

Nothing could have been more majestically grandiloquent than Dennison's manner while making this statement, and his two friends gazed admiringly at him in speechless approval.

"This state of things," he went on, "must be remedied. All the unloved, miserable, hysterical women who have lately taken to cackling about their rights and wrongs, are doing it, I believe, out of sheer malice and envy, in an effort to make happy wives discontented. The upheaval and rending of home-affections must be stopped. Our wives, for example, appear to have no conception of our admiration and affection for them —— — —"

"Perhaps," interposed Fairfax, "*they* think that *we* have no conception of their admiration and affection for us!"

"Oh! I say, that won't do, old fellow," murmured Adair. "Admiration for *us* is no go! You don't suppose Laura, for instance, admires *me?* Not much; though I believe she used to. Of course Mrs. Fairfax may admire you—"

Here a faint smile began to play about his mouth, which widened into an open laugh as he surveyed Fairfax's broad, good-natured countenance — a laugh in which Fairfax himself joined so heartily that the water came into his eyes.

"No; of course it's ridiculous," he said, recovering himself at last. "She couldn't admire me. She's too pretty herself. All she sees is a redfaced man coming home punctually to dinner. However, she admires Bibi."

"Bother admiration," struck in Dennison sharply. "I didn't suggest that our wives should *admire* us; I said that they should reverence and respect us; and I also said I thought they appeared to be quite indifferent to the admiration and affection we have for them."

"That's true!" said Fairfax gloomily. "It's a positive fact."

"Well, then," went on Dennison, "as they don't seem to want us, let's clear out."

"Agreed!" said Adair. "Gold coast and fever for me!"

"Same for me," said Fairfax. "I don't want a healthy climate!"

"All right. I'll see to that!" and Dennison stood up, smiling a grim smile. "We'll take the worst part of the coast, where even the natives die! *Of course I shall tell my wife where I am going.*"

This with dreadful emphasis.

"And I shall tell mine," said Fairfax.

"And I mine," sighed Adair.

"Now come and look at the maps and the days of sailing," went on Dennison. "We can easily start in a fortnight."

They left the smoking-room for the reading-room, and were soon absorbed in the discussion of their plans.

That evening, when Adair went home, he found his wife dressed for a party, and looking radiantly youthful and lovely.

"Going out somewhere to-night, Laura?" he inquired languidly, as his eyes took in every detail of her graceful figure and really beautiful face.

"Yes," she replied. "Only round the corner to the Jacksons. They have an 'at home.' Will you come?"

"No, thanks," he said, as he sat down to dinner. "I hate crushes."

She made no comment, but simply took her place at table and smiled upon him like a beneficent angel. He, meanwhile, was thinking within himself that she was the very prettiest woman he had ever seen; but he considered that if he ventured to express that thought aloud she would laugh at him. A husband to compliment his wife? Pooh! the thing was unheard of! Besides, the butler was in the room — a civil man in black, of high repute and decorous character — and he would have been truly shocked had his master made any remark of a personal nature during the course of his attendance at dinner. When this dignified retainer had departed, leaving husband and wife alone to dessert, the impulse to say pretty things to his better half was no longer dominant in Adair's mind, so instead of a compliment he made an announcement.

"Laura, I am going away."

She looked at him straightly, her soft violet eyes opening a little more than usual.

"Are you?"

"Yes. I want a change," he said, keeping his gaze riveted on the table-cloth, and trying to work himself up to the required pitch of melodramatic feeling, "a change from this hum-drum society life where — where I am not wanted. You see, I don't get enough to do here in London. I'm sick of town life. I'm not necessary to *you*" — this with a touch of bitterness. "You can do the social round well enough without me, and I — I'm going to try roughing it for a time."

Had he looked up that moment, he would have seen his wife's face growing pale, and he might also have noted that her breath came and went quickly, as though she were trying to suppress some strong emotion; but he did not look — not just then; he only heard her speak, and her voice was both cheerful and calm.

"What fun!" she said. "It will do you a world of good!"

He looked up this time, and his expression was one of reproachful astonishment.

"Fun!" he echoed. "Well, I don't know about that I am going to the Gold Coast with Jack Dennison. It's full of fever, and even the natives die. I don't suppose I shall escape scot-free."

"Why do you go, then?" she asked, with a smile, rising from her chair and preparing to put on her evening cloak. Adair rose also, and taking the mantle from her hands, put it round her.

"Why do I go?" he echoed, with just the slightest suspicion of a tremor in his voice. "Well, if *you* can't guess, Laura, *I* can't explain. I couldn't be rough with you for the world, and it might sound rough to say that I know you're sick of me, and that I'm better out of your way for a time. Married people ought to separate occasionally; it's quite natural you should get bored seeing me every day of your life. You wouldn't take to the 'Pioneers' if you weren't in need of a change of some sort from the monotony of my company. If I go off to Africa, I shall have the pleasure of hoping you'll be glad to see me back. It'll give you time to be glad. At present you can't be glad, because you see too much of me. You don't mind my going?"

"Not in the least!" she answered, and to his secret indignation he fancied he saw almost a laugh in her eyes. "I think it will be jolly for you. And Jack Dennison is going, is he?"

"Yes; and George Fairfax."

"Really! How nice! You three were always such good chums. I expect you'll have a perfectly lovely trip. When are you thinking of starting?"

"In a fortnight."

"Delightful! We must have a little dinnerparty before you go to wish you all luck! I hope you mean to bring me some nuggets and any amount of queer necklaces and bracelets and barbaric ornaments. Ta-ta for the present! I must be off or I shall be late at the Jacksons. Don't sit up for me!"

She floated gracefully out of the room like a sylph on wings, giving him a dazzling smile as she went. When she had quite disappeared he flung himself into a chair and said, "Damn it! very gently. Then he lit a big cigar, and meditated.

"She doesn't care a bit!" he reflected. "That hint about even the natives dying didn't affect her in the least. She is quite callous. Ah! this is what comes of social faddists and problemists, and the artificial 'tone' at which life is taken nowadays. All humbug and sham, and no time for sentiment. Love? — pooh! — that's over and done with; there's no such thing. Upon my life, I believe if I were dead, Laura would only squeeze a couple of tears out of those pretty eyes of hers, and then set about considering the newest fashions for mourning."

While he sat thus absorbed in solitary musings of a sufficiently dreary and despondent character, his friend George Fairfax had likewise gone home to dinner, and had, in quite another sort of fashion, broken the news of his intended departure to *his* wife, an exceedingly pretty, lively little woman, with a quantity of fair hair and dancing, laughing, roguish blue eyes.

"Well, I sha'n't be here for the Dog Show!" he remarked abruptly, shooting out the words with fierce emphasis, and casting an indignant glance at a tiny Yorkshire "toy" terrier that was curled up in its mistress's lap like a ball of fine spun silk. "I shall be thousands of miles away. And if you want to 'wire' me any of Bibi's triumphs you'll find it expensive."

"Really!" and Mrs. Fairfax looked up sweetly, stroking her pet the while. "Why, where are you going?"

"To Africa!" replied her husband solemnly. "To the Gold Coast — to the worst part, where fever rages, and *where even the natives die!*"

He pronounced the last words with particular emphasis. But she remained perfectly placid; she only bent over Bibi, and murmured with an ecstatic chuckle, "Oh, zoo ducky 'ittle sing!"

George stared very hard at her without producing any impression, and in a deeply injured tone he resumed: "Yes; I am going out with Jack Dennison. I find it necessary; in fact, imperative to go —— — —"

"Ah, yes, agricultural affairs *are* in a bad way!" she said sympathetically. "Do you know, I *thought* you would have losses this year on the lands — rentals are going down so much, and everything is so hopeless for the farmers; I really think you are wise to try and recuperate. I suppose Dennison has got a mine or something?"

He favoured her with a look that was meant to be scornful, but which only succeeded in being plaintive.

"You mistake the position, Belle," he said, with severe politeness. "I have had *no* losses, I do not need to recuperate, and Dennison has *no* mine. I am going because I *wish* to go; because, as I have had occasion to mention to you before, I do not appear to be wanted here. You are too much absorbed in — in your 'kennel' duties to attend to me and here he gave vent to what he considered a culminating burst of sarcasm. "Yes, I feel in the dog's way. The dog is master here — I am not. You have several dogs, I know; but *the* dog, the one I mean at present in your lap, is the chief object of your consideration, tenderness, and interest. He always takes prizes; he deserves attention. I do not take prizes; I cannot compete with him. Therefore I am going away for a change — a change from society and dog shows. It will do me good to grapple with danger and death" — here he looked as tragic as his amiable round face would allow him—" and when I return home again, after many adventures, you will be glad, perhaps, to see me."

His wife's eyes twinkled prettily like sapphires as she surveyed him.

"Of course I shall be glad," she said frankly; "but I quite agree with you in thinking that the trip will do you all the good in the world. I have thought for some time that you've been a little out of sorts — a trifle hypochrondriacal — or a touch of the spleen, because you say such funny things." ("Funny things!" George was speechless.) "And Dennison will make a splendid travelling companion. When do you go?"

"In a fortnight," he answered feebly, utterly bewildered at her cool way of taking what he thought would prove a startling and fulminating announcement.

"Oh, then I must see to your flannel shirts," she observed. "They wear flannel next to the skin as a preventive of fever in Africa."

"Ah! there's no preventive against *that* fever," he muttered, morosely, adding almost under his breath, "Even the natives die!"

"Oh, I should think quinine and flannel would be useful," she responded cheerfully. "The natives don't know how to take care of themselves, poor things! Englishmen do. I sha'n't be a bit anxious about *you.*"

"Won't you? No, I don't suppose you will;" and Fairfax began to feel rather snappish. "It isn't as if I were Bibi. Adair is going, too."

"Is he really? Can he bear to leave his lovely Laura?"

"His lovely Laura will get on very well without him, I dare say," retorted Fairfax. "By the time he comes back she'll very likely be in knicker-bockers, playing football with the Pioneers!"

With this parting shot he marched out of the room in haste, disappointed and indignant at his wife's indifference. She, left alone, lay back in her chair and indulged in a hearty laugh, which had the effect of rousing the pampered "Bibi" to such a pitch of wonder that he found it necessary to rise on his hind legs and apply his cold, wet nose to his mistress's chin with a mild sniff of inquiry. She caught the pretty little animal up in her arms and kissed its silky head, still laughing and murmuring, "Oh, Bibi! men *are* funny creatures! ever so much funnier than dogs! You can't imagine how nice and funny they are, Bibi!"

After a while she became serious, though her eyes still danced with mirth. Putting her little dog down, she began to count on her fingers.

"In a fortnight — well, I must see Laura, and find out what *she* thinks about it. Then we'll both go and consult Mrs. Dennison. The boys are at school — so *that's* all right. I wonder what the steamer is? We can easily find out. Dear old George! what a silly he is! And John Dennison and Frank Adair are equally silly — three of the dearest old noodles that ever lived! I must see Laura to-morrow."

Meanwhile a conversation more or less similar had taken place between Mr and Mrs. Dennison. John was a man of action, and prided himself on the swift (and obstinate) manner in which he invariably made up his mind. His wife did not consider herself behind him in resolution; she was a handsome woman of about thirty-eight, with a bright expression and a frank, sweet smile of her own which proved very attractive to her friends, who came to her with all their troubles, and gave her their unbounded confidence. She was active, strong, and energetic, and never wasted a moment in useless argument; so that when, her husband said quite suddenly, "I am going to Africa," she accepted the statement calmly as a settled thing, and merely inquired —

"When?"

He eyed her severely.

"In a fortnight," he answered, jerking out his Words like so many clicks of a toy-pistol. "Gold Coast. Bad place for fever. Even the natives die."

Mrs. Dennison's tender heart was touched at once, but, as her husband thought, in quite the wrong way.

"Poor things!" she said, pityingly; "I dare say their notions of medicine are very primitive. You must take a double quantity of quinine with you, John, dear, and you may be able to save many lives."

He stared at her, his face reddening visibly.

"God bless my soul, Mary, I shall have enough to do in taking care of my own life," he snapped out, "without bothering after the natives. You don't seem to think of that!"

"Oh, yes, I do," responded Mary, very tranquilly. "But you are a strong, healthy man, John, and very sensible; you know how to look after yourself — no one better; and I should indeed be silly if I felt any anxiety about you. May I ask what you are going to the Gold Coast for? or is it a secret?"

Now, John Dennison was, on the whole, a good fellow; honest, honorable, and true to the heart's core; but with all his virtues he had a temper, and he showed it just then.

"No, it is not a secret, madam!" he burst forth, trembling from head to foot with the violence of his emotions. "If I were to speak quite plainly, I should say the reason of my going is an open scandal! Yes, that is what it is! Oh, you may look at me as if you thought me a troublesome lunatic — you have that irritating way, you know — but I mean it. I may as well be a wanderer and a vagabond on the face of the earth, for I have no home. What *should* be my home is turned into a meeting-place for all the crack-brained faddists in London, who form 'societies' for want of anything better or more useful to do. It *may* be very interesting to talk and make speeches about the necessity of feeding the people on nourishing bread instead of non-nourishing alum stuff, but it has nothing to do with *Me! I* don't personally care what the people eat, or what they don't eat. I ought to care, I suppose, but I don't! When I was a hard-working lad, I ate what

I could get, and was thankful; no nice ladies and gentlemen met in draw-ing-rooms to assert that I was badly fed, and that I ought to be looked after more tenderly. 'Fads' were not in fashion then; people fought for themselves manfully, as they should do, and came up or went down ac-cording to their own capabilities; and there wasn't all this cosseting and coddling of the silly and incompetent. It is quite ridiculous that in an age like ours a 'society' should be formed for the purpose of teaching the ma-jority what sort of bread to eat. By the Lord Harry! if they're such con-founded idiots that they can't distinguish between good bread and bad, they deserve to starve. Even the dullest monkey knows the difference be-tween a real turnip and a sham one. I've given you my opinion on these sort of subjects before. I'm against all 'Leagues' and 'Bodies' and 'Working Committees.' I hate them. *You* like them. That's where we differ. *You*, in your Anti-Corset League, want to make girls give up tight-lacing; now, *I* say, let them tight-lace till they split in half, if they like it; there'll only be so many feminine fools the less in the world. And as for the 'Social Reformation' business — pah! that's not fit for a decent woman to med-dle with. If women would only begin to 'reform' themselves, and make their husbands happy, society might be purified to a great extent; but so long as households are looked upon as a nuisance, husbands a bore, and children a curse, nothing but misery can come of it. And the reason I am going away is this — that I do not feel myself the master of my own house; there are too many 'Committees' accustomed to meet in it at their own discretion; *your* time is entirely taken up with laudable efforts to improve the community" — here he indulged in a mild sneer—" so much so that I have become nothing but an unnecessary appendage to the im-portance of your position. Now" — and he grew fierce again—" I do not choose to play second fiddle to any one, least of all to my own wife. So I shall clear out and leave you to it. George Fairfax and Frank Adair feel the domestic wretchedness of their positions as keenly as I do, and they are going out to the Gold Coast with me. I shall provide you amply with means — and *they* will do the same on behalf of *their* wives — and we shall be absent for a considerable time. In fact, who knows whether we may ever come back at all?" — here his voice became sepulchral. "Fortu-nately, our wills are made!"

He ceased. Throughout his somewhat lengthy tirade, his wife had sat quite still, patiently listening, her hands reposefully folded over a book on her knee, her eyes regarding him with a clear steadfastness in which there was a soft lurking gleam of something like compassion. Now that he had finished what he had to say she spoke, in gentle deliberate accents.

"I am to understand then, my poor John," she said, almost maternally, "that you are leaving home on account of your dislike to the way I try to employ myself (very ineffectually I admit) in doing good to others?"

He gave a short nod of assent and turned his eyes away from her. It rather troubled him to be called "my poor John!"

"And Mr. Adair finds equal fault with his beautiful girl-wife Laura!"

"Poor Adair has equal reason to find fault," was the stem reply. "A man may very well become crusty when he finds the woman he loves to adoration deliberately rejecting *his* affection for that of a Pioneer!"

A curious little trembling appeared to affect Mrs. Dennison's full white throat, suggestive of a rising bubble of laughter that was instantly suppressed.

"Mr. Fairfax, you say, is going also?" she murmured gently.

"He is. Not having the necessary qualifications for a dog-trainer, he is not required in his home," replied her husband with intense bitterness. "Dogs now occupy Mrs. Fairfax's whole time to the total exclusion of her domestic duties."

Mrs. Dennison was silent for a little while, thinking. Then she put the book she held carefully down on a side-table, and rose in all her stately height and elegance, looking the very *beau ideal* of a handsome English matron. Crossing over to where her husband stood, she laid her plump pretty hand, sparkling with rings, tenderly on his bald spot, and said in the sweetest of voices —

"Well, John, dear, all I can say is that I am delighted you are going! It will do you good; in fact it's the very best thing possible for all three of you. I think you've all been too comfortable and lazy for a long time; a voyage to the Gold Coast will be the very tonic you require. Of course I'm sorry you've no sympathy with me in my humble efforts to do a little useful work among my fellow-women during my leisure days, and while the children are at school, but I don't blame you a bit. Of course you have your ideas of life just as I have mine, and there's no need for us to be rude to each other or quarrel about it. An ocean-trip will be just splendid for you. I'll see to your things. I know pretty well what you will want in Africa. I fitted out a poor fellow only the other day, who was convicted of his first theft; the gentleman he robbed wouldn't prosecute, because of the sad circumstances. It's too long a story to tell now, but we got him a place out in Africa with a kind farmer, and I fitted him out. So I know just the kind of flannels and things required."

"Exactly!" said "Dennison, quivering and snorting with repressed wrath and pain. "Fit me out like a convicted thief! Nothing could be better! Suit me down to the ground!"

His wife looked at him with that kind maternal air of hers and laughed. She had a very musical laugh.

"Oh, you dear old boy!" she said cheerfully. "You must always have your little joke, you know!"

And with that she moved in a queen-like way across the room and out of it.

Left alone, John sank into a chair and wiped his fevered brow.

"Was there ever such a woman!" he groaned within himself despairingly. "To think that she once loved me! and now — now she takes my going to a malarial climate as coolly as if it were a mere trip across Channel and back! What a heart of stone! These handsome women (she *is* a handsome woman) are as impervious to all sentiment as — as icebergs! And as for tact, she has none. Fancy bringing that convicted thief into the conversation. Almost as if she thought I resembled him. Oh, the sooner I'm out of England the better. I'll lose myself in Africa, and she can get up an 'Exploration Fund' with a working committee, and pretend to try and find me. And then when she *hasn't* found me, she can write a book of adventure (made up at home) entitled *How! Found my Husband*. That's the way reputations are made nowadays, and by the Lord Harry, what devilish humbug it all is!"

Plunging his hands deep in his pockets he sat and stared at the pattern of the carpet in solitary reverie, angrily conscious, through all his musings, of having "felt small" in the presence of his wife, inasmuch as throughout their conversation *she* had maintained her wonted composure and grace, and *he*, though of the "superior" sex, had been unwise enough to lose his temper.

Two or three days later Mrs. Dennison, Mrs. Fairfax, and Mrs. Adair had what they called "a quiet tea." They spent the whole afternoon together, shut up in Mrs. Adair's elegant little boudoir, and spoke in low voices like conspirators. The only witness of their conference was Bibi, who took no interest whatever in their conversation, he being entirely absorbed in the contemplation of a tiger-skin rug which had a stuffed and very life-like head. Desiring, yet fearing, to spring at the open throat and glittering teeth of this dreadfully-alive looking beast, Bibi occupied his time in making short runs and doubtful barks at it, and quite ignored the occasional ripples of soft and smothered laughter that escaped from the three fair ones seated round the tea-table, because he thought, in his "prize-terrier" importance, that their amusement was merely derived from watching his cleverness. It never entered into his head that there could be any other subject in the world so entertaining and delightful as himself. So he continued his dead-tiger hunt, and the ladies continued their *causerie*, till the tiny Louis Seize clock on the mantelpiece tinkled a silvery warning that it was time to break up the mysterious debate.

"You're quite agreed then?" said Mrs. Dennison, as she rose and drew her mantle round her in readiness to depart.

"Quite!" exclaimed Laura Adair, clasping her hands in ecstasy, "it will be glorious!"

"Simply magnificent!" echoed Belle Fairfax, with rapture sparkling in her blue eyes, then suddenly perceiving her Liliputian dog nigh upon actually getting bodily in to the elaborately-modelled throat of the tiger-head, she caught him up, murmuring, "Zoo naughty sing! zoo sail go too; rocky-pocky, uppy-downy, jiggamaree!"

"Good heavens, Belle," cried Mrs. Dennison, putting up her hands to her ears in affected horror, "no wonder your husband complains if he hears you talk such rubbish to that little monster!"

"He isn't a monster!" protested Belle indignantly. "You can't say it; you daren't! Just look at him!"

And she held Bibi up, sitting gravely on his haunches in one little palm of her hand. He looked so absurdly small and quaint, and withal had such a loving, clever, bright, wee face of his own, that Mrs. Dennison relented.

"Positively he *is* a darling!" she said, "I'm bound to admit it. Landseer might have raved over him. No wonder your husband's jealous of him!"

All three ladies laughed gaily, though Laura had something like tears in her beautiful eyes.

"I think," she said softly, "that as far as I am concerned, Frank *may* have a little cause to feel himself neglected. You see when one goes very much into society as I do, one falls unconsciously into society's ways, and one gets ashamed of showing too decided a liking for one's own husband. It is a false shame, of course, but there it is. — And I am really so deeply in love with Frank, that when we were first married people remarked it, — and other women made fun of me, and then — then I joined the Pioneers out of a silly notion of self-defence. The Pioneers, you know, are all against husbands and the tyrannies of men generally — even the loving tyrannies; and I thought if I was a Pioneer nobody would tease me any more for being too fond of my own husband. It was very stupid of me, yet when I once got among them I felt so sorry for them all; they seemed to have such topsy-turvy notions of marriage and life generally that I set my-self to try and cheer up some of the loneliest and most embittered of the members, and do you know I *have* succeeded in making a few of them happier, but Frank sees it in the wrong light—"

She stopped, and Belle Fairfax kissed her enthusiastically.

"You are a dear!" she declared. "The prettiest and sweetest woman alive! The upshot of it all is, that if *we* have made mistakes with the dear old boys, so have they made mistakes with us, and we've hit upon the best plan in the world for proving how wrong they are. All we've got to do now is to carry out our scheme thoroughly and secretly."

"Leave that to me!" said Mrs. Dennison, smiling placidly, "only you two girls be ready — the rest is plain sailing."

The following week Mr and Mrs. Dennison gave a little dinner-party. The company numbered six, and were the host and hostess, Mr and Mrs. Adair, and Mr and Mrs. Fairfax. It was a "farewell" feast; the ladies were in high spirits, the gentlemen spasmodically mirthful and anon depressed.

Bright Mrs. Fairfax, at dessert, made a telling little speech, proposing the healths of "Our Three dear Husbands! A pleasant trip and a safe return to their loving wives!" Laura smiled sweetly, and looked volumes as she kissed her glass and waved it prettily to Adair. Mrs. Dennison nodded smiling from the head of the table to her husband sitting glumly at the foot thereof, and Mrs. Fairfax openly wafted a kiss to the silent George, whose face was uncommonly red, and who, moreover, had evidently lost his usual excellent appetite. As a matter of fact the Three Wise Men were very uncomfortable. Their wives had never seemed to them so perfectly fascinating, and they themselves had never felt so utterly "small" and embarrassed. However, they were all too obstinate to confess their sensations one to another; their resolve was made, and there was no going back upon it without, as they considered, a loss of dignity.

The days flew on with incalculable speed, and the evening came at last when they all said "goodbye" to the fair partners of their lives, and started for Southampton. They had purposely arranged to leave London on the evening before the steamer sailed, in order that during the silence and solitude of night each wife might have ample opportunity for mournful meditation and the shedding of such repentant tears as are supposed to befit these occasions. But up to the last moment the fair ones maintained their aggravating cheerfulness; they were evidently more inclined to laugh than to cry, and they bade farewell to their husbands "with nods and becks and wreathed smiles" suitable to festal jollity. There was no sentiment in their last words either; Mrs. Dennison tripped out of her house to see her husband into his hansom, and pitching her "sweet soprano" in its highest key cried, "Remember, your things for the voyage are in the yellow portmanteau! The *yellow* portmanteau, mind! Good-bye!"

"Good-bye!" growled John. Then gathering himself up into a heap in one corner of the cab, he said, "*Damn* the yellow portmanteau!"

"Good-bye, Frank, dear!" Laura Adair had chirruped like some pretty tame bird, as she raised herself on tip-toe to kiss her tall and handsome spouse. "All I ask is, *do* try not to get your nose sunburnt! It *is* so unbecoming. Such a lot of African travellers have a peeled nose!"

"I'll do my best, Laura," returned Frank, with melancholy resignation. "If I live, I will take care of — my — nose. If I die—"

"Oh, but you won't die!" declared Laura vivaciously. "You will come home and bring me *heaps* of nuggets."

Then the cab had driven off with him, and Laura had run into the house like a wild creature to cry over the chair where he had lately sat, and to kiss the stump of cigar he had left in the ashtray, and roll it up in paper like a precious relic. Laughing and crying together, she behaved like a lunatic for about five minutes; then becoming rapidly sensible, she murmured "*Darling!* It will soon be all right," and went quietly upstairs to finish something she had to do in the way of packing.

George Fairfax had to kiss the dog Bibi as well as his wife when he left, and his parting words were gruff and husky. He loved the bright little woman with the blue eyes who stood watching him off with her little toy-terrier in her arms — loved her with all the tenderness of a strong man's heart and once or twice he was tempted to break his promise to Dennison and throw up the whole business. But he fought obstinately against his rising sentiment, and said, "Ta-ta, Belle!" as if he were going to the club for an hour, and she laughed, waved her hand, and said, "Ta-ta!" also. When he had actually gone, however, she, like her friend Laura, cried, and kissed things of his which she found lying about; then she, too, became composed and practical, and drying her eyes, went in *her* turn to finish something *she* had to do in the way of packing.

Next morning the Three Wise Men stood together on the deck of the great ship outward bound, and mournfully watched the shores of England receding rapidly from their view. They had been almost the last to come on board, for having carefully told their wives at what hotel in Southampton a telegram would find them, they had, each one secretly, hoped against hope that some urgent message from home might have forced them (much against their wills, of course) to return in haste to London. But no such "reprieve" had been granted; no news of any kind had arrived, and so there they were — perfectly free to carry out their plans, and steaming away as fast as possible from the land they held dearest and fairest in all the world. They were very silent, but they thought a good deal. The captain of the ship, a jolly man, with a pleasant twinkle in his eye, spoke to them now and then in passing, and told them casually that there were several very pleasant ladies among the saloon passengers.

They heard this with stoical indifference, verging on bilious melancholy. As the English coast vanished at last into a thin blue line on the edge of the horizon, George Fairfax broke the "dumb spell" by a profane "swear."

"Damn it! I think Belle might have wired to say good-bye!"

"I confess I am surprised," murmured Adair slowly, "that Laura never thought of it."

"Women are all alike," snapped Dennison. "Court them and they're all romance; marry them, and they're dead to feeling."

And grumbling inaudibly he went below. The other two followed him in gloomy resignation, angry with themselves and with all their surroundings. When, later on, they took their places at the dinner-table, they were so unsocial, morose, and irritable that none of the passengers cared to talk to them or attempted to "draw them out." As for the women—" I see no pretty ones," said Adair.

"All old frumps!" grunted Fairfax.

"Women's rights and men's lefts!" snarled Dennison.

Three seats at table were empty, "Those three ladies who came on board early this morning are dining below?" inquired the captain cheerfully of the steward.

"Yes, sir."

Towards evening the wind freshened, and presently blew a heavy gale. The waves ran high, and many a bold heart began to sicken at the giddy whirl of waters, the nervous plunging of the ship, the shuddering of her huge bulk as she slipped down into the gulfs and climbed up again on the peaks of the foam-crested and furious billows. Next day, and the two next after that, the storm went on increasing, till, in the Bay of Biscay, the clamour and confusion of the elements became truly appalling. All the passengers were kept below by the captain's orders. The Three Wise Men lay in their berths because it seemed better to lie there than try to stand upright, and be tumbled about with the risk of breaking bones. Adair, too, was grievously seasick, and so reduced to utter mental and bodily misery, that he thought nothing, knew nothing, and cared nothing, though the heavens should crack. One night the wind sank suddenly, the waves continued to run into high hills and deep hollows with dizzy pertinacity; but there was a comparative calm, and with the calm came a blinding close grey sea-fog. The steamer's speed was slackened: the dismal fog-horn blew its melancholy warning note across the heaving waste of waters; and partially soothed by the deadly monotony of the sound, and the slower pace at which the ship moved, all Three Wise Men dropped off into a profound and peaceful slumber — the deepest and most restful they had enjoyed since they came on board. All at once, about the middle of the night, they were startled up and thrown violently from their berths by a frightful shock — a huge crash and cracking of timber. All the lights went out; then came roarings of men's voices, whistlings, and faint shriekings of women, accompanied by the rush and swirl of water.

"What's the matter?" shouted Dennison, picking himself up from the floor of his cabin.

"Collision, I should say!" returned Adair, out of the darkness. "Get your clothes on. Where's George?"

"Here!" answered Fairfax. "I am standing in a pool of water. Our window's smashed in — the sea's pouring through the port-hole."

They threw on what clothes they could find, and made the best of their way on deck, where they at once learned the extent of the disaster. A large foreign steamer had borne down upon their vessel in the fog, making a huge rent in the hull through which the water was pouring, and the prospect of sinking within half an hour seemed imminent. The foreign liner had gone on her way, as usual, without stopping to learn what damage she had done; all the passengers and crew were assembled on deck, the former quiet and self-possessed, the latter engaged in actively lowering the boats; and the captain was issuing his orders with the customary coolness of a brave Englishman who cares little whether his own lot be death or life so long as he does his duty.

"By Jove!" exclaimed Dennison as he surveyed the scene: "we're in for it! They're beginning to fill the boats; women and children first of course. If there's no room for us, we'll have to sink or swim in grim earnest!"

His two friends, Fairfax and Adair, looked on at the scene for a moment in silence. What each man thought within himself concerning the comfortable homes they had left behind cannot here be expressed — they kept their feelings to themselves, and merely went forward at once to proffer their assistance to the captain.

"Oh, you will take care of *me*, I'm sure!" sud' denly said a sweet plead-ing voice behind Adair, while a face, fair as an angel's, shone full upon him out of the storm and darkness, "I shall not be at all frightened with *you!*"

Adair turned sharply round, "*Laura!*" he gasped.

She slipped her arm through his, and smiled bravely up at him.

"Yes, it's me!" she said. "You didn't suppose I was going to part with you for such a long, uncertain time, did you? Oh no, darling! How *could* you think it! Are we going to be drowned? I don't mind, if I stop with you, and you hold me very tight as we go down. I'm so glad I came!"

He caught her in his arms, and kissed her with the frenzied passion of a Romeo. Indeed it would have been difficult even for a Shakespeare to de-pict the tragic tumult then raging in this "modern" husband's soul — the love, joy, terror, remorse, and reverence that centred round this delicate and beautiful creature who loved him so well that she was ready to con-front a horrible death for his sake! Meanwhile a little blue-eyed woman was clinging to George Fairfax, sobbing and laughing together.

"Oh, are we going to die?" she inquired hysterically, "Dear George, are we going to die? Do let us keep together, and poor Bi-bi with us! I've brought Bi-bi!"

"Heaven bless Bibi!" cried George fervently, hugging little woman and little dog together. "Oh, my darling Belle! who would have thought of seeing you here! *Why* did you come?"

"To take care of you, of course!" she replied, her blue eyes full of tears. "I didn't mean to show myself till we got to that horrid place in Africa, where you said the natives die of fever and things. Oh, dear, are we to get into boats? I won't go without you, George; nothing shall induce me!"

"My dearest, women and children *must* go first," said the unhappy George. "Oh, what fools we were to leave England! To think we should have brought you to this! Why, there's Mrs. Dennison!"

There she was indeed, calm, and almost smiling in the midst of danger. She held her husband's arm, for bluff John Dennison was completely tak-en aback and unnerved, and made no attempt to hide the tears that filled his eyes and rolled down his cheeks.

"It's all my fault," he said huskily. "If it hadn't been for me, Fairfax and Adair would never have started on this unlucky journey, and you dear women would not have got into this danger. As it is, God help us all! I believe we are doomed."

"Oh let us hope not," answered Mrs. Dennison softly and cheerily, "and if we are, it's not a hard death if we can only keep together. Look! there's the captain beckoning us now; come, girls!"

And how it happened none of them could ever quite realise, but certain it is, that within the next few minutes, the Three Wise Men found themselves in a small open boat, with their three wives, rocking up and down in the wallowing trough of the sea, the dog Bibi being the only other passenger. Fortunately, the clearance of the living freight from the sinking steamer had been effected with such promptness and method, that every soul on board got safely away before she began to heel under, and the pale light of morning showed the little fleet of boats riding high on the crests of the still uproarious billows. But as the hours went on, and the sun rose, these boats began to part company, and by ten o'clock in the morning, the little skiff containing the Three Wise Men and their fair partners was the only object visible on the shining expanse of the sea. The steamer had sunk.

Slowly and heedfully the Three pulled at their oars, and many a loving and anxious look did each man cast at the soft bundled-up figures in the stern, huddled together for warmth and support. All three women slept, out of sheer exhaustion, and the morning sunshine beamed full on the sweet face of the beautiful Laura, her peacefully closed eyelids making her look like some dreaming saint, while the fresh wind ruffled the bright uncovered locks of Belle Fairfax, whose tiny dog, curled close against her breast, was not asleep, but, on the contrary, was watchfully observing, with sharp eyes and attentively quivering nose, every wave that threatened to disturb his mistress's slumbers. Presently John Dennison essayed a remark.

"They're too good for us."

The silence of his friends gave tacit consent. Encouraged, he offered another opinion.

"If we drown we shall deserve it. We've been fools."

Again silence implied agreement. Then all three bent to the oars more earnestly, now and then turning their heads to scan the ocean in search of some home-returning ship which might offer them rescue. The sun rose higher and higher, the great sea sank to smoothness and turned to liquid gold, and at about midday Belle awoke. At first she looked frightened; but, meeting her husband's fond eyes, she smiled.

"Well, we're not dead yet!" she said briskly. "But I'm afraid we shall soon be hungry!"

"I'm afraid so too!" responded George dejectedly.

Laura sat up just then, whereupon Mrs. Dennison spoke as if she herself had not been asleep at all.

"I have some biscuits and some brandy," she said, in her bright clear voice. "We can hold out for a little while on that."

"Of course," said Belle; then mournfully, "If the worst comes to the worst, we must eat Bibi!"

At this a smile came on every face. Bibi himself, always alert at the mention of his own name, seemed much interested at the direful proposal; and presently, despite anxiety and danger, they all laughed outright.

"I'd cut off my own hand and eat it rather than eat Bibi," declared George emphatically. "Besides, poor little chap, he would hardly be a mouthful for a hungry man."

"Oh, but he would be better than nothing!" said Belle, bravely, winking away the tears that *would* come at the thought of the possible end of her small favourite. "I would rather he were eaten than that anybody should suffer—"

As he spoke the distant heavy throbbing of engines across the water was heard. Adair sprang up in the boat, shading his eyes from the sun.

"Here comes a liner!" he cried, "bearing straight down upon us, by Jove! Here, let us wave something; they're sure to see us!"

Quick as thought Mrs. Dennison slipped off a dainty white petticoat she wore, and handed it to her husband to serve as a signal of distress. Tied to an oar, its lace frills fluttered to the breeze, and in less time than it takes to relate they were perceived and rescued. The vessel that took them on board was bound for Southampton, and in due time the Three Wise Men, with their wives and Bibi, were landed on their native shore, none the worse, though much the wiser, for their little experience. The rest of the shipwrecked passengers, together with the captain and crew, were similarly rescued.

About a week after their safe return to London, Mr and Mrs. Dennison gave another little dinnerparty. The same number sat down to table as before, and the party was composed of the same persons. It was a very blithe and festive gathering indeed, and the Three Wise Men were much merrier than most wise men are supposed to be.

Healths were proposed of a strange and wild character by both the ladies and the gentlemen.

"Here's to Bibi!" cried George Fairfax, enthusiastically. "Long may he hold his own as the smallest and prettiest of Yorkshires!"

Loud applause ensued, accompanied by wild yapping on the part of the toasted canine hero, who, in due consideration of his having been shipwrecked and run the risk of being eaten, was on a velvet cushion within kissable distance of his mistress, Then Mrs. Adair got up, glass in hand.

"I beg to propose the continuance of lovemaking between husbands and wives!" she said, blushing divinely. "Kind words never do harm, — tender nothings are more than learned somethings! Pretty courtesies save many misunderstandings; and, coupled with my toast, I will ask you to drink to the womanlier and happier enlightenment of my friends the Pioneers!"

Amid loud clappings the toast was drunk; and, on silence being restored, John Dennison rose to his feet, and, in a voice somewhat tremulous with feeling, said —

"My dear boys — Frank Adair and George Fairfax, I have only one toast to propose, the only one in my opinion worth proposing — our wives! The dear women who have patiently borne with our humours, who have allowed us to have our own way, who followed us in faithful devotion, when out of a mere fit of the spleen we left them, and who proved that they were ready and willing to die with us if death had come. We imagined they were faulty women — just because they endeavoured to find some useful employment for themselves while we were wasting our time at our clubs and billiard-rooms; but we have discovered that the biggest fault we can accuse them of is their love for us! My boys, we don't deserve it, but we may as well try to. Any man who has won for himself the treasure of a good woman's entire love, should do his level best to make himself as worthy of it as he can. We're all lucky men; we've got three of the best women alive to share our fortunes with us; we behaved like fools in leaving them, and they behaved like angels in coming after us, and now we're all together again there's nothing more to say, but here's to them with all our hearts. Our love to them! our devotion! our reverence!"

The applause here was somewhat subdued because too deeply felt; and Belle Fairfax was crying a little out of sheer happiness. Mrs. Dennison thought it was time to make a diversion, and rose to the occasion with her usual spirit.

"John, dear!" she said, smiling at him across the table, "do you know when we were all in that little boat in mid-ocean, uncertain whether we should be rescued, or killed with starvation and exposure, I was irresistibly reminded of the old nursery jingle about the Wise Men of Gotham. Do you remember it? —

> 'Three wise men of Gotham
> Went to sea in a bowl —
> If the bowl had been stronger
> My song might have been longer!'

"You know, dear, you were all so like those wonderful men! You went to sea — you *would* go to sea — in your own bowl of a theory! Now, if that bowl had been stronger, why the song might have been longer! As it is—"

"It is finished," said John, with a smile, coming round from his place and openly kissing her where she sat. "And I defy any man to show me a better ending!"

ANGEL'S WICKEDNESS

"I hate God!" said Angel.

And having made this un-angel-like statement, she folded her short arms across her breast and surveyed her horrified audience defiantly.

It was a cold December Sunday afternoon, and the Reverend Josiah Snawley was superintending a Bible-class in a small, white-washed, damp and comfortless schoolroom in one of the worst quarters of the East End. He was assisted in his pious task by the virginal Miss Powser, a lady of uncertain age, tall and lanky of limb, with sandy locks much frizzled, and a simpering smile. The children ranged in a forlorn row before these two charitable persons were the miserable offspring of fathers and mothers whose chief business it was in life to starve uncomplainingly. And Angel — such was the odd name given her by her godfathers and godmothers in her baptism — was one of the thinnest and most ragged among all the small recipients of the Reverend Josiah's instructions, which had that day consisted of well-worn mild platitudes respecting the love of God towards His wretched, selfish and for ever undeserving creation. She had usually figured as rather a dull, quiet child, more noticeable perhaps than others of her condition, by reason of her very big dark eyes, small sensitive mouth, and untidy mass of chestnut-golden hair; but she had never come prominently to the front, either for cleverness or right-down naughtiness till now, when she boldly uttered the amazing, blood-curdling declaration above recorded.

"Was that Angel Middleton who spoke?" inquired the Reverend Josiah, with bland austerity. "Say it again, Angel! but no, no!" Here he shook his head solemnly. "You will not *dare* to say it again!"

"Yes, I will!" retorted Angel, stubbornly. "I hate God! There!"

A terrible pause ensued. The other children stared at their refractory companion in stupefied amazement; they did not quite understand who "God" was, themselves being but poor little weak, physically incapable creatures, who were nearly always too hungry to think much about Infinite and Unreachable splendours; but they had a dim idea that whoever the "Unknown Quantity" in Creation's plan might be, it was very wrong to hate Him! Dreadfully wrong! Frightfully wicked, and alarming from all points of view. After staring at Angel till they could stare no more, some of them put their fingers to their mouths and stared at Miss Powser. What did *she* think of it? Oh, *she* was limp with horror! — her eyes had grown paler, greener, and more watery than ever. She had clasped her hands, and was looking plaintively at the Reverend Josiah, as indeed it was her frequent custom to do. He meanwhile laid down the Testament he held, and surveyed the whole class with a glance of righteous indignation.

"I am shocked!" he said slowly, "shocked, and pained, and grieved! Here is a child — one who has been taught Bible-lessons Sunday after Sunday — who tells me she hates God! What blasphemy! What temper! Stand forward, Angel Middleton! Come out of the class!"

Whereupon Angel came out as commanded, and fully declared herself. Like a small alien on strange soil, she stood in advance of the other children, her worn, bursting shoes showing the dirty-stockinged feet within, her patched skirt clinging scantily about her meagre little figure, her arms still folded across her chest, and her lips set in a thin, obstinate line. Something in her look and attitude evidently irritated the Reverend Mr. Snawley, for he said sharply —

"Unfold those arms of yours directly!"

She obeyed; but though the offending limbs dropped passively at her sides, the little grimy hands remained firmly clenched.

"Now!" and the clergyman drew a deep breath, and taking up his Testament gave a smart rap with it on the desk in front of him. "Explain yourself! *What* do you mean by such wicked conduct? *Why* do you hate God?"

Angel looked steadily on the floor, and her lips quivered.

"Because I *do*!" she replied resolutely.

"That's no answer!" And the reverend gentleman turned to his lady-assistant in despair: "Really, Miss Powser, you should not have admitted such a child as this into the Sunday class. She seems to me quite incorrigible; a mere insolent heathen!"

Miss Powser appeared quite crushed by the majesty of this reproach, and feebly murmured something about a "mistaken idea of character," adding as a bright suggestion that the child had better be dismissed.

"Dismissed? Of course, of course!" snorted the Reverend Josiah angrily. "She must never come here again. Such a bad example to the other children Do you understand what I say, Angel Middleton? You must never come here again!"

"All right," said Angel, calmly; "I don't care."

"Oh, Angel! Angel!" moaned Miss Powser faintly. "I am so sorry to see this. I had hoped for much better things from you. Your father—"

"That's it," interrupted the girl suddenly, her breast heaving. "That's why I hate God. You teaches us that God does everything; well, then, God is killing father. Father never did any harm to anyone; and yet he's dying. I know he is! He couldn't get work when he was well, and now there isn't enough to eat, and there's no fire, and we're as miserable as ever we can be, and all the time you say God is good and loves us. I don't believe it! If God won't care for father, then I won't care for God."

The words rushed impetuously from her lips with a sort of rough eloquence that almost carried conviction; her way of reasoning seemed for the moment surprising and unanswerable. But the Reverend Mr. Snawley was equal to the emergency.

"You are a very wicked, ignorant child," he declared sternly. "If your father can't get work, it is most probably his own fault. If he is ill and incapable there is always the workhouse. And if God doesn't take care of him as you say, it must be because he's a bad man."

Angel's big eyes flashed fire.

"Yer lie!" she said steadily. "He's worth a dozen such as you, anyway."

And with this she turned on her heel and left the schoolroom, her proud step and manner indicating that she metaphorically shook the dust of it for ever from her feet. Her departure was watched in absolute silence by her startled companions, the insulted and indignant clergyman, and the pathetic Miss Powser; but when she had fairly gone, Mr. Snawley, turning to the rest of the class, said solemnly —

"Children, you have seen to-day a terrible exhibition of the power of Satan. No one that is not possessed of a devil would dare to express any hatred of God! Now remember, never let me see any of you playing with Angel Middleton; keep away from her altogether, for she's a bad girl — thoroughly bad — and will only lead you into mischief. Do you hear?"

A murmur, which might have meant either assent or dissent, ran through the class, and the Reverend Josiah, smoothing his vexed brow, took up his Testament and was about to resume his instructions, when a little shrill, piping voice cried out —

"Please, sir, I want to leave the class, sir!"

"*You* want to leave the class, Johnnie Coleman!" echoed the clergy-man—" what for?"

"Please, sir, 'cos Angel's gone, sir!" and Johnnie stumped his way to the front and showed himself — a small, bright, elfish-looking boy of about twelve. "Yer see, sir, I can't anyways promise not to speak to Angel, sir; she's my *gal!*"

A gurgling laugh of evident delight rippled along the class at Johnnie's bold avowal, but a stem look from Mr. Snawley rapidly checked this ebul-lition of feeling.

"Your *gal!*" and the good clergyman repeated the words in a tone of shocked offence; "John Coleman, you surprise me!"

John Coleman, ragged, blue-eyed and dirty, seemed to care but little as to whether he surprised the Reverend Josiah or not, for he resumed the thread of his shameless argument with the most unblushing audacity.

"'Iss, sir. She's my gal, an' I'm her bloke. Lor' bless yer, sir! we've bin so fur years an' years — ivver since we wos babbies, sir. Yer see, sir, 'twouldn't do fur me to go agin Angel now— 'twouldn't be gentleman-like, sir!"

Evidently John Coleman knew his code of chivalry by heart, though he was only a costermonger's apprentice, and was not to be moved by fear from any of the rules thereof, for, gathering courage instead of alarm from the amazed and utter speechlessness of wrath with which Mr. Snawley regarded him, he proceeded to defend the cause of his absent ladye-love after the fashion of all true knights worthy of their name.

"I spec's Angel's hungry, sir. That's wot riles her wrong-like. Don't yer know, sir, what it is to 'ave a gnawin' in yer inside, sir? Oh, it's orful bad, sir! really 'tis, sir — makes yer 'ate everybody wot's got their stummicks full. An' when Angel gets a bit 'ere an' there, she gives it all to 'er father, sir, an' niver a mossul for 'erself; an' now e's a going to 'is long 'ome, so they sez, an' it's 'ard on Angel anyways, and—"

"That will do!" burst out Mr. Snawley loudly, and suddenly interrupting the flow of Master Johnnie's eloquence, and glaring at him in majestic disdain; "you can go."

"'Iss, sir. Thank-ye, sir. Much obleeged, sir." And, with many a shuffle and grin, Johnnie departed cheerfully, apparently quite unconscious of having committed any breach of good manners in the open declaration of his sentiments towards his "gal," and entirely unaware of the fact that, apart from the disgust his "vulgarity" had excited in the refined mind of the Reverend Josiah, he had actually caused the pale suggestion of a blush to appear on the yellow maiden-cheek of Miss Powser! Immoral John Coleman! It is to be feared he was totally "unregenerate" — for once out of the schoolroom he never gave it or his pious teachers another thought, but, whooping and whistling carelessly, started off at a run intending to join Angel and comfort her as best he might, for her private and personal griefs as well as for her expulsion from the Bible-class. For once, however, he failed to find her in any of those particular haunts they two were wont to patronize.

"S'pose she's gone home!" he muttered discontentedly. "An' she won't thank me for botherin' round w'en 'er father's so bad. Never mind! I'll wait near the alley in case she comes out an' wants me for ennythink."

And with this faithful purpose in view, he betook himself to the corner of a dirty back slum, full of low tenement houses tottering to decay, in one of which miserable abodes his "gal" had her dwelling; and, sitting down on an inverted barrel, he began to con over a pictorial alphabet, a present from Miss Powser, which, though he knew it by heart, always entertained him mightily by reason of the strange coloured monstrosities that adorned every separate letter.

Meanwhile, as he imagined, Angel had gone home—" home" being a sort of close cupboard, dignified in East End parlance by the name of "room," where on a common truckle-bed, scantily covered, lay the sleeping figure of a man. He was not old — not more than forty at most — but Death had marked his pale, pinched features with the great Sign Ineffaceable, and the struggle of passing from hence seemed to have already begun, for as he slept his chest heaved labouringly up and down with the rapid breath that each moment was drawn in shorter gasps of pain and difficulty. Angel sat close by him, and her big soft eyes were fixed with passionate eagerness on his face — her whole little loving, ardent soul was mirrored in that watchful, yearning gaze.

"How can I?" she murmured to herself, "how can I love God, when He is so cruel to father?" Just then the sick man stirred, and opening his eyes, large, dark and gentle, like those of his little daughter, he smiled faintly.

"Is that you, Angel?" he asked whisperingly.

"Yes, father!" And taking his thin hand in her own, she kissed it. His glance rested on her lovingly.

"Ain't you been to class, dearie?"

"Yes, father. But—" She paused — then seeing he looked anxious and inquiring, she added—" But they don't want me there no more."

"Don't want yer there no more!" her father echoed in feeble wonder. "Why, Angel—"

"Don't ye worry, father!" she burst forth eagerly, "it's all my fault; 'tain't theirs! I said I hated God, and Mr. Snawley said I was wicked, an' I s'pose I am, but I can't help it, and there's all about it! I'm sick of their preachin' an' nonsense, an' it don't make you no better nor me, an' we're all wretched, an' if it's all God's doing then I *do* hate God, an' that's the truth!"

A flickering gleam of energy came across the suffering man's face, and his large eyes shone with preternatural light.

"Don't ye, Angel! Don't ye hate God, my little gel! ye mustn't — no, no! God's good; always good, my dear! It's all right wi' Him, Angel; it's the world that forgets Him that's wrong. God does everything kind, dearie. He gave me your mother, and He only took her away when she was tired and wanted to go. All for the best, Angel! All for the best, little lass!

Love God, my child, love Him with all your heart, an' all your soul, an' all your mind."

His voice died in indistinct murmuring, but he still kept his gaze fixed wistfully on his daughter's half-ashamed, half-sullen little face. She, continuing to fondle his hand, suddenly asked, "Why was I called Angel, father?"

He smiled, a very sweet and youthful smile.

"Just a fancy o'mine an' your mother's, my dear, that's all! We was young an' happy-like then, an' work was easier to get; an' such a dear sweet baby lass ye were when ye were born, with gold curls all over your head and bonnie bright eyes, that we said ye were like a little angel. An' so we named ye Angel for the sake of the pleasantness of it an' the sound of it, an' ye must *be* an angel, dearie, Angel by name and angel by nature. Yes, yes! it's all right! God gave ye to me, an' He knows all — all the trouble an' worry an' fret—"

He broke off suddenly, and sat up straight in his bed, while Angel, terrified by a strange expression in his face that she had never seen there before, cried out sharply, "Father! Father! what is it?"

He did not answer her; his eyes were full of radiance, and seemed to be looking at something his frightened child could not see.

"Angel!" he said, presently, in a faint hoarse whisper, "look! There's your mother! I knew she'd come! Don't ye hate God, my little gel! He's sent her for me. God's as good as good can be; it's the world that's wrong — the world—"

He paused; his breathing almost stopped, and he still stared steadily before him.

"Father! Father!" sobbed Angel, sinking on her knees in a passion of grief and fear. "Oh, father!"

His hand wandered feebly to her bent head, and lay coldly on her warm soft hair.

"Don't ye — hate — God — Angel," he gasped brokenly. "Love Him! — an' — an' He'll take care of ye!" Then, all at once, with a rich manly ring in his voice, such as his poor forlorn daughter had seldom heard, he exclaimed, "All right, my lass, I'm coming!"

Starting up at the sound and chilled to the heart with dread, Angel gave one wild look at him; and lo! while she yet gazed, he fell back heavily; a solemn shadow crossed his face — a shadow, which passing as swiftly as it had descended, left the features smooth and young; every line of care and perplexity vanished as if by magic; a smile settled on the lips, and all was over. With a shriek of agony the desolate child flung herself across the bed by her father's stiffening corpse, unable to realise his death, and out of the very acuteness of her despair sank for the time being into merciful insensibility.

Late on that same evening Johnnie Coleman, sleepy and disappointed, prepared to leave the corner of the alley where he had kept faithful vigil all the afternoon, and set himself to return to the dirty piece of matting on the floor in his master, the costermonger's, abode, which matting he, being an orphan, accepted as bed and lodgement. Suddenly his eyes were attracted by a bright glare in the sky, and hardly had he had time to receive the impression of this when the cry of "Fire! Fire!" resounded through the street, and set him running off at racing speed for the exciting scene of the disaster. It was some distance away, and as he ran he was quite unaware that another fleet-footed figure pursued him — no other than his "gal," Angel Middleton. She had crept out of her wretched dwelling, poor child, sick with hunger and stupefied with grief, and perceiving her ragged boy-friend waiting for her at the corner, had come towards him slowly and languidly, and had been just about to call him by name, when off he had rushed at the pace described, not seeing her, whereupon she, in the mere nervous impulse of the moment, followed. Soon the two, running thus, were merged and lost in a great crowd of people, who stood looking up at a wreath of brilliant flames that darted from the roof and walls of a small shop and dwelling in one — the house of a general grocer and dealer in oil and household provision. Owing to the inflammable nature of the goods kept in the store, the fire grew fast and furious, and though the engines rapidly arrived it was evident that very little could be done to save the perishing building. The owner of the place threw himself from one of the windows and escaped by a miracle without injury; but when his wife, half-suffocated with smoke, was dragged out from the burning walls more dead than alive, she struggled frantically to rush back again into the heart of the flames.

"My children! my baby!" she screamed and wailed. "Save them! Oh! save them! Let me go! — let me die with them!"

"Steady, mother!" said one of the pitying firemen, holding her arm in a tight grip. "'Tain't no use frettin'. Leave the little 'uns to God!" Yes, truly to God, and — His "Angel"! For suddenly the crowd parted; a little girl, whitefaced and dark-eyed, with golden-brown hair streaming behind her like a comet, rushed through and made straight for the burning house. There was a horrified pause; then Johnnie Coleman's shrill voice, rendered shriller by terror, cried out—" It's Angel! Angel Middleton!"

"Angel Middleton!" roared the crowd, not knowing the name, but catching it up and echoing it forth like a cheer in responsive excitement. "Hooray for Angel! There's a brave gel for ye! See; she's got the baby!"

And, sure enough, there at one of the burnt-out windows, with smoke and flame eddying around her, stood Angel, holding a tiny infant in her arms, the while she looked anxiously down into the street below for some further means of rescue. Several people rushed forward, holding an extended sheet which had been hastily procured, and, fearing lest she should be stupefied into inaction by the smoke, they shouted —

"Throw it, Angel! Never fear! Throw it down!"

Whereupon Angel threw the child; it was caught in safety, and she, the rescuer, vanished. Only to reappear again, however, at the same window with two more small children, of about two and four years of age, at sight of which such a thunder of acclamation went up as might have been heard at the furthest holes and corners of degraded Whitechapel. She meanwhile, leaning far out over the charred and smoking window-frame, demanded in clear, ringing tones —

"Are there any more children? Are these all?"

"Yes, yes!" shrieked the frantic mother, running forward with her just-restored baby clasped to her breast— "All! — You've saved them all! God love you, dear!"

Once more the protecting sheet was outspread, and without any haste or alarm for her own safety, Angel let one child after another drop straightly and steadily from her hold; they were caught and saved, uninjured. Then all interest became centred on the girl-heroine herself; and as the wall on which she had her footing tottered to and fro, a great cry went up from the crowd.

"Quick, quick, Angel! Jump!"

A smile crossed her pale face for a moment; she looked to right and left, and was just about to leap from her perilous position, when, with a sickening crash the brickwork beneath her gave way and crumbled to ruins, while up roared a new and fierce pyramid of fire. Quickly and courageously all hands went to the rescue of the rescuer, and in a few minutes, which, to the pitying onlookers seemed long hours, they dragged her forth, cruelly burnt but not disfigured; crushed and dying but not dead. Lifting her tenderly, they carried her out of the reach of the smoke and laid her down — one gentle-hearted fireman supporting her little golden head against his arm, while the mother, whose children she had saved, fell on her knees beside her, weeping and blessing her, and kissing her poor charred hands. She was quite conscious, and very peaceful.

"Don't ye mind," she said placidly; "father's gone, and 'twould ha' bin no use for me to stay. Why, Johnnie, are you there?" And her wandering eyes rested smilingly on a small doubled-up object close by that looked more like a bundle of rags than a boy. —

"'Iss," sobbed Johnnie. "Oh, Angel! I've bin waitin' for ye all the afternoon. I wouldn't stop in class arter they wouldn't 'ave ye no more — an' I wanted to see ye an' tell ye as how it wouldn't make no change in me, an' now — now—"

Tears prevented the faithful Johnnie's further utterance; and Angel, with an effort, made a sign that she wished him to come nearer. He came, and she put up her lips to his.

"Kiss me, Johnnie," she whispered. He obeyed; the great drops rolling fast down his grimy cheeks, while the crowd, reverently conscious of the solemn approach of death, circled round these two young things and watched their parting with more passionate though unspoken sympathy than could ever have been expressed by the noblest poet in the noblest poem.

"I was wicked," said Angel softly, then. "You must tell them all, Johnnie — at class — that I was wicked, and — that I am — sorry I said I hated

God; I didn't understand. It's all for the best — father's gone, and I'm goin' — an' I'm so glad, Johnnie — so happy! Bury me with father, please; — and tell everybody — everybody — that I love God — *now*."

There was a silence. The fireman supporting the girl's head suddenly raised his hand with suggestive gravity, and those who wore hats in the crowd reverently lifted them. The smothered sobbing of tender-hearted women alone broke the stillness; the stars seemed to tremble in the sky as the Greater Angel descended and bore away the lesser one on wings of light to heaven.

And the East End turned out from every grimy hole and squalid corner all its halt and blind, and maimed and miserable, and bad and good, to attend at Angel's funeral. The East End has a rough heart of its own, and that heart had been touched by an Angel's courage, and now ached for an Angel's loss. She and her father were buried together in the same grave on Christmas Eve; and the Reverend Josiah Snawley, realising perhaps for the first time the meaning of the words— "*Let your light so shine before men, that they may see your good works, and glorify your Father which is in heaven*" read the Burial Service with more emotion than was usual with him. Poor Johnnie Coleman, wearing a bit of crape in his hat, and carrying three penny bunches of violets, to throw upon his little sweetheart's coffin, was the most sincerely doleful of all chief mourners; desperately rubbing and doubling his dirty fists into his eyes he sobbed incessantly and refused to be comforted.

"Worn't she my gal?" he blubbered indignantly to a would-be consoler. "An' ain't I to be sorry at losin' 'er? I tell ye there ain't no one left alive as good as she wos!"

Even Miss Powser forgot for the nonce that she was a lonely spinster, whom nobody, not even Mr. Snawley, seemed disposed to marry; and, only remembering simple womanliness, shed tears unaffectedly, and spent quite a little fortune in flowers to strew over the mortal remains of the "mere insolent heathen" — the rebellious child who had said she "hated God." For in this one thing was the sum and substance of Angel's wickedness; she hated what seemed to her poor unenlightened mind the wanton cruelty of the inexorable Fate that forced her father to starve and die! Forgive her! — pity her, good Christians all! You who, comfortably fed and clothed, go to church on Christmas Day and try to shut out every suggestion of misery from your thought, forgive her as God forgives — God who knows how often His goodness is mistaken and misrepresented by the human professed exponents of Divine Law; and how He is far more frequently portrayed to His most suffering, ignorant and helpless little ones as a God of Vengeance rather than what He is — a God of Love!

THE DISTANT VOICE

"After long sleep, to wake up in heaven to the sound of a beautiful voice, singing!..."

The sick man muttered these words aloud, and, turning on his pillows, opened his eyes to meet the cold, grey, passionless ones of his physician who bent over him, watch in hand.

"Delirious, eh?" said the doctor, observing him narrowly. "This won't do at all. How's the pulse?" The patient extended his wrist. "H'm! Not so bad! You were talking nonsense just now, Mr. Denver."

"Was I?" Denver smiled faintly, and sighed. "I was dreaming, I think; a strange dream, about" — he paused a moment, then went on—" about heaven."

The doctor put his big watch back in its pocket, and looked about for his hat and gloves.

"Ah, indeed!" he murmured abstractedly. "Very pleasant, no doubt! Dreams are often exceedingly agreeable. You must go on with the medicine, Mr. Denver; it will alleviate pain, and it is all I can do for you at present. If you could pick up your strength, we might try an operation; but it's no use just now."

Denver's sad dark eyes rested on him wistfully.

"Stop a moment, doctor," he said; "I should like to ask you a question. I'm not delirious; I'm quite myself — at least as much as I shall ever be. I know mine is a hopeless case; cancer is bound to kill, sooner or later. Still, you're only mortal yourself, and the time must come when you will have to go the same way I am going. I'm on the verge of the grave, so it's not worth while deceiving me. Now, tell me honestly, do you believe in heaven?"

The doctor had found his hat and gloves by this time, and was ready for departure.

"Dear me, no!" he answered; "certainly not! That is, if you mean a supernatural heaven. The only heaven possible to the human being is the enjoyment of a certain set of brain sensations which elevate him into a particular mood of happiness; hence the saying that 'heaven is not a place but a state of mind.'"

"Then," went on Denver slowly, "you do not think there is any sort of conscious or individual life after death?"

"My dear sir," replied the doctor, somewhat testily — he was a great man in his profession and had a number of distinguished patients waiting for him that morning—" these are questions for the clergyman of the parish, not for me. I really have no ability to argue on such abstruse matters. I can only say, as a man who has studied science to some extent, that I personally am convinced that death is the natural and fitting end of the diseased or superannuated human being, and that when he dies, he is beyond all doubt absolutely dead and done for."

John Denver still looked at him earnestly.

"Thank you!" he said at last, after a pause. "You are a clever man, doctor, and you ought to know. I am an ignorant fellow, always was ignorant, I'm afraid. But when I worked for my living as a lad down in the mines, and looked up from the darkness of that deep earth, to the round bit of blue sky that shone in thick with stars above me, I used to believe heaven was there and God in the midst of it. It was nonsense, I suppose, but I wish I had the old faiths now. I think I should be able to bear my trouble better."

The doctor was slightly embarrassed and perplexed. It was the old story; he had no drug wherewith to "minister to a mind diseased." Patients often bored him in this way with troublesome questions. If John Denver had been a poor man instead of a rich one, he might not have even answered him; but millionaires are not met with every day, and Denver was a millionaire.

"Why do you not see your clergyman?" he asked. "It is possible he might reinstate you in your beliefs—"

Denver's brows clouded.

"My clergyman?" he echoed, a trifle sorrowfully. "My clergyman is far too much occupied with the comforts of earth to think over deeply concerning the joys of heaven. The last time I saw him, he urgently begged me to leave something to the church in my will. 'I am sorry to hear your disease is hopeless,' he said, 'but I am sure you would wish a part of your wealth to be of some benefit to the Almighty.' As if any man's money could really 'benefit' the Creator of all things! No, doctor! My clergyman has no support to give me in the trial I am passing through. I must bear it quite alone. Don't let me detain you any longer. Good-morning, and again thank you!"

The physician muttered a hasty response, and made his exit, glad to escape from what he considered the "fads" of a fanciful invalid.

Left to himself, John Denver stared wearily into the vacancy of the great room in which he lay. It was furnished simply, yet richly, and through the large bay window set half open, he could see the verdant stretches of park and meadow land of which he was the owner. He thought of the years of patient toil he had endured to amass his present wealth, of his life out in the "far West," of the sudden discovery of silver ore which had made him one of the richest men in the world, and of all the glamour and glitter of slavish society which had attended him ever since his attainment to fortune. He thought of the pretty woman he had married — a fresh, lively girl when he had first met her, and one whom he had fondly fancied loved him for himself alone; but who was now no more than a frivolous *mondaine,* for whom nothing was sacred but social conventionalism, and whose heart had steadily hardened under the influence of boundless wealth till she was as soulless as a fashion-plate. He thought of his children who had never loved him with really disinterested affection, of his son, who only looked upon him as the necessary provider of his yearly allowance, of his daughter, who was running the rounds of society in search of some titled noodle for a husband, almost, if not utterly indifferent to the fact that her father was dying of an incurable disease, and as memory after memory chased itself through his tired brain, a sudden rush of tears blinded him, and he groaned aloud, "O God! what has my life been worth! What worth has any life if death must be the end?"

At that moment a slight tap came at his door, and before he had time to say "Come in!" the intending visitor abruptly entered.

"I thought I should find you at home, John Denver," he said, in singularly slow, musical tones; "I met your wife in the garden, and she told me the doctor had just left you."

Denver nodded a faint assent. He was weary and exhausted; and in the presence of this particular friend of his, was always strangely disinclined to speak. Truth to tell, Paul Valitsky, known to many as a great painter, and suspected by some of being a dangerous Russian Nihilist, was a rather remarkable-looking man, possessed, too, of a certain fascination which attracted some people and distinctly intimidated others. Though small of stature and somewhat bent, he was not old; his face, pale and rather angular, was beautified by a pair of fine eyes, greenish-grey in hue, with an occasional changeful light in them like that which plays on opals. These eyes were his chief feature; they at once captivated and held all who met their fiery iridescent glances, and as he turned them now on Denver, a great kindness softened them — an expression of infinite tenderness and regard, which was not lost upon the invalid, though he lay still and apparently unmoved to any responsive feeling by that gentle and searching scrutiny.

"So the fiat has gone forth, and we must die!" said Valitsky presently, in almost caressing accents. "Well, there are worse things in life than death."

Denver was silent.

"You dislike the idea?" resumed his visitor after a slight pause. "The quiet of the tomb is not an agreeable prospect? You seem discomposed; but you are a brave man — you surely cannot be afraid!"

"No, I am not afraid," replied Denver steadily. "I am only — sorry!"

"Sorry! And why?"

"Well, in the first place I am sorry to have made so little good use of my time. All I have done has been to amass money, and what is that! — a delusive quest and an unsatisfactory gain, for I profit nothing by my life's work — my gold cannot cure sickness or keep back death. In some unfortunate way, too," he paused and sighed, "I have missed love out of all my fortunes, and now, here at the last, I am left alone to, meet my fate as best I can, and my 'best' is a bad attempt. Yes; I am sorry to die; I am sorry to leave the world, for it is beautiful; sorry to lose the sight of the sun and the blue sky—" he broke off for a moment, then went on, "But I tell you, Paul, if I could believe in another life after this one, as you do, and if the dream I had an hour ago were a truth, then I should not be sorry; I should be glad!"

"Ay, ay!" and Valitsky nodded sympathetically. "And what was this dream?"

"I dreamed I was in heaven," said Denver, his troubled face lighting up with an inward rapture. "But not such a heaven as the parsons preach of; it was a world somewhat resembling this one, only vaster and more beautiful. I seemed to myself to have wakened suddenly out of a deep sleep, and as I woke I heard a voice — the loveliest and tenderest voice imaginable! — singing a sweet song; and I swear to you, Paul, I thought I knew and loved the unseen singer!"

Valitsky rose from the chair he had occupied near the window, and, approaching the bed, laid his fine, nervous hand on Denver's wrist, fixing him at the same time with his strange iridescent eyes.

"So you have heard a voice from the other world, my friend!" he said. "And yet you doubt! You know what *I* am — you know that for me, at times, the portals of the Unseen are set open. Men call me artist, idealist, madman, judging me thus because I know the touch of higher things than are common to ordinary eating, drinking, breeding, perishing clay; but let them call me what they will, at death my faith will bridge the tomb, where their materialism shrinks away in fear and horror. That voice you heard — listen and tell me — was it at all like this?"

He held up his hand with a warning gesture — and, through the silence, a faint, delicious sound of song came floating distinctly — clear, yet far off, as though it fell from the regions of the upper air, "My God!" cried Denver, starting up in his bed. "It is the same — the very same! Paul, Paul! What does it mean?"

"It means," answered Valitsky steadily, "that you are on the verge of the Eternal, my friend; and that I, a poor unworthy medium of communication, am bidden to assure you of the fact. The heaven you dreamed of is a real heaven; the voice you hear is a real voice; and the One who sings awaits your coming with all the love you have missed in your life till now.

Believe me or not as you will, I speak the truth. Death, or what mortals call death, will bestow upon you such joy as is incapable of human comprehension or expression, but at the same time it is but fair to you to say that you can have your choice; knowing what I have told you, you yet have the privilege given to you to decide whether you will die or live on."

Denver stared amazedly. "You talk in riddles, Paul! Live on? I? My doom is sealed; I know that well enough. You can do nothing, spiritualist and idealist though you are, to hinder it."

"If you choose to live, you shall live!" said Valitsky firmly. "I will guarantee it, for so I have been commanded. Cancer shall not kill nor any other evil cut the thread of your existence. But, were I you, I would die rather than live." Denver had grown very pale.

"You — *you* will guarantee my life if I choose to live?" he asked, in low, tremulous tones. "*Can* you guarantee it?"

"I can and will. I swear it! I came here today on purpose to tell you so. But think well before deciding! — the barriers of the unseen world are lifted now, ready for your admission. If by your own choice they close again, the Voice you heard will sing to you no more."

With a wild, searching glance Denver scrutinised his strange friend's pale countenance. It was passionate and earnest — only the eyes sparkled with an intense, fiery gleam. Uncertain what to believe, and yet strongly impressed by Valitsky's steadfast manner, knowing him, too, for a man who was credited, rightly or wrongly, with singularly occult powers, he suddenly made up his mind and spoke out impetuously.

"I will live!" he said. "The next world may be a dream, the sweet voice that stole away my heart may be a delusion, but *this* world is real, a tangible fact, a place in which to move and breathe and think in. I will stay in it while I can! If you indeed have the force you seem to possess, why use it upon me and give me life — *this* life? I choose, not heaven but earth; I will live on!"

Slowly Valitsky withdrew from the bedside, and, standing a few paces away, surveyed Denver with an intense expression of mingled scorn and compassion.

"Be it so," he said. "Live, and try to find joy, peace, or love in what life brings you. You have chosen badly, my poor friend! You have rejected a glorious reality for a miserable delusion. When you are tired of your choice let me know. For the present, farewell!"

The door opened and closed softly — he was gone. For hours John Denver lay still with wide-open eyes, going over and over every detail of the strange conversation he had had with this strange man, and wondering whether it was true that he was granted a new lease of life, or whether it was mere fantastic boasting on Valitsky's part. Finally he slept a sound and dreamless sleep. The next day, on awaking, he was free from pain, and during the ensuing week he was so far recovered as to be able to leave his bed and resume his ordinary occupations. The great physician who attended him was completely taken aback, the supposed cancerous ailment appeared after all to have no existence, and for the thousandth time an apparently infallible doctor was proved wrong. John Denver lived, as Valitsky had sworn he should do. He lived to see his son in the criminal's dock for forging a friend's name; he lived to see his daughter married to a vicious "nobleman," whose days were passed in gambling and nights in drinking; he lived to know that his wife had been faithless to him for years, and that she had hoped for his death and was furiously disappointed at his continuance of life; he lived to entertain flatterers who fawned upon him for his wealth alone, to feed servants who robbed him at every turn, to realise to the full the cruelty, hypocrisy, meanness, and selfishness of his fellow-creatures, till, at last, after seven tedious summers and winters had passed away, a great weariness came over him and a longing for rest. Conscious of the failure and futility of his life, he sat all alone one evening in his great library, looking vaguely out on the misty moonlit lawn, and unbidden tears rose to his eyes as he thought, "If I could only dream again that dream of heaven, and wake to hear the sound of that beloved and beautiful voice singing."

On a sudden impulse, he drew pen and paper towards him, and wrote to Paul Valitsky, whom he had only very rarely and casually seen since that strange personage had offered him the choice of life or death.

"MY FRIEND, — You told me when I was tired to let you know. I am tired now. Life offers me nothing. I made, as you said, a bad choice. If you believe in a heaven still, will you assure me of it? If that voice I once heard is real, if it is the voice of one who is pitiful, and true, and tender, may I not hear it again? Certain mysteries are unveiled to you, certain faiths are clear to you; if to your potent secret force I owe the gift of longer life, take it back I entreat you, and let me find myself where I was seven years ago, on the verge of the Eternal, with the golden gates ajar!"

Several days elapsed before he received any reply to this letter, and he was growing restless, feverish, and impatient, when at last it came, its characteristic brevity quieting him into a strange and passive peace. It ran thus: "Heaven has not altered its design or changed its place, my friend, because blind Earth doubts its beauty. Your seven years is a little seven minutes to the dwellers in that higher sphere — a mere pause in the song you heard!

Be satisfied, on the night you receive this letter the song shall be continued and the Singer declared."

Dreamily John Denver sat at his open window, with this missive in his hand; the glory of a rosy sunset bathed all the visible country, and a thrush, swaying to and fro on a branch of pine, piped a tender little evening carol. He listened to the bird with a vague pleasure; he was quite alone, alone as he had been for many months since his wife had fled from him with her latest lover. He was conscious of a singular sensation, an impression of *duality*, as though he, John Denver, were the mere frame or casing for another individual and intelligent personality, a creature that until now had been pent up in clay, suffering and resentful, but that at the present moment was ready to break loose from imprisonment into a vast and joyous liberty.

"And yet," he murmured, half aloud, "if there is a heaven, what right have I to enter it? I have done nothing to deserve it. I have honestly striven to do my best according to my poor knowledge; but that is of no account. I have missed love on earth, it is true; but why should I expect to find it in another world? Valitsky declares that all God's work is founded on pure equity, and that every human soul has its mate either here or elsewhere; if that were true — if that could be true — perhaps by the very law of God which knows no changing, I may meet and love the singer of that heavenly song!"

At that very moment a sound, sweet and penetrating, pierced the silence — the full, delicious cadence of a melody more dulcet than ever came from the throat of any amorous lark or nightingale; and John Denver, the weary and world-worn man of many cares and many disappointments, stood up alert, pale and expectant, peering wistfully yet doubtfully into the gathering shadows of his room. Earth and earth's gains had proved delusions — would the hope of heaven prove equally vain?

"The voice divine!" he whispered rapturously. "The same beloved voice I heard before!... it sings again! So sweet a voice could not deceive. I will accept it as assurance of the truth of God!" With straining sight he still gazed into the deepening darkness... Was it fancy? or did he see there an angel-figure, and face fairer than that of any pictured vision? — a face luminous as a star, and full of tenderest appeal, love, and ecstasy. He stretched out his arms blindly... wonderingly... with a supernal sense of joy.

"It is true!" he said. "God is just, and heaven exists, despite all narrow, worldly doubtings! What has been missed shall be found; what has been lost shall be gained; and even to the poorest, the most sinful, and most ignorant shall consolation be given. For death is not death — but Life!" He staggered a little — his breath failed him — and falling back in his chair he closed his eyes. The mystic voice sang on, flooding the silence with exquisite music; he smiled, listening.

"After long sleep, to wake up in heaven to the sound of a beautiful voice singing!" he murmured — and then was still.

And even so John Denver slept the sleep of death; and, if all faiths are not frenzies, even so he woke!

THE WITHERING OF A ROSE

I

Immediately above the picturesque town of Lucerne there is a towering eminence clothed with pines, to the summit of which the exploring and aspiring tourist can ascend by one of those ingeniously contrived "funicular" railways, now so common in all the mountainous districts of Switzerland.

The little passenger-car is worked by the cog-wheel-and-water system, and jogs slowly up a precipitous incline, which, surveyed from the bottom, appears to slant at about an angle of ninety degrees. But it is not so perilous as it seems. The journey is easy and safe enough; and those who are troubled with "nervous sensations," and who insist on closing their eyes firmly while travelling up in the strange conveyance, which, when observed from a sufficient distance, certainly somewhat resembles a squat kind of blue-bottle clinging to a wall, will have their full consolation and reward on arriving at the top.

For there one of the most glorious landscapes in the world is spread before the enraptured sight; the lovely "Lake of the Four Cantons" glitters below in all its width of vasty blue, surrounded by kindly mountains, the peaks of which, even in the height of summer, still keep on their sparkling diadems of virginal snow; on either hand a forest of tall pine-trees stretches away for miles, a forest where one may wander in solitude for hours, walking on a thick carpet of the softest moss strewn with the brown and fragrant "pine needles," scarcely hearing one's own footsteps, and seeing nothing but the arching cathedral-like splendour of solemn green gloom, flecked through here and there by the blue of the sky and the bright rays of the sun.

At the entrance of this forest stands one of the prettiest of rustic hotels known as the "Pension Gutsch," a house built in the true Swiss style, with picturesque gabled roofs and wide wooden verandahs — its charming seclusion and simplicity offering a delightful contrast to the garish glories of the "Schweizerhof" and the other monstrous Americanized hotels of Lucerne, where the main object of every one concerned, from the *portier* down to the smallest paying guest, appears to be to forget as completely as possible the fact that Switzerland, as Switzerland, exists, and to live solely for the enjoyment of the *table-d'hote*, dress, flirtation, and lawn-tennis.

It is a singular fact, but true, that all the big hotels in Lucerne have their *table-d'hôte* dinner served precisely at the sunset-hour — the very time when grand old Mount Pilatus is gathering around his frowning brows strange and mystic draperies of crimson and gold and green — when the lake looks like melted jewels, and all the lovely hues of heaven are merging by delicious gradations into the cool, pearly grey of such pure twilight as is never seen save in countries where the air is rarefied by the presence of perpetual snow. For this very reason persons of a fanciful and romantic turn of mind, who prefer scenery to soup, frequently do battle with their nerves to the extent of being lifted — like little frightened children in a basket — up the precipitous "Gutsch" where, at the unpretentious, spotlessly clean and fragrant hotel bearing that name, they can do pretty much as they like, and have the supreme comfort of quiet rooms and refreshing sleep, luxuries completely denied them at all the large hotels in the town.

Moreover, by making a special arrangement and paying a little extra, they can have their meals served at their own stated hours, all of which sensible management and forethought on the part of the proprietor has the result of making his house a favourite resort of artists, poets, and dreamers generally. The frivolous and empty-headed would not care for such a place — it offers nothing but repose and beauty; it is not a suitable abode for golfers or tomboy tennis-players — they do well to remain in Lucerne and cling to the noisy and overcrowded "Schweizerhof." But it is eminently fitted for lovers in the first stage of sentimental ardour, and it is an ideal nook wherein to spend a happy honeymoon.

When, on one dazzling afternoon in early July, a gentleman with black moustaches got out of the little "funicular" car, and assisted a charmingly attired and very young lady with fair hair to alight also, and when these twain were followed by a Valet, a maid, and the porter bearing some very new-looking luggage, none of the people already staying at the "Gutsch" had any difficulty in classifying them. They were newly married; their very appearance betrayed them. One of the regular *habitues* of the place, a dark-eyed young man clad in carelessly-fitting tweeds, said as much to the landlord, who, having bowed the couple in, now stood on his doorstep benevolently surveying the prospect.

"On their wedding tour, I suppose?" he observed, with a smile.

"It is possible," replied mine host discreetly. "The lady is young. Not so young the gentleman. They have engaged the best rooms."

"Ah! Plenty of money about, then?"

"It is to be thought so," replied the proprietor, as he continued to smile blandly at the scenery. "The lady has a maid, the gentleman a valet. Every-thing" — and he spread out his hands expressively—" is *de luxe.* They are English people — evidently well bred. Perhaps you know the name — Allingham — Mr and Mrs. Allingham, of Dunscombe Hall, Norfolk?"

The dark-eyed artist thought a moment, then said "No." A vague idea was in his mind that he had seen a sketch or photograph somewhere of Dunscombe Hall, but he was not sure. And mine host being called away at the moment, the conversation was broken off.

The new arrivals had their meals served to them privately in their own apartments; so any curiosity felt concerning them among the *table-d'hôte* company at the "Pension Gutsch" was not destined to be largely gratified. One morning, however, Mr. Francis Fane, the dark-eyed artist, already mentioned, met Mrs. Allingham walking by herself in one of the lonelier and more outlying paths of the pine forest, and was quite taken aback by her extremely childish appearance. She was so small and light on her feet, she had such a young, wistful, wondering face, and her figure was cast in such a dainty and delicate mould, that, as she passed him silently by, in her simple white morning dress, tied round the waist with a knot of blue ribbon, she looked like a little girl just fresh from school, and it seemed impossible, almost absurd, to consider her as a married woman.

"Why, she can't be more than fifteen or sixteen!" he mentally ejaculated, staring after her bewilderedly. As a matter of fact she was twenty, and had seen two "seasons" in town; but things of the "world worldly" had as yet left no trace on her fair features, and her eyes still held their dreams of innocence unsullied, — hence, though a woman, she was still a child.

"Mrs. Allingham, of Dunscombe Hall, Norfolk!" repeated Frank Fane to himself, with a short gruff laugh. "By Jove! It seems preposterous!"

It did seem, if not preposterous, a little strange; and Rose Allingham herself sometimes thought so. She had been married just a fortnight, and had not yet got over the novel sensation of having a big thick wedding-ring on the tiny third finger of her little white hand. She would turn it round and round with a whimsical solemnity, and now and then she secretly polished it up with a small bit of chamois leather kept in her jewel-case for the purpose. And as she regarded her wedding ring even so she regarded her husband. The well-dressed gentleman with the perfectly irreproachable manner, even features, and well-groomed moustache, was Harold Brentwood Allingham, of Dunscombe Hall, Norfolk; and she was Mrs. Harold Brentwood Allingham, of Dunscombe Hall, Norfolk.

It all seemed very interesting, and new, and important. She was never tired of going over and over the events which had, in their sequence, led her up to this lofty position of matrimonial dignity. She had left school to be "brought out" and "presented" — oh, that presentation! Would she ever forget the misery of it? The bother of her long train — the nasty, spiteful behaviour of the ladies who pushed her, pinched her, and generally "scrimmaged" for entrance into the Throne-room; the bitter cold of the weather, and the horrible draughts that blew all over her uncovered neck and arms; the disappointment of there being no Sovereign to receive her when she made her pretty curtsey (practised for three weeks under the tuition of one of the best mistresses of deportment in London) but only one of the Princesses; the extreme hunger and thirst from which she suffered during the long "wait;" then, her utter prostration and sinking into a dead faint when she got home, and having beef-tea put down her throat in hot spoonfuls by her anxious mother; all this was perfectly fresh in her mind.

Then came the memory of several balls and dances, at many of which she had met th goodlooking and rich Mr. Harold Brentwood Ailingham, and had danced with him — he was a splendid dancer — then Henley, where the same Harold Brentwood Allingham had invited her to his house-boat, and given her flowers and bon-bons; then, a visit to a beautiful country house in Devonshire, where she had found him installed as one of the house-party; then, that afternoon when he had discovered her alone in the rose-garden, reading poetry, and taking the book out of her hands, and begun to make love to her. Such funny love! Not at all like the love the poets write about — nothing in the least like it. There was no nonsense about "breaking hearts" and "wild despairs" and "passionate tinglings" in Mr. Harold Brentwood Allingham. He was a very self-complacent man — he thought marriage a sensible and respectable institution, and was prepared to enter upon it in a sensible and respectable manner.

So, without verbiage, or what is called "high-flown" sentiment, he had put his case kindly and practically. He had said "Rose, would you like to marry me?" And she had surveyed him in such astonishment that he was quite amused.

"I have spoken to your parents," he had then continued, taking her hand, and patting it encouragingly; "and they approve — very highly. You are a charming, unspoilt girl; and though I am some years older than you, that is just as it should be. I am sure we shall be very happy together. You know I can give you anything you want.

My wife" — and here his back had stiffened slightly—" would naturally occupy an enviable position in society." And Rose had trembled all over with nervousness.

"I know!" she had faltered. "But I am not sure that I — I love you, Mr. Allingham."

He had laughed at this. "Oh, but I am sure," he had replied, "I know you better than you do yourself. There is no one else you care for, is there?"

"Oh, no," she answered earnestly, which indeed was true. She had often reflected on the fact — rather desolately. No one had shown her any special kindness or attention since she "came out" except this Mr. Allingham.

"Then let us consider it settled," he had said, and had kissed her, and led her out of the rose garden; and later on in the day had given her a wonderful engagement ring of the most superb diamonds. And so things had drifted on, and the preparation of her trousseau had been a great excitement, and her marriage day another excitement, and now, here she was, fast wedded, and on her honeymoon in Switzerland, with the irreproachable gentleman, whose black moustache would henceforth have to command her wifely admiration, year after year, till it turned grey. Somehow she had not realised the weight and seriousness of marriage till it was consummated; she had read many love-stories, many love-poems, in which all the heroes and heroines raved and swore in exquisitely choice language, and ended by killing themselves or somebody else with the dagger, pistol, or poison bowl, but the even prosaicness of married life had not been set before her in similarly graphic style.

Now and then she was a little afraid of herself — afraid that she was not as happy as she ought to be. She could not analyse her own feelings very well, but occasionally she caught herself sighing and murmuring uneasily, "I wonder if I really love him?" The doubt made her uncomfortable, for she had a tender heart and sensitive conscience. The relations between herself and her husband had, up till now, been more formal than passionate; for among his other idiosyncrasies, Mr. Allingham had a nervous horror of ridicule, and in consequence of this, had endured positive torments during their journey up the Rhine into Switzerland. He suspected everyone he met of the crime of knowing he was on his honeymoon "tour," and the unpleasant scowl he assumed for would-be friendly strangers, frequently remained on his brows for the benefit of his young wife, who was thereby rendered constrained and depressed.

Arrived at the "Pension Gutsch," he adopted an equally severe and distrustful demeanour towards the good-natured landlord, who made a dreadful mistake one morning by becoming too friendly, and venturing to suggest a drive, which he humbly considered would be a charming excursion for *une jeune mariée*. Mr. Allingham gave him a look that ought to have transfixed him, if looks had any such power, and told him curtly that he did not care about "excursions," and that "Madame" would please herself as to a choice of walks or drives. After this, the humiliated landlord took care to avoid giving further offence by any undue exhibition of personal interest in his best paying guests, and the days rolled slowly on in a long sunshiny stretch of perfect calm, without any change to vary or break their peaceful monotony. Days of delicious weather they were — pure and balmy as spring, though it was full summer — happy days they might have proved to Rose Allingham if they had not also been days of ever-deepening perplexity. She was a very loving little creature — quick to respond to kindness — and she troubled herself desperately in secret as to why she could not, though she tried, be altogether loving to her husband. Something held her back from him — there was some impalpable barrier between his nature and hers that kept them singularly apart, though to all appearances united. The veriest trifles helped to emphasise this curious state of things. One evening, strolling together in the pine-woods, she began to think of all the dainty love-poems she used to read and be so fond of, and bringing to mind their dulcet teachings, she suddenly took her husband's hand, and gently slipped it round her waist, leaning her fair little head confidently back against the shelter of the arm thus encircling her. Then, looking up, with shy, sweet eyes and a ravishing blush, she said softly —

"There! Isn't that nice?"

He regarded her with a gentlemanly amazement.

"Certainly not! It is not 'nice.' It is anything but nice! I am surprised at you, Rose! I really am! Suppose anyone were to meet us walking along in this ridiculous position! Why, they would take us for Cook's tourists — a Cockney 'Arry and 'Arriet out for a stroll! Nothing could be more vulgar and degrading!"

He withdrew his arm in haste, and walked beside her stiffly erect, scenting the piney air in virtuous indignation. His young wife said not a word, but walked on also, with crimsoning cheeks and downcast eyes, her little feet moving somewhat wearily. Presently he glared down upon her with an air of relenting condescension.

"Surely you know that demonstrations of affection in public are very bad form?" he inquired.

She looked up, her soft eyes flashing for once with something very like scorn.

"Where is the public?" she asked. "We are quite alone; alone with the forest and the sunset — and with God! But I am sorry if my action offended you."

"Dear me, I am not offended — why should I be?" he retorted pettishly. "You meant it well, no doubt. But wherever we are, alone or before witnesses, we must avoid even the appearance of vulgarity. And pray do not quote poetry to me, I hate it. 'Alone with the forest and the sunset, and with God!' What rubbish that is!"

"Is it?" and she gave a little sigh. "It is not poetry at any rate. It is only me!"

"Only you!" he repeated. "What do you mean?"

"I mean that I said it — they are my own words; just as they came into my head. Very silly, of course."

He eyed her with dignified wonder.

"Silly!" he echoed. "I should think so, indeed. Nothing could be sillier. They remind me of the style which the newspaper critics condemn as 'forcible feeble.'"

He smiled, and stroked his black moustache. All at once she looked up at him with an expression of pathetic pleading in her young face.

"Harold," she said, in a low uncertain voice, "are you sure — I mean — do you really love me?"

At this he felt seriously vexed; she was going to be hysterical or something, he was sure — women were all alike.

"My dear Rose," he replied, with laborious politeness, "I think if you will take into consideration the fact that I have married you, you will scarcely need to ask such a very foolish question. If I had not loved you I should not have made you my wife. That you are my wife ought to be sufficient for you — the deepest feelings, as you know, have the fewest words. I hope," here his voice became distinctly aggrieved in tone, "I hope you are not going to cry. Nothing is more childish; but perhaps you are over-tired, and had better go indoors. Pray remember that we are living more or less under public inspection, and that an hotel is not the place to make a 'scene' in."

She raised her eyes to his. They were dry and bright and cold.

"Do not be afraid," she said. "I am not crying, and I shall make no scene."

And, turning from him, she entered the hotel in silence. He did not follow her, but remained sauntering up and down on the turf outside, smoking a cigar.

The next morning Mr. Francis Fane was out in the woods with his easel and sketching-block, bent on finishing a rather powerful study of a tall pine-tree split through by lightning. He had been hard at work for more than an hour before he became aware that there was a small white bundle lying, apparently thrown, on the moss at some little distance off. He could not make it out very distinctly, for the shadows of the pines were so long and wide, and presently, moved by curiosity, he got up and went to see what it was. As he approached, it resolved itself into a figure — a slight little figure clad in white with a blue ribbon round its waist — and stopping abruptly in his advance, he caught the smothered sound of low sobbing.

"By Jove!" he muttered—" Mrs. Allingham!"

Indescribably pained and uncomfortable at this discovery, he was about to step noiselessly back to his easel without uttering a word, when the girl suddenly raised her head, and perceiving him, started up, nervously trying to control herself.

"I — I beg your pardon!" he stammered. "I — I came out here to make a sketch—"

"Not of me, I hope!" she said, with a little tremulous smile; then without the least pretence or affectation, she dried her eyes with a tiny lace handkerchief and began to laugh, though a trifle forcedly.

"I came out here, not to sketch, but to cry," she confessed naively. "You know it's very nice to have a little weep all to oneself sometimes."

"Is it?" and he reddened foolishly. "I should have thought—" But he could not devise any fitting end to the sentence; and she looked at him with a touch of wistfulness in her dewy eyes.

"May I see your sketch?" she said, picking up a large pine-cone from the ground and studying its pretty polished divisions with intense interest. "I have often noticed you wandering about with your easel and paint-box. You are Mr. Francis Fane, are you not? and you are staying at the same hotel as we are?"

To all this he assented, walking beside her dreamily, and always thinking what a child she looked. As they drew near the spot where he had left his easel, he woke up to consciousness of prosy etiquette, and endeavoured to realise that his companion was not a woodland sylph as she seemed, but a "married lady" of position.

"I'm afraid my poor sketch is hardly worth your looking at, Mrs. Allingham," he began formally. She interrupted him by a little gesture.

"Oh, you know I am Mrs. Allingham?" she queried, smiling.

"Of course I do!" he answered, somewhat amused and surprised at her tone. "Everybody at the 'Pension Gutsch' knows you by sight."

She mused a little, still intent on the mathematical partitions of the pine-cone she held. Suddenly she looked up.

"And what do they say of me?" she asked.

Fane was quite taken aback by the directness of the question. Meeting her eyes, however, and noting the inquiring candour and sweet innocence of their expression, he answered out and manfully —

"They say you are very young, and very pretty. You could hardly expect them to say or to think anything else, could you?"

She smiled and blushed.

"Oh, I don't know!" she said. "You see, I thought they might think me — well — funny!"

He stared.

"Funny?"

"Yes. Because it does seem funny, doesn't it, for such a little thing as I am to be a married woman? Some people must think it curious. Fancy — a married woman! Oh, I am quite old enough — I am twenty — but I don't seem to be tall enough or big enough!" and she spread out her pretty hands expressively and with a charming smile. "I don't know quite where I got all my silly ideas from, but when I was at school I used to think a married woman meant somebody fat and important-looking, who always wore a cap at breakfast, and a bow of velvet on the exact top of her head by way of full dress at dinner. I did, really!" and her eyes sparkled at the sound of Fane's joyous laughter. "Of course, I know better now, but then —— —" here she broke off as she saw the easel just in front of her with the unfinished sketch upon it. She looked at it long and earnestly, and Fane watched her, feeling somewhat curious to know what sort of criticism this baby-faced creature would pass upon it. She studied it from every point with close attention, and her eyes grew soft and serious.

"It is very human!" she said, at last. "The poor split tree tells its own history. You can see it did not know anything — it grew up quite happily, always looking at the sky and believing that no harm could befall it — till all at once the lightning struck it to the heart and killed it. And in this picture of yours it seems to ask was it my fault that I fell? Of course, you mean it as an emblem of some noble ruined life, do you not?"

He heard her with a certain wonder and reverence — her voice was so very sweet and grave.

"I cannot say I ever thought of it in the way you see it," he answered, "but I am very glad — and proud, that you find so much poetry in my poor effort."

"Poetry? — oh, no. I am not at all poetical!" she said quickly, and almost shamefacedly. "I used to be rather fond of reading Keats and Byron, but I never do that now — my husband does not like it—"

"Indeed!" murmured Fane vaguely, wishing he could make a picture of her as she stood before him in her little white gown, with a picturesque, broad-brimmed hat resting on the sunny curls of her abundant hair.

"No," she went on, confidingly, "he thinks it such nonsense. You see, he is a very clever man, and very scientific. He reads all the heavy magazines, and thinks it is very silly to waste time on studying verse, when one can have so much prose."

"Yes, there certainly is a good deal of prose about," said Fane.

At that moment a shadow crossed the sunlight in which they stood, and Mr. Allingham suddenly made his appearance.

"Why, Harold!" exclaimed his wife, springing towards him, "I thought you had gone into the town!"

"I have been into the town," he replied frigidly, "but I returned a few minutes ago. Perhaps you are not aware it is nearly our lunch hour?" Then, with a stand-offish yet would-be patronising air, addressing himself to Fane, "You are an artist, sir?"

"I do a little in that way," replied the young man, modestly. "Mrs. Allingham happened to pass by while I was at work, and she has been kind enough to look at my sketch."

"Ah — yes — er — yes! Very good indeed!" murmured Mr. Allingham, scarcely glancing at the picture as he spoke. "Rose, it is time we went in. You are staying at our hotel are you not, Mr. — er — Mr. —— — ?"

"Fane," said that gentleman mildly.

"Fane, oh! ah — yes. I think I have heard of you in London. You have exhibited, have you not?"

"Frequently."

"Oh, yes, er — I remember! Charmed — charmed to meet you! Are you coming our way now?"

"No!" said Fane, rather brusquely, "I must finish my work."

And he raised his hat courteously as husband and wife in their turn saluted him and walked away together. He looked after them for some minutes, noting with an artist's eye the swaying youthful grace of the woman's dainty figure and the stiff uncompromising squareness of the man's.

"Ill-matched in every way," he said to himself. "She is too young; and he is too — conceited."

That same evening he was somewhat surprised when Mr. Allingham came up to him with almost an air of cordiality, and invited him to take coffee, and a smoke afterwards, in that private part of the "Gutsch" verandah which had been specially partitioned off for the sole use and benefit of the newly-wedded pair. He went, and was shyly welcomed by Mrs. Allingham, who looked more like a small lost angel than ever, attired in a loose tea-gown of silky white, adorned with old lace, and sleeves of delicate chiffon. She sat a little apart, looking out through the creepers which festooned the verandah at the full moon, sailing slowly through white clouds over the heights of Sonnenberg.

"Mrs. Allingham does not object to 'smoke'?" said Fane courteously, before lighting his cigar. She turned her head, surprised; her husband laughed.

"Well, I never asked her," he said. "Rose, do you hear? Do you object to smoke?"

"Object? I? Oh, no," she faltered. "Not at all!"

Her husband laughed again and passed the liqueurs to his guest, who, however, helped himself very sparingly. Allingham drank *off* some cognac, and began to talk, and presently brought round the conversation to the subject of his place in Norfolk — Dunscombe Hall.

"I have been looking," he said, with a pompous air, "for a competent person to make sketches of the place. Now, I believe, if I am not mistaken, that you are on the staff of one of the pictorials?"

Fane admitted the fact.

"Then you would be the very man for me. I should not at all mind giving you the job if you would care to undertake it."

It was on the tip of Fane's tongue to say that he would see him — first, for the man's tone was so bumptious and patronizing as to be distinctly offensive. But, glancing at the delicate profile of the girl who leaned out among the clambering vines, looking at the solemn beauty of the night, he restrained himself by an effort.

"If my engagements will allow me to accept any extra work I shall not object," he answered, stiffly, "but I should have to communicate with my editor first."

"Oh, certainly, certainly," said Mr. Allingham complacently. "Only if you do it at all you must do it in October. If you can't arrange that I must get somebody else. Dunscombe Hall is a very fine subject for an artist's pencil. It used to be a monastery, and there are still some ruins of the old cloisters in the grounds. And there is a showy bit of sketching always at hand in the Haunted Mere."

"Is it haunted?"

"Well, they say so," replied Allingham, lighting his cigar. "I've never seen the ghost myself, but I am told that whenever there is to be a death in the family a lady appears in a boat on the water and beckons the departing spirit. All nonsense, of course. But I rather like a family ghost."

"And you?" asked Fane of Mrs. Allingham, seeing that she had turned towards them and was listening attentively.

"I cannot quite tell whether I do or not," she said slowly, and he fancied he saw her tremble. "I have never been in a haunted house to my knowledge, and, of course, it will be a new experience." She forced a little smile. "I did not know Dunscombe Hall had a ghost."

"Well, you know now," said her husband cheerfully. "But it is a ghost that never comes indoors. And the Haunted Mere is a mile off from the house, so no one is likely to make its acquaintance. You will let me know in good time, Mr. Fane, as to whether you can undertake my commission or not?"

"Certainly."

The conversation then changed to other matters, and when they parted for the night Fane thought Mrs. Allingham looked very tired and sad. A great pity filled his heart for the winsome little creature who seemed made for special tenderness and care, and who, despite the fact of her married dignity, had such an air of pathetic loneliness about her.

"Poor little woman!" he murmured, as he strolled out by himself in the warm moonlight, before going to bed. "She has got a perfectly irreproachable, commonplace prig for a husband — he will never do her any harm openly — never grudge her anything — never scandalise her in the least — and yet—"

He did not pursue the train of his reflections — he glanced at the moon, the tall straight pine-trees, the dewy turf — then, with a sigh over what he, as a modern pessimist, was disposed to consider the "fairness and futility" of creation generally, forgot everything in a sound and dreamless sleep.

II

During the rest of their stay at the "Pension Gutsch" Mr. Fane saw a good deal of the Ailinghams. Moved by the consideration that the artist was a man not unknown to fame, Mr. Ailingham unbent towards him as much as so important a person could be expected to unbend, and even condescended to take a few "excursions," such as he had once declared he hated, in his new acquaintance's company. They parted in August — Mr and Mrs. Allingham to return to England, and the stately attractions of Dunscombe Hall, Norfolk, and Fane to make a climbing tour in the Tyrol. They left the "Gutsch" all together on the same day, jogging down the steep declivity for the last time in the odd little cog-wheel car.

"It is like coming down from heaven!" said Rose Allingham, looking wistfully up at the receding pine-trees, bending to and fro like tall plumes on the height.

"Let us hope we are not going to the 'rival region'!" laughed Fane. "You liked the 'Gutsch,' then, Mrs. Allingham?"

"Very much," she answered.

"It is a fairly pleasant place for a short sojourn," said her husband disparagingly. "Very monotonous, of course. I should never care to go there again."

"Wouldn't you?" murmured Rose timidly. "Oh, I should."

"No doubt!" retorted her husband, with a hard smile. "But then, you see, I shouldn't."

And he began to read a London paper two days old, which had arrived for him that morning.

At Lucerne station they said good-bye to Fane, Mr. Allingham expressing his hope in language that savoured more of command than entreaty, that the artist would undertake his "commission" in October to sketch the various beauties of Dunscombe Hall.

"As to terms," he said loftily, "I think we need not mention them, as nothing of that sort will stand in your way or mine. Whatever you choose to fix I shall very willingly agree to."

The young man flushed a little, but said nothing. Shaking hands again with Mrs. Allingham, he presented her with a pretty bunch of Alpine blue gentians and edelweiss as a parting "souvenir," and lifting his hat, remained uncovered till the train had steamed off.

"If it were not for her," he mused, "I would see Dunscombe Hall and its priggish owner at Jericho before I'd go near either of them. As it is — well — I'll think about it."

September passed in a glorious blaze of beauty and perfect weather; and by the time October was a week old, his "thinking about it" had resolved into a definite course of action. So that, on one solemn and shadowy evening, when the smell of falling leaves was in the air, and the indefinable melancholy of autumn darkened the landscape even as a sad thought darkens a bright face, he was driven under the frowning and picturesque gateway of Dunscombe Hall, and up the fine-but rather gloomy avenue of ancient elms that led to the stately building. The carriage had been sent to meet him at the station, and when he finally arrived and got out at the door of the house, he was received by a dignified man-servant in dark livery, who informed him that Mr. Allingham had been obliged to go out for an hour, but that Mrs. Allingham was "waiting tea" for him in the drawing-room. To the drawing-room he was therefore shown; and such was the size and antique splendour of that vast apartment, that for a moment he could scarcely perceive his young hostess, who at the announcement of his name came forward to meet him. And when he did realise her presence, such a shock of pain went through him that he could scarcely speak. The change wrought in her during a space of barely two months was so terrible, that he could only stammer out some unintelligible words, press her small cold hand and gaze at her wonderingly. She meanwhile met his pitying, inquiring regard with a gentle patience in her own eyes.

"I see," she said, with a faint smile, "you think I am looking ill, don't you? — Yes — everybody does. It is quite true I am not well — I fancy sometimes this place" — and a light shiver ran through her—" does not agree with me. It is very, very big" — here she laughed— "and I am very small. I am sure a little woman ought to live in a little house to be comfortable. But I have a very good doctor — so kind and clever — he says it is only want of tone and a little heart-weakness — that's all. Come and have some tea — there's a fire at this end of the room."

She led the way to a sort of "cosy corner," where light and warmth were concentrated near a tea-table set out with Queen Anne silver and Sèvres china, and sitting in a low chair opposite her, Fane watched her in compassionate silence.

If she had looked a child before, she seemed more than ever one now — she had grown so thin and pale and fragile, that it seemed as if the merest puff of wind would blow her out of existence altogether. Her little hands, waxen-white and delicate, were scarcely equal to the task of lifting the teapot to pour out the tea, but as she busied herself with her hospitable duties, a faint colour came into her cheeks, and her eyes sparkled more brightly.

"Isn't this a huge room?" she said, as she passed Fane his cup. "It's meant for hundreds of people, you know — people in powdered wigs and court suits. I don't think it accommodates itself to modern life at all."

"It is indeed enormous!" and Fane glanced up and down and round about him. "The ceiling appears to be frescoed."

"Oh, yes, it is wonderful. Quite horrid, in my opinion — but Mr. Allingham says it is marvellous. Any number of fat goddesses and Cupids. You will see it much better by daylight. We have no gas in this room, because it would spoil the fresco — that is why it is always so dark — to light it up. We should have to put candles in all those four big Venetian chandeliers; and each one of them holds two hundred lights."

"No economy in candles there!" said Fane, laughing.

"No, indeed! But, of course, we never have occasion to light it up — we never give parties; there are not enough people in the neighbourhood to come to them if we did."

"How far are you from Sandringham?" he inquired.

"Oh, a long way. We are just conveniently out of the reach of everybody worth knowing, and everything that is going on."

And she laughed, a trifle bitterly.

"It must be rather dull at times," he said, studying her changed face attentively. "You should get some friends to come and stay with you — a jolly house-party."

"Oh, Mr. Allingham would never hear of such a thing," she said quickly. "He cannot bear to have a number of people about him. My mother came down for a short time in September, but she declared the house was damp and gave her rheumatism. She went back to London after about a week, and then I fell ill."

"What was the matter with you?" he asked sympathetically.

She shrugged her shoulders.

"All sorts of things — fainting-fits, weakness, nerves — disagreeableness generally. Here is Harold."

She broke off her conversation with Fane directly her husband entered the room, and seemed to shrink into herself like a sensitive plant too roughly handled. Allingham himself was the same as ever — irreproachable in dress, demeanour, and what is understood by a portion of society as "gentlemanliness." He greeted Fane with exactly the correctly measured air of cordiality — namely, that of the wealthy host and encouraging patron — and it was an air that galled the young artist's pride considerably, though he was careful for Mrs. Allingham's peace and comfort to show no offence. He certainly could not complain of his entertainment. A suite of rooms to himself, and perfect liberty of action; he breakfasted, lunched, and dined at a table appointed with the costliest luxuries; a carriage was at his disposal whenever he needed it; and Mr. Allingham had, furthermore, given him the choice of any horse in his stables, should he care for riding. He had engaged to make two dozen sketches of Dunscombe Hall from all the different points of view, and when once he began his work he became almost entirely engrossed in it.

The place was undoubtedly a fine object for any artist's study — its architecture was well-nigh perfect, and all the surroundings were eminently picturesque, though indubitably of a solitary and melancholy character. He did not see as much of Mrs. Allingham as he could have wished; she was often ailing, and though she invariably exerted herself to appear at dinner, there were times when she was not equal even to the effort, and her husband, seated in solitary state at his glittering board, would make formal excuses for her absence.

"My wife is very young," he would explain ponderously, "and is therefore inclined to give way to any trifling ailment. The doctor assures me she is suffering merely from a little want of tone, and the autumnal air depresses her; there is nothing at all serious the matter."

"She looks extremely ill," said Fane impulsively. "You think so?" and Mr. Allingham smiled indulgently. "I expect you are not accustomed to the ways of women; they put their looks on and off as easily as their gowns. In her present nervous condition of health it quite depends on

Mrs. Allingham's own humour as to whether she looks well or ill — it has nothing whatever to do with any actually real organic mischief."

Fane swallowed a glass of wine hastily to keep down the angry remark that rose to his lips, for the cold callousness of his host was almost more than he could bear. Reflecting quickly, however, that it was not his business to interfere, and that the less he said the better for Mrs. Allingham, he was silent.

"You have not tried your hand yet at the Haunted Mere?" inquired Mr. Allingham presently.

"No. I — er — the fact is — I have not yet had time to go and look at it."

"True — you have been very much occupied with the house itself," and Mr. Allingham nodded approvingly—" and your work is admirable — quite admirable! But I should suggest your visiting the Mere before the foliage quite falls. I fancy you will find it well worth your study." —

"I will go to-morrow," said Fane.

And on the morrow he went. He started early in the morning, one of the gardeners directing him as to which path to follow. When he came in full sight of the glittering sheet of water he could scarcely refrain from uttering a cry of rapture. It was so mystically beautiful; the deep solitude surrounding it was so intense and unbroken, that he no longer wondered at the reputation it had of being "haunted." Grand old willow-trees, with gnarled trunks and knotty stems bent above its glassy surface, and beyond it in the distance the land rolled away in gentle undulations of green and brown, relieved here and there with a clump of stately elms or a tangle of bright yellow furze. The place was so still that not even the twitter of a bird broke the breathless calm — and, powerfully impressed by the whole scene, Fane took a rapid pencil sketch in outline to begin with, his ultimate intention being to make a large picture of it, with a view to exhibition in one of the London galleries. Returning rapidly to the house, to finish what he had commenced the previous day, he met Mrs. Allingham walking slowly to and fro on the terrace.

"Have you been to the 'Haunted Mere'?" she asked, smiling.

For a moment he could not speak. The very pathos of her young face, the fatigue of her soft eyes, the listless expression of her very figure, all this went to his heart, and made him pity her as he had never pitied any woman. He felt her to be no more than a little tired-out child — a child longing to be taken up in tender arms and gently carried home. There was a slight tremble in his voice as he answered, with an effort at playfulness —

"Yes, I have seen the Mere, but not the ghost. Do you know, Mrs. Allingham, I begin to think you must be the ghost — you look like one this morning."

"Do I? I'm sorry. I hate to be ill — my husband doesn't like it. I wish I could get strong more quickly."

"Are you feeling worse, then, to-day?" asked Fane, with a touch of real anxiety in his tone, which made her look at him in grateful wonder.

"Oh, no," she said. "I am only a little 'run down,' as the doctor says, and weak. Harold declares it is all woman's nonsense, and thinks I don't exert myself to get well; but indeed I do. It is very kind of you to take so much interest—"

"Kind!" echoed Fane, almost irritably; then, glancing about him to make sure there was no one in sight, he approached her more closely.

"Look here, Mrs. Allingham, do forgive me if I seem officious or impertinent, but I can't help asking you this one question — are you quite happy?"

She glanced up at him almost affrightedly, and meeting his friendly eyes, her own filled with sudden tears.

"No, I am not," she faltered. "But it is wicked of me to say so, because you see it is quite my own fault. I ought to be happy — I have everything I want."

"Except — love!" said Fane, in a half whisper, struggling mentally with the insane desire that had suddenly seized him, to take this pale little child-woman in his arms and show her what the tenderness of love could be.

She looked at him almost reproachfully.

"I think you mistake," she said gently, with a curiously sad little old-world air of dignity. "Harold loves me very much in — his own way. He is not of a demonstrative nature."

Fane was silent. Presently she resumed in the same gentle accents.

"It is not his fault, indeed, it is nobody's fault that I do not feel as happy as I ought to do. It is something in my own temperament. I fancy that perhaps I am too young to be married; not in years I mean, but in feeling and education. You see, being quite small and slight as I am, I have always been treated as more or less of a child. Even when I came home from being presented at the Queen's Drawing Room, and fainted away all in a heap on the stairs, my mother called me a 'poor baby.' You remember what I told you at the 'Gutsch'?

— how I had always imagined that married women must be big and fat, and important? Well, really they are, as a rule, and I am so different! All the married ladies in this neighbourhood, for instance, look upon me as quite an absurdity."

"Then they are very impudent and ill-bred," said Fane hotly.

"Oh, no, they're not," and she laughed a little. "They come and call on regular days, and ask me if I am equal to the management of such a large house? Do I not find the servants a great trial? Have I a strong constitution? One lady always surveys me mournfully through her pince-nez, and says, 'You are very young to have secured such a magnificent establishment.' And that is quite true! Dunscombe Hall is magnificent — don't you think so?"

They paused on the terrace just at a point which faced the extensive left wing of the grand old pile. Carved escutcheons, flying buttresses and heraldic devices were all thrown up into sharp prominence by the mellow rays of the autumnal noonday sun, and immediately opposite them was the sculptured figure of a warrior-saint in a Gothic niche, festooned with clambering white roses, whose delicate blossoms surrounded and softened the statue's frigid aspect of frozen prayer.

Fane shivered slightly. "Yes," he said in a tone of one who makes reluctant admission. "It is a fine old place. But its character is distinctly melancholy. It is not a Beethoven 'Sonata' or a Mendelssohn 'Lied' — it is one of Chopin's most mournful 'Nocturnes.'"

Rose Allingham gave him a quick glance of perfect comprehension, but said nothing in reply. Moving in her light, bird-like way across the terrace, she gathered one of the roses that hung near the statue in the niche and gave it to him. He had scarcely taken it from her before its leaves fell in a white fragrant shower at his feet. She smiled a little forcedly.

"I was afraid of that," she said. "They are all on the very point of falling. I will not give you another from that tree. This afternoon — or tomorrow — I will get you one from the rosery; they are in better condition there. Now I must not detain you from your work any longer; you want all the daylight possible. Have you got this old stone saint in any of your sketches yet?"

"Not yet," he answered abstractedly, looking first at her and then at the petals of the fallen rose.

"Oh, I hope you will put him in somewhere!" she exclaimed, almost playfully. "He is such a dear old thing! You seem quite melancholy over that wasted rose."

"I am," he admitted. "I hate to see any beautiful thing perish."

"But then so many beautiful things do perish," she said, with a musing regret in her eyes. "One must get accustomed to that. You recollect your picture of the great pine-tree on the 'Gutsch,' split through by lightning? That suggested to me the ruin of a noble life. Well, all these little white roses that fall so easily at a touch, they are to me the emblems of just such a number of little lives; quite little lives, you know, of no actual use to anybody; only just pretty and fragrant and harmless, that at a rough touch or hasty misunderstanding drop to pieces and sink into the ground unnoticed and unmissed. I believe each little rose has its own little secret sadness."

She smiled and waved her hand to him, and she moved away slowly and re-entered the house.

When she was quite out of sight Fane, moved by some odd sentiment which he could not himself analyse, picked up every one of the fallen rosepetals and put them in his pocket-book. Then he set about sketching the ancient sculptured saint, while the sun was still bright on its weather-beaten features and piously folded hands.

The next day was the first of November, the "Feast of All Saints." The weather was beautifully clear and warm, and Fane went out early, without even seeing his host and patron as usual, in order to profit by the clearness of the atmosphere and get a long day's steady work. When he returned in time for the late dinner he heard that Mrs. Allingham had been seized with a succession of fainting-fits, and that the doctor had been sent for. Greatly disconcerted by this news he entered the dining-room full of eager and sympathetic inquiries, but found his host so bland and calm, and so perfectly satisfied that there was no cause whatever for anxiety as to his young wife's condition, that he felt it would be deemed odd and out of place if he, as a visitor and "paid artist," had exhibited any unduly great concern.

"It was mere weakness and nervous prostration," said Mr. Allingham, drinking his champagne with relish as he spoke, "and in these cases fainting-fits are a relief rather than a danger. I am sorry Rose has allowed herself to run down in this way. I am afraid it will necessitate my going with her to the sea-side for a short time. It would be particularly inconvenient to me just now — but if it must be done it must."

Fane could not speak. He gulped his food and wine down hastily with such a sense of impotent rage as almost choked him. He could scarcely bear to look at the composed, sleek, self-satisfied man beside him, attired as was his usual evening custom in irreproachable dress-suit, starchy shirt and white tie — he would have liked to knock him down and trample on him. As soon as dinner was ended, he left the room with a muttered hasty excuse about "having letters to write," and went out in the soft night air to smoke by himself and "cool down," as he inwardly expressed it, for his feelings were in a perfect tumult. Pity and anxiety for Mrs. Allingham, and contempt for her husband, struggled for the mastery in his mind; and he walked on and on through the grounds under the light of a full moon, not heeding where 'he was going to in the heat of his wrath and excitement.

"I can't stand it!" he said, half aloud, at last. "I'll leave the place tomorrow! I can finish the sketches at home now, I've got enough material to go upon. If I stay here any longer I shall come to fisticuffs with that egotistical prig, or — or — otherwise make a fool of myself."

A sudden shiver ran through him; and conscious of a certain dampness and unpleasant chill in the air, he stopped abruptly to see whither he had come.

To his amazement, right in front of him stretched the "Haunted Mere," glittering like polished steel in the silver rays of the moon. Something there was in the weird aspect of the still water and the twisted willows that impressed him with a sense of awe; and, as though a cold hand had been laid upon his heart, his anger died away into a dull, aching pain. He stood like one hypnotised, staring vaguely at the Mere, disinclined to move, and scarcely capable of thought. And as he remained thus, waiting for he knew not what, he saw distinctly a pale shadow fall like the reflection of a cloud across the shining width of water — a shadow that darkened slowly and grew, as it were, palpably into the shape of a small boat with a curved and curiously luminous prow; straining his eyes he watched, every nerve in his body throbbing with fear. The boat began to move out of shadow into moonlight, and as it moved it showed its spectral occupant — a woman's figure veiled completely in misty white, that stood erect and waved its arms beckoningly towards the turret of Dunscombe Hall. Reaching the very middle of the Mere where the moonlight shone broadest and brightest, the ghostly skiff paused on the water motionless. Again and yet again the veiled phantom waved its arms appealingly, commandingly; then, like a wreath of mist or smoke, it vanished!

Released from the terrible tension of his nerves, Fane uttered a loud cry; it was echoed among the dark woods and answered by the mournful hooting of owls. All at once he remembered the legend — that the ghost of Dunscombe Hall was said only to appear when death threatened some member of the family.

"My God!" he exclaimed, "can it be possible!"

And without waiting to think another moment he turned and ran, ran as though he were running a race for life, straight back to the Hall. Breathlessly rushing through the dark antiquated porch, he jostled against a man coming out.

"Mr. Allingham," he began.

"I am not Mr. Allingham," said the stranger, "I am Dr. Dean."

"The doctor? Oh, then—" And he leaned back against a pillar of the porch to recover breath and equanimity; "Mrs. Allingham is—"

"Dead," said the doctor gently.

NEHEMIAH P. HOSKINS, ARTIST

"They," said Mr. Hoskins, "made up my mind that this 'Daphne' will be the picture of the year — that is, so far as visitors to Rome are concerned. I do not exhibit at the French Salon, nor at the English Academy. I find" — and Mr. Hoskins ran his hand through his hair and smiled complacently—" that Rome suffices me. My pictures need no other setting than Rome. The memories of the Caesars are enough to hallow their very frames! Rome and Nehemiah Hoskins are old friends. What?"

This "What?" was one of Mr. Hoskins's favourite expressions. It finished all his sentences interrogatively. It gracefully implied that the person to whom he was speaking had said, or was going to say, something, and it politely expressed Mr. Hoskins's own belief that no one would or could be so rude as to hear his eulogies of himself without instantly corroborating and enlarging them. Therefore, when, on the present occasion, Mr. Hoskins said "What?" it was evident that he expected me to respond, and make myself agreeable. Unfortunately, I had no flatteries ready; flattery does not come easy to me, but I was able to smile. Indeed, I found it convenient to smile just then: the intimate association of the two names, "Rome" and "Hoskins," moved me to this pleasantness. Then, without speaking, I took up a good position in the studio, and looked at the "Daphne."

There was not the least doubt in the world that it was a very fine picture. Drawing, grouping, colouring, all were as near perfection as human brain and hand could possibly devise. The scene depicted was the legended pursuit of Daphne by Apollo. It was an evening landscape; a young moon gleamed in the sky, and over a field of nodding lilies came the amorous god, with flying feet and hair blown backward by the wind, his ardent poetic face glowing with the impatience and fierceness of repulsed passion. Pale Daphne, turning round in fear, with hands uplifted in agonised supplication, was already changing into the laurel; half of her flowing golden tresses were transformed into clustering leaves, and from her arched and slender feet the twisted twigs of the tree of Fame were swiftly springing upward. The picture was a large one; and for ideality of conception, bold treatment, and harmony of composition would have been considered by most impartial judges, who have no "art-clique" to please, a marvellous piece of work. Yet the wonder of it to me was that it should have been painted by Nehemiah P. Hoskins. The "Daphne" was grand, but Hoskins looked mean, and the contrast was singular. Hoskins, with his greased and scented hair, his velveteen coat, his flowing blue tie, and his aggressive, self-appreciative, "up-to-date" American "art" manner, clashed with the beauty of his work discordantly.

"I presume," he said, twirling his moustache with a confident air, "that picture is worth its price. What?"

"It is very fine — very fine, indeed, Mr. Hoskins!" I murmured. "What are you asking for it?"

"Fifteen thousand dollars is my price," he answered jauntily. "And cheap it is at that. My friends tell me it is far too cheap. But what matter? I am not hampered by mercenary considerations. I work for the work's sake. Art is my goddess! Rome is my altar of worship! I will not debase myself or my profession by vulgar bargaining. When I first set this picture up on the easel for exhibition I said fifteen thousand dollars would content me. Since that time my countless admirers have reproached me, saying, 'You ask too little, Hoskins; you are too modest, you do not realise your own greatness. You should demand a hundred thousand dollars!' But no! Having said fifteen thousand, I stick to it. I know it is cheap, ridiculously cheap, but never mind! there are more ideas still left in the brain that produced this work. What?"

"Indeed, I hope so," I said earnestly, endeavouring to overcome my dislike of the man's personality. "It is a magnificent picture, Mr. Hoskins, and I wish I could afford to purchase it. But as I cannot, let me say at least

how warmly I congratulate you on the possession of so much true genius."
Mr. Hoskins bowed complacently.

"A word of appreciation is always welcome," he observed grandiloquently. "Sympathy is, after all, the best reward of the inspired artist. What is money? — Dross! — When a friend comprehends the greatness of my work and acknowledges its successful accomplishment, my soul is satisfied. Money can only supply the vulgar necessities of life, but sympathy feeds the mind and rouses anew the divine fires! What?"

I really could not find any words to meet his interrogative "What?" this time. It seemed to me that he had said all there was to say, and more than was necessary. I took my leave and passed out of the studio, vaguely irritated and dissatisfied. The "Daphne" haunted me, and I felt unreasonably annoyed to think that one so vulgar and egotistical as Nehemiah P. Hoskins should have painted it. How came such a man to possess the all-potent talisman of Genius? I could now comprehend why the American colony in Rome made such a fuss about Hoskins; no wonder they were proud of him if he could produce such masterpieces as the "Daphne"! Still thinking over the matter perplexedly, I re-entered the carriage which had waited for me outside the artist's studio, and should have driven away home, had it not been for the occurrence of one of those apparently trifling incidents which sometimes give the clue to a whole history. A little dog was suddenly run over in the street where my carriage stood — one of its forelegs was badly cut and bled profusely, but otherwise it was not seriously injured. The driver of the vehicle that had caused the mishap came to me and expressed his regrets, thinking that I was the owner of the wounded animal, as, indeed, I seemed to be, for it had limped directly up to me, yelping pitifully, as though appealing for assistance. I raised the small sufferer in my arms, and seeing that it wore a plain brass collar inscribed "Mitû, 8, Via Tritone," I bade my coachman drive to that address, resolving to restore the strayed pet to its owner or owners. It was a pretty dog, white and fluffy as a ball of wool, with soft brown eyes and an absurdly small black nose. It was very clean and well kept, and from its appearance was evidently a favourite with its master or mistress. It took very kindly to me, and lay quiet on my lap, allowing me to bind up its wounded paw with my handkerchief, now and then licking my hand by way of gratitude.

"Mitû," said I, "if that is your name, you are more frightened than hurt, it seems to me. Somebody spoils you, Mitû, and you are affected! Your precious paw is not half so bad as you would make it out to be!"

Mitû sighed and wagged his tail; he was evidently accustomed to be talked to, and liked it. When we neared the Via Tritone he grew quite brisk, perked up his silky ears, and looked about him with a marked and joyful recognition of his surroundings; and when we stopped at No. 8 his excitement became so intense that he would certainly have jumped out of my arms, in complete forgetfulness of his injured limb, had I not restrained him. The door of the house was opened to us by a stout, good-natured-looking lady, arrayed in the true Italian style of morning *déshabille*, but who, in spite of excessive fat and slovenliness, possessed a smile sunny enough to make amends for far worse faults.

"Oh, Mitû! Mitû!" she cried, holding up her hands in grave remonstrance, as she caught sight of the little dog. "How wicked thou art! Well dost thou deserve misfortune! To run away and leave thy pretty signora!"

Mitû looked honestly ashamed of himself, and tried to hide his abashed head under my cloak. Curious to see the "pretty signora" alluded to, I asked if I might personally restore the stray pet to its owner then and there.

"But certainly!" said the smiling padrona, in mellifluous tones of Roman courtesy. "If you will generously give yourself the trouble to ascend the stairs to the top — the very top, you understand? — of the house, you will find the signora's studio. The signora's name, Giuletta Marchini, is on the door. Ah, *Dio!* But a minute ago she was here weeping for the wicked Mitû!"

Plainly, Mitû understood this remark, for he gave a smothered yelp by way of relieving his feelings. And to put him out of his declared remorse, suspense, and wretchedness as soon as possible, I straightway began to "generously give myself the trouble" of climbing up to his mistress's domicile. The stairs were many and steep, but at last, wellnigh breathless, I reached the topmost floor of the tall old house, and knocked gently at the door, which directly faced me, and on which the name "Giuletta Marchini" was painted in neat black letters. Mitû was now trembling all over with excitement, and when the door opened and a fair woman looked out, exclaiming in surprised glad accents "Oh, Mitû! *caro* Mitû!" he could stand it no longer. Wriggling out of my arms he bounced on the floor, and writhed there with yelps and barks of mingled pain and ecstasy, while I, in a few words, explained to his owner the nature of his misadventure. She listened, with a sweet expression of interest in her thoughtful dark eyes, and a smile lighting up one of the most *spirituelle* faces I ever saw.

"You have been very kind," she said, "and I do not know how to thank you enough. Mitû is such a dear little friend to me that I should have been miserable had I lost him. But he is of a very roving disposition, I'm afraid, and he is always getting into trouble. Do come into the studio and rest — the stairs are so fatiguing."

I accepted this invitation gladly, but scarcely had I crossed the threshold of the room than I started back with an involuntary exclamation. There, facing me on the wall, was a rough cartoon in black and white of the "Daphne" as exhibited by Nehemiah P. Hoskins!

"Why!" I cried, "that is a sketch of the picture I have just seen!"

Giuletta Marchini smiled, and looked at me attentively.

"Ah! you have been visiting the American studios?" she asked.

"Not all of them. This morning I have only seen Mr. Hoskins's work."

"Ah!" she said again, and was silent.

Impulsively I turned and looked at her. She was attending to Mitû's injured paw. She had placed him on a cushion and was bandaging his wound carefully, with deft, almost surgical skill. I noticed her hands, how refined they were in shape, with the delicate tapering fingers that frequently indicate an artistic temperament — I studied the woman herself. Young and as slight as a reed, with a quantity of fair hair partially lifted in thick waves from a broad intelligent brow, she did not bear any semblance to that type known as an "ordinary" woman. She was evidently something apart from the commonplace. By and by I found out a certain likeness in her to the "Daphne" of Hoskins's wonderful picture, and, thinking I had made a discovery, I said —

"Surely you sat to Mr. Hoskins for the figure of Daphne?"

Smiling, she shook her head in the negative.

I felt a little embarrassed. I had taken her for a model, whereas it was possible she might be an artist herself of great talent. I murmured something apologetic, and she laughed — a clear, sweet, rippling laugh of purest mirth and good-humour.

"Oh, you must not apologise," she said. "I know it must seem to you very singular to find the first sketch of the 'Daphne' here and the finished picture in Mr. Hoskins's studio. And it is really such an odd coincidence that, through Mitû, you should come to me immediately after visiting Mr. Hoskins that I feel I shall have to explain the matter. But, first, may I ask you to look round my studio? You will find other things beside that 'Daphne' cartoon."

I did look round, with ever-growing wonder and admiration. There were "other things," as she said, things of such marvellous beauty and genius as it would be difficult to find in any modern artstudio. In something of incredulity and amazement I instantly asked —

"These studies are yours? — you did them all yourself?"

Her level brows contracted a little — then she smiled.

"If you had been a man I should have expected that question. But, being a woman, I wonder at your suggesting it! Yes — I do my work myself, every bit of it! I love it! I am jealous of it while it remains with me. I have no master — I have taught myself all I know, and everything you see in this room is designed and finished by my own hand — *I am not Mr. Hoskins!*"

A sudden light broke in upon me.

"You painted the 'Daphne'!" I cried.

She looked full at me, with a touch of melancholy in her brilliant eyes.

"Yes, I painted the 'Daphne.'"

"Then how — why—" I began excitedly.

"Why do I allow Mr. Hoskins to put his name to it?" she said. "Well, he gives me two thousand francs for the permission — and two thousand francs is a small fortune to my mother and to me."

"But you could sell your pictures yourself!" I exclaimed. "You could make heaps of money, and fame!"

"You think so?" and she smiled very sadly. "Well, I used to think so, too, once. But that dream is past. I want very little money, and my whole nature sickens at the thought of fame. Fame for a woman in these days means slander and jealousy — no more! Here is my history," and with a quick movement of her hand she drew aside a curtain which had concealed another picture of great size and magnificent execution — representing a group of wild horses racing furiously onward together, without saddle or bridle, and entitled "I Barberi."

"I painted this," she said, while I stood lost in admiration before the bold and powerful treatment of so difficult a subject, "when I was eighteen. I am twenty-seven now. At eighteen I believed in ideals; and, of course, in love, as a part of them. I was betrothed to a man — an Austrian, who was studying art here in Rome. He saw me paint this picture — he watched me draw every line and lay on every tint. Well, to make a long story short, he copied it. He brought his canvas here in this studio and worked with me — out of love, he said — for he wished to keep an exact fac-simile of the work which he declared would make me famous. I believed him, for I loved him! When he had nearly finished his copy he took it away, and two days afterwards came to bid me farewell. He was obliged to go to Vienna, he told me, but he would return to Rome again within the month. We parted as lovers part — with tenderness on both sides — and when he had gone I set to work to give the last finishing touches to my picture. When I had done all I thought I could do, I wrote to a famous dealer in the city and asked him to come and give me his judgment as to the worth of my work. Directly he entered this room he started back, and looked at me reproachfully. 'I can do nothing with a copy,' he said; 'I have just purchased the original picture by Max Wieland.'"

I uttered an exclamation of indignation and compassion.

"Yes," continued Giuletta Marchini, "Max Wieland was my lover. He had stolen my picture, he had robbed me of my fame. I do not quite know what happened when I heard it. I think I lost my head completely for a time — my mother tells me I was ill for months. But I myself have no remembrance of anything but a long blank of hopeless misery. Of course, I never saw Max again. I wrote to him; he never answered. I told the picture-dealer my story, but he would not believe it. 'The design of "I Barberi"' he said, 'is not that of a feminine hand. It is purely masculine. If Max Wieland is your *damo,* you do him a great and cruel injustice by striving to pass off your very accurate copy as the original. It will not do, my dear little sly one, it will not do! I am too old and experienced a judge for that. No girl of your age was ever capable of designing such a work — look at the anatomy and the colouring! It is the *man's* touch all over — nothing *feminine* about it.' And then," went on Giuletta slowly, "the story got about that I had tried to steal Max Wieland's picture, and that he had broken off his engagement with me on that account. My mother, who is old and feeble, grew almost mad with anger, for she had witnessed his work of copying from me — but no one would believe her either. They only said it was natural she should try to defend her own daughter. Then we were poor, and we had no money to appeal to the law. No dealer would purchase anything that bore my name — as an artist I was ruined."

Here the dog Mitû, conscious that his mistress's voice had rather a sad tone in it, limped across to her on his three legs, holding up his bandaged paw. She smiled, and lifted him up in her arms.

"Yes — we were ruined, Mitû!" she said, resting her pretty rounded chin on his silky head. "Ruined as far as the world and the world's applause went. But one cannot put a stop to thoughts — they will grow, like flowers, wherever there is any soil to give them root. And though I knew I could not sell my pictures, I continued to paint for my own pleasure; and to keep my mother and myself alive I gave drawing-lessons to children. But we were poor — intolerably, squalidly poor — till one day Mr. Hoskins came."

"And then?" I inquired eagerly.

"Why, then — well!" and the fair Marchini laughed a little. "He made me a curious proposal. He said he was an American artist who desired to establish himself in Rome. He could only paint landscapes, he told me, and he knew he would require to have 'figure-pictures' in his studio to 'draw.' He said he would pay me handsomely to do these 'figure-pictures' if I would sell them to him outright, let him put his name to them, and ask no more about them. I hesitated at first, but my mother was very ill at the time, and I had no money. I was driven by necessity, and at last I consented. And Mr. Hoskins has kept his word about payment — he is very generous — and my mother and I are quite well off now."

"But he is asking fifteen thousand dollars for the 'Daphne,'" I cried, "and he only gives you two thousand francs! Do you call that generous?" Giuletta Marchini looked thoughtful.

"Well, I don't know!" she said sweetly, with a plaintive uplifting of her eyebrows; "you see it costs him a great deal to live in Rome; he entertains numbers of people and has to keep a carriage. Now it costs us very little to live as we do, and we have no friends at all. Two thousand francs is quite as large a sum to me as fifteen thousand dollars is to him."

"And you will never make any attempt to secure for yourself the personal fame you so well deserve?" I asked in astonishment.

She shrugged her shoulders.

"I think not! What is the use of it — to a woman? Celebrity for our sex, as I said before, simply means — slander! A man may secure fame through the vilest and most illegitimate means, he may steal other people's brains to make his own career, he may bribe the critics, he may do anything and everything in his power, dishonourably or otherwise — provided he succeeds he is never blamed. But let a woman become famous through the unaided exertions of her own hand and brain, she is always suspected of having been 'helped' by somebody. No, I cannot say I care for fame. I painted my picture, or, rather, Mr. Hoskins's picture" — and she smiled—" out of a strong feeling of sympathy with the legend. The god approaches, and the woman is transformed from a creature of throbbing joys and hopes and passions into the laurel — a tree of bitter taste and scentless flower! I am happier as I am — unknown to the world — while Hoskins 'is an honourable man'!" she finished, making the Shaksperian quotation with a bright laugh, as she dropped the curtain over the great canvas of "I Barberi," the picture that had been the cause of so much sorrow in her life.

After this adventure I visited Giuletta Marchini often, and tried to argue with her on the erroneous position she occupied. I pointed out to her that Nehemiah P. Hoskins was making out of her genius a fraudulent reputation for himself. But she assured me there were many struggling artists in Rome who made their living in the same way as she did — namely, by painting pictures for American "artists" who had no idea of painting for themselves. I discussed the matter with her mother, a dried-up little chip of an old woman with black eyes that sparkled like jewels, and I found her quite as incorrigible on the subject as Giuletta herself.

"When a girl's heart is broken, what can you do?" she said, with eloquent gestures of her head and hands. "The Austrian devil is to blame — Max Wieland; may all evil follow him! Giuletta loved him. I believe, if she would only confess it, she loves him now. Her character is not a changeful one. She is one of those women who would let her lover kill her and kiss the hand that dealt the blow. She has genius — oh, yes! Genius is not rare in Italy. It is in the blood of the people, and we do not wonder at it. Things are best as they are. She is not happy, perhaps, but she is at peace. She loves her work and we are able to live. That is enough, and all we want in this world. And for Giuletta, a woman does not care for fame when she has lost love."

And from her I could get no other verdict. She had, however, a strong sense of humour, I found, and fully recognised the art-fraud practised on his patrons by Nehemiah P. Hoskins, but she could not see that her daughter was either affected or injured by it. At Giuletta's own earnest request I therefore refrained from any immediate interference with Nehemiah's prosperity and growing reputation. He was quite the "lion" in Rome that year, and entertained whole embassies at tea. The "Daphne" was purchased at his own price by one of the wealthiest of his countrymen (a former "navvy," who now keeps "secretaries" and buys historical land in England), who has had it carefully "hung" in the most conspicuous part of his new picture-gallery, and who calls Hoskins "the American Raphael."

Meanwhile, at my suggestion, Giuletta Marchini is painting a work which she intends to submit to some of the best judges of art in Paris; and, judging from its design so far as it has proceeded, I think it is possible that in a couple of years Nehemiah P. Hoskins will be found to have "gone off" in a singular manner, while Giuletta Marchini will have "come up," to be received, no doubt, with the usual mixture of abuse and grudging praise awarded to work that is known to be woman's, instead of the applause that frequently attends the inane productions of pretentious and fraudulent men. In truth, it would sometimes seem that it is better, as this world goes, to be a man and an impostor, than a woman and honest. And concerning American artists in Rome, it is well known how many a one has there enjoyed a brief but dazzling reputation for "genius," which has suddenly ended in "smoke," because the gifted Italian who has played "ghost" behind the scenes has died, or emigrated, or gone elsewhere to make a name for himself. This rapid and apparently mysterious failure has attended the career of one Max Wieland, upon whom the Viennese journals now and then comment in terms of reproach and disappointment. His great picture, they say, of "I Barberi," had led the world of art to expect works from him of the very highest order, but, strange to say, he has done nothing since worthy of remark or criticism. Giuletta knows this, but is silent on the subject, and for herself, is certainly more alarmed than pleased at the prospect of winning her deserved fame.

"To be censured and misunderstood," she says, "is it pleasant — for a woman? To be pointed out as if one were a branded criminal, and regarded with jealousy, suspicion, and even hatred — is it worth fighting for? I myself doubt it. Yet if the laurel must grow from a human heart I suppose it cannot but cause pain."

And even while she works steadily on at her new picture, she tells me she is quite contented as she is, and happier than she thinks she is likely to be as an art "celebrity." In the interim, Nehemiah P. Hoskins, the "American Raphael," is triumphant; accepting homage for genius not his own, and pocketing cash for work he has not done; while he is never so magnificently convincing, so grandiloquently impressive, as when, surrounded by admiring male friends, he discourses complacently upon the "totally mistaken" vocation of "woman in art"!

AN OLD BUNDLE

"She's a reg'lar old bundle — she is; more worry than she's wuth!"

The speaker was a buxom laundress of some thirty-five or forty years of age, with à plump, merry face, a twinkling eye, and an all-round comfortable, kindly manner; and her words, though in themselves apparently harsh, were uttered in such a tone of genuine, if half-playful, affection, as robbed them of every suspicion of ill-humour. She was ironing out some dainty articles of feminine apparel profusely trimmed with lace, and though her attention was chiefly bent on her work, she glanced every now and then, with a curious mingling of wearied patience and keen anxiety, to the chimney-corner of her ironing-room, where, in a large chair, propped up by a large pillow, sat the "old bundle" alluded to.

"She *will* come in here on ironin' days; it ain't no good tryin' to prevent 'er. She can't see a bit how the things is bein' done; but she fancies she can, an' that's just as good for'er. Lor', now! Look at 'er, all droopin' forward fit to break 'erself in two! Here, granny! Hold up!"

And thus exclaiming, she hurried to the chair, and, with tender zeal, lifted the "bundle" into a better sitting posture, thereby disclosing to view a little old woman with a nut-brown wrinkled face like that of some well-preserved mummy. Two very small, very dim eyes peered up at her as she settled the pillow, and a weak wheezy voice piped out —

"That's 'er! That's my little Betty, my youngest grandarter! I knows 'er — I knows 'em all — fine-grown boys an' gels, for sure! Betty, she's a good hand at frills, but she can't do 'em as I could when I was a gel. Lor'! when I was a gel — eh, dearie, dearie me—" Here the voice sighed away into indistinct murmurings, and ceased.

Her "youngest grandarter" looked round with a matronly smile.

"That's the way old folks alius' goes on," she observed indulgently. "I 'xpect I'll do the same if I'm ever 'er age. She's a wonderful one for 'er time of life — ninety-five come Christmas. Such a memory as she's got! A bit mixed now an' then, but there's a'most nothing she can't remember. She was a married woman with a family before the Queen was crowned; an' once she was somewhere nigh Windsor Park an' saw the Prince o' Wales carried about as a baby. Didn't ye, granny?" Here she raised her voice to something between a shriek and a whistle. "Didn't ye see the Prince o' Wales in long clothes?"

A galvanic shock appeared to go through the "old bundle," and two skinny hands were thrust forth tremblingly in the air.

"Ay, that I did!" wheezed the weak voice again. "He wor the dearest little dear, as rosy as rosy — Lor' bless his 'art! I seed 'im on his marriage-day, too — me an' my 'usband; we were a'most killed in the crowd, so we was, but I seed 'im, an' he smiled at me — so did the beautiful princess from Denmark, she smiled, too — just straight at me. It's truth I'm tellin' — both on 'em smiled at me just straight an' pleasant like — it's truth I'm tellin'—"

"No one's doubtin' ye, granny," said the comely Betty, shaking out the ethereal-looking lace petticoat she had just finished, and unrolling another preparatory to further operations. "You were a fine, handsome woman still, then, worn't ye, eh?" This with a sly wink round.

"Ah, worn't I, worn't I?" screamed granny, now becoming wildly excited. "You ask William what I wor! He'll tell ye! He used to say, 'You'll never get old, my dear; that's what it is, you'll never get old.' Where's William? You ask 'im — he's the man to talk o' my looks; he thought a deal o' them — he'll tell ye. It ain't for me to praise mysell" — and here an odd chuckle and creak came from the chair, whereby it became dimly manifest that the "old bundle" was laughing— "it ain't for me — you fetch 'im an' ask 'im — he'll tell ye—"

"That's poor grandfather she's chattering about now," said Betty very softly. "He's been dead these twenty years."

She went on ironing, meditatively, for a few minutes, and then said —

"It's queer how some folks never get quite what they want in this world. Now she" — jerking her head in the "old bundle's" direction—"

she's had a particular wish all 'er days, an' it's never been given to 'er — now and again she do harp on it till she wears a body out. In all 'er terrible long life she's never seen the Queen, an' that's 'er craziness. She takes it awful badly. We've tried all we know to manage it for 'er, an' it seems as if there was a fate against it. She could never manage it for 'erself when she was well an' strong, an' now it's more 'ard than ever. We took 'er with us on Jubilee day, an' she began to cry at the sight of the crowd, an' got nervous like; then we took 'er when the Imperial Institute was opened, an' that worn't no use neither, she was too feeble to stand the pushing an' scrambling. We've done our best, but something alius comes in the way, so I expect it's no good trying any more."

At that moment granny lifted herself up with a good deal of energy and peered at the ironing-board.

"What are ye doin' with them frills?" she demanded. "You ain't 'arf a hand at them. When I was a gel, I could do frills fit for the Queen to wear. Ah! *she* must be a fine leddy, the Queen of England, with 'er gold crown on 'er head an' 'er great jewels on 'er breast; an''er grand robes all round an' about 'er, an' trailing yards on the ground. Eh, dearie, dearie, dearie, me!" — and she shook a sort of eldritch wail out of herself—" I'll never be at peace till I see 'er — never! I've seen the Prince of Wales many a time, God bless 'im! — an' the princess — an' they've smiled at me — but Lor'! the Queen is like the Lord Almighty — we've got to believe in 'er without seein' 'er!"

Her granddaughter looked gravely shocked.

"*Lor'*, granny, you shouldn't talk so — it sounds as blasphemous as if ye were in church," she said, with a most curious irrelevance. "I'm just surprised at you — a decent, God-fearing body like yourself. Surely there's no such need for us to see the Queen; it's enough to know that she's there."

"'Tain't!" shrieked the "old bundle" vehemently. "'Tain't, I tell ye! She's *there*, is she? *Where? Where* is she, ye silly gel? Don't make me a fool nor yourself neither! *Where* is she?"

"Why, granny, in 'er palaces, for sure!" replied Betty soothingly.

"Don't she never come out o' them palaces?" expostulated granny, getting shriller and shriller. "Don't she never take no air? Then it's a shame to the country to let 'er be stifled up an' hidden away from the people who would love to see 'er with 'er robes an' crown on 'er 'ead, poor pretty dear! I call it just disgraceful, I do! Get 'er out of it — yes, you tell William what I say; the country ain't got no business to' keep 'er shut up first in one prison an' then another — an' I tell ye, Betty, there's something very queer about the way they send 'er to Scotland for such a long time— 'tain't right, Betty! — you mark my words, 'tain't right! — it's a plot to keep 'er away from us, you see if it ain't! Lor'! she's a young woman yet — just lost 'er 'usband too! it's 'ard on 'er to shut 'er up — it's powerful 'ard—"

Here granny sank back exhausted, her withered head shaking to and fro involuntarily with the violence of her emotions.

"Lor'! bless 'er 'eart!" cried Betty, running to her, and tenderly caressing what now truly appeared to be nothing but a sunken heap of clothes. "How she do mix up things, to be sure! She can't get 'em right nohow. She ain't forgotten nothing, an' yet she can't sort 'em straight. Hullo, granny! Lord love 'er! If she ain't cryin' now!"

"They ain't got no right," whimpered granny dolefully, burying her wrinkles in her granddaughter's ample bosom, "to shut up the Queen. Let us 'ave a look at 'er, I say — we all loves 'er, and we'll 'earten 'er up a bit—"

"Don't you worrit, granny," said the buxom Betty consolingly. "She isn't shut up — don't you think it! She can go out whenever she likes."

"Can she?" and the "old bundle" lifted her tear-stained, aged face, with a faint hope expressed upon it.

"Ah, well, if it's the truth you're speakin', I'm glad to 'ear it. I'm glad an' thankful she can come out o' them palaces. But I've never seen 'er, an' I wish — I wish" — here came a prolonged and dismal snuffle—" I wish I could see 'er with my own eyes afore" — a long pause— "afore I die."

The poor "old bundle" was by this time completely done up, and meekly submitted to be put comfortably back on her pillow, where in a few minutes she was sound asleep. The kind-hearted Betty resumed her ironing, and, glancing up once wistfully at the interested visitor who had witnessed the little scene, remarked —

"It do seem a pity that she can't 'ave what she wants! She won't last long!"

The visitor agreed sympathetically, and presently withdrew.

It was then the "season" in town, and in due course it was announced in the papers that the Queen would visit London on a certain day to hold a special "drawing-room," returning to Windsor the next afternoon. Betty was told of this, and was also informed that if she got a bath-chair for her "old bundle," and started early, a friendly constable would see that she was properly placed outside Buckingham Palace in order to view the Queen as she drove by on her arrival from the station, and before the carriages for the Drawingroom commenced to block the thoroughfare. There would, of course, be a crowd, but the English crowd being the best-natured in the world, and invariably kind to aged persons and little children, no danger to "Granny" need be anticipated. The joy of the old lady, when she was told of the treat in store for her, was extreme, though her great age and frail health made her nervous, and filled her with fears lest again she should be disappointed of her one desire.

"Are you sure I shall see the Queen, Betty?" she asked, twenty times a day. "Is there no mistake about it this time? I shall really see 'er; 'er own darling self? God bless 'er!"

"Quite sure, granny!" responded the cheery Betty. "You'll be just at the Palace gates, an' you can't help seeing 'er. An' I shouldn't wonder if she smiled at you like the Prince o' Wales!"

This set the "old bundle" off into a fit of chuckles, and kept her happy for hours.

"Like the Prince o' Wales!" she mumbled; then nodding to herself mysteriously: "Ah, he *do* smile kind! Everybody knows that. He *do* smile!"

The eventful morning at last arrived, ushered in by the usual "Queen's weather" — bright sunshine and cloudless skies. The "old bundle" was wrapped up tenderly and carried into a comfortable bath-chair, wheeled by an excessively sympathetic man, with an extremely red face, who entered *con amove* into the spirit of the thing.

"A rare fine old lady she be," he remarked, as he fastened the leather apron across his vehicle. "Ninety-five! Lord bless me! I hope I'll have as merry an eye as she has when I'm her age! See the Queen? To be sure she shall; and as close as I can manage it. Come along, mother!"

And off he trotted with his charge, Betty bringing up the rear, and enjoying to the full the fresh beauty of the fine sunny spring morning. Outside Buckingham Palace a crowd had commenced to gather, and a line of mounted soldiery kept the road clear. Betty looked around anxiously. Where was the friendly constable? Ah, there he was, brisk and businesslike, though wearing a slightly puzzled air. He joined her at once and shook hands with her, then bent kindly towards the aged granny.

"Lovely morning, mother," he said, patting the mittened hand that lay trembling a little on the apron of the bath-chair. "Do you a world of good."

"Yes, yes," murmured the old woman; "an' the Queen?"

"Oh, she's coming," returned the "Bobby," looking about him in various directions; "we expect her every minute."

"The fact is," he added, in an aside to Betty, "I can't rightly tell which gate of the Palace Her Majesty will enter by. You see, both are guarded; the crowd keeps to this one principally, just about where we are, so I suppose it will be this one, but I couldn't say for certain. It is generally this one."

"Is it?" said Betty, her heart sinking a little. "Shall granny be placed here then?"

"Yes, you can wheel her as far as here," and he designated the situation. "If the Queen drives in by this gate, she will pass quite close; if she goes by the other, well — it can't be helped."

"Oh, surely she won't!" exclaimed the sensitive Betty. "It would be such a disappointment."

"Well, you see, Her Majesty doesn't know that—" began the constable, with an indulgent smile.

"But the crowd is *here* — outside *this* gate," persisted Betty.

"That's just why she *may* go in at the other," said the guardian of the peace, thoughtfully. "You see, the Queen can't abear a crowd."

"Not of 'er own subjects?" asked Betty; "when they love 'er so?"

"Bobby" discreetly made no answer. He was busy instructing the man who wheeled the bath-chair to place it in a position where there would be no chance of its being ordered out of the way. Once installed near the Palace gates, the "old bundle" perked her wizened head briskly out of her wrappings, and gazed about her with the most lively interest. Her aged eyes sparkled; her poor wrinkled face had a tinge of colour in it, and something like an air of juvenility pervaded her aspect. She was perfectly delighted with all her surroundings, and the subdued murmur of the patiently waiting crowd was music to her ears.

"Ain't it a lovely day, Betty?" she said, in her piping, tremulous voice. "And, ain't there a lot of nice good-looking people about?"

Betty nodded. There was no denying the fact. There were "nice good-looking" people about — an English crowd respectfully waiting to see their Sovereign is mostly composed of such. Honest hard-workers are among them, men of toil, women of patience; and all loyal to the backbone — loyal, loving, and large-hearted, and wishful to see their Queen and Empress, and cheer her with all the might of wholesome English lungs as she passes them by.

"It's lucky it's a fine day," said a man standing close to Betty, "else we shouldn't see the Queen at all — she'd be in a close carriage."

"She won't be in one to-day," said Betty confidently.

"I don't think so. She may. Let's hope not!" Again Betty's faithful heart felt an anxious thrill, and she glanced nervously at her "old bundle." That venerable personage was sitting up quite erectly for her, and seemed to have got some of her youth back again in the sheer excitement of hope and expectation. Presently there was a stir among the people, and the sound of horses' hoofs approaching at a rapid trot.

"Here she comes!" exclaimed the bath-chair attendant, somewhat excitedly, and Betty sprang to her grandmother's side.

"Here she comes, granny! Here comes the Queen!"

With an access of superhuman energy the old woman lifted herself in the chair, and her eyes glittered out of her head with a falcon-like eagerness. Nearer and nearer came the measured trot of the horses, a murmur of cheering rose from the outskirts of the crowd. Betty strained her eyes anxiously to catch the first glimpse of the royal equipage, then — she shut them again with a dizzy sense of utter desolation — it was a *closed* vehicle, and not the smallest glimpse could be obtained of England's Majesty.

The Queen, no doubt fatigued, sat far back in the carriage, and never once looked out. The horses turned in at the very gate near which the "old bundle" waited, alert — and in an almost breathless suspense — trotted past and were gone.

"We must go now, granny," said Betty, the tears rising in her throat. "It's all over."

The old woman turned upon her fiercely.

"What's all over?" she demanded quaveringly. "Ain't I come here to see the Queen?"

"Well, you've seen 'er," answered Betty, with an accent of bitterness which she could not help, poor soul. "You've seen all anybody has seen. That was 'er in that carriage."

Granny stared in vague perplexity.

"In the carriage?" she faltered. "That was 'er? Who? Who? Where? There worn't nothin' to see — nobody—"

"Get home, mother; you'll get mixed up in the crowd if you don't. We'll be having all the carriages along for the Drawing-room presently," said the friendly constable kindly. "The Queen's in the palace by now."

At this, the poor old dame stretched out her trembling hands towards the palace walls.

"Shut up again!" she wailed. "Poor dear — poor dear! Lord help ye in your greatness, my lovey! God bless ye! I'd a' given the world to see your face just once — just once — eh, dearie, dearie, dearie me! It's a cruel day, an' I'm very cold — very cold — I shall never see — the Queen, now!"

The constable gave a startled glance at Betty, and sprang to the side of the bath-chair.

"What, what, mother! Hold up a bit!" he said. "Here, Betty — I say — be quick!"

Two or three bystanders clustered hurriedly round, while Betty caught the drooping venerable head, and, laying it against her bosom, burst out crying.

"Oh, granny, granny dear!"

But "Granny" was dead. Betty's "old bundle" had been suddenly moved out of her way, leaving empty desolation behind, and an empty corner never to be filled. Some of the crowd, hearing what had chanced, whispered one to another —

"Poor old soul! She wanted to see the Queen just once before she died. She'd never seen her, they say. Ah, well, the Queen has a rare kind heart — she'd be sorry if she knew."

And there was many a wistful, upward glance at the windows of the palace, as the "old bundle" was reverently covered and borne home, giving place to the daintier burdens of rich-robed beauty and jewels brought freely to "see the Queen" on Drawing-room day.

MADEMOISELLE ZEPHYR

A vision of loveliness? A dream of beauty?

Yes, she was all this and more. She was the very embodiment of ethereal grace and dainty delicacy. The first time I saw her she was queen of a fairy revel. Her hands grasped a sceptre so light and sparkling that it looked like a rod of moonbeams; her tiny waist was encircled by a garland of moss rosebuds, glittering with dew, and a crown of stars encircled her fair white brow. Innocent as a snow-flake she looked, with her sweet serious eyes and falling golden hair; yet she was "Mademoiselle Zéphyr" — a mere *danseuse* on the stage of a great and successful theatre — an actress whose gestures were simple and unaffected, and therefore perfectly fascinating, and whose trustful smile at the huge audience that nightly applauded her efforts startled sudden tears out of many a mother's eye, and caused many a fond father's heart to grow heavy with foreboding pity. For "Mademoiselle Zéphyr" was only six years old! Only six summers had gilded the "refined gold" of the little head that now wore its wreath of tinsel stars; and scarcely had the delicate young limbs learned their use, than they were twisted, tortured, and cramped in all those painful positions so bitterly known to students of the "ballet."

"A very promising child," the wealthy manager of the theatre had said, noticing her on one of the "training" days, and observing with pleasure the grace with which "Mademoiselle" lifted her tiny rounded arms above her head, and pointed her miniature foot in all the approved methods, while she smiled up into his big fat face with all the fearless confidence of her age and sex.

And so the "promising child" advanced step by step in her profession, till here she was, promoted to the honour of being announced, on the great staring placards outside the theatre, as "Mademoiselle Zéphyr," the "Wonderful Child-Dancer!" and, what was dearer far to her simple little soul, she was given the part of the "Fairy Queen," in the grand Christmas pantomime of that year — a rôle in which it was her pride and pleasure to be able to summon elves, gnomes, witches, and flower-sprites with one wave of her magic wand. And she did it well too; never could wand or sceptre sway with prettier dignity or sweeter gravity; never did high commands issuing from the lips of mighty potentates sound so quaintly effective as "Mademoiselle Zéphyr's" tremendous utterance —

"You naughty elves! begone to you dark wood!
You'll all be punished if you are not *dood!*"

This word "*dood*," pronounced with almost tragic emphasis in the clearest of baby voices, was perhaps one of the greatest "hits" in Mademoiselle's small repertoire of "effects though I think the little song she sang by herself in the third act was the culminating point of pathos after all. The scene was the "Fairies' Forest by Moonlight," and there Mademoiselle Zéphyr danced a *pas seul* round a giant mushroom, with stage moonbeams playing upon her long fair curls in a very picturesque manner. Then came the song — the orchestra was hushed down to the utmost softness in order not to drown the little notes of the tiny voice that warbled so falteringly, yet so plaintively, the refrain —

"*I see the light of the burning day*
Shine on the hill-tops far away,
And gleam on the rippling river, —
Follow me, fairies! follow me soon,
Back to my palace behind the moon,
Where I reign for ever and ever!"

A burst of the heartiest applause always rewarded this vocal effort on the part of little "Mademoiselle," who replied to it by graciously kissing her small hands to her appreciative audience; and then she entered with due gravity on the most serious piece of professional work she had to do in the whole course of the evening. This was her grand dance — a dance she had been trained and tortured into by an active and energetic French ballet-mistress, who certainly had every reason to be proud of her tiny pupil. "Mademoiselle Zéphyr" skimmed the boards as lightly as a swallow — she leaped and sprang from point to point like a bright rosebud tossing in the air — she performed the most wonderful evolutions, always with the utmost grace and agility; and the final attitude in which she posed her little form at the conclusion of the dance, was so artistic, and withal so winsome and fascinating, that a positive roar of admiration and wonderment greeted her as the curtain fell. Poor little mite! My heart was full of pity as I left the theatre that night, for to give a child of that age the capricious applause of the public instead of the tender nurture and fostering protection of a mother's arms, seemed to me both cruel and tragic. Some weeks elapsed, and the flitting figure and wistful little face of "Mademoiselle Zéphyr" still haunted me, till at last, with the usual impetuosity that characterizes many of my sex, I wrote to the manager of the theatre that boasted the "Wonderful Child-Dancer," and, frankly giving my name and a few other particulars. I asked him if he could tell me anything of the "Zéphyr's" parentage and history. I waited some days before an answer came; but at last I received a very courteous letter from the manager in question, who assured me that I was not alone in the interest the talented child had awakened, but that he had reason to fear that the promise she showed thus early would be blighted by the extreme delicacy of her constitution. He added *en passant,* that he himself was considerably out of pocket by the "Zéphyr's" capricious health; that she had now been absent from the boards of his theatre for nearly a week; that on making enquiries, he had learned that the child was ill in bed and unable to rise, and that he had perforce stopped her salary and provided a substitute, an older girl not nearly so talented, who gave him a great deal of trouble and vexation. He furthermore mentioned in a postscript that the "Zéphyr's" real name was Winifred M — , that she was the daughter of a broken-down writer of *libretti,* and that her mother was dead, her only female relative being an elder sister whose character was far from reputable. He gave me the

"Zéphyr's" address, a bad street in a bad neighbourhood; and assuring me that it was much better not to concern myself at all with the matter, he concluded his letter. His advice was sensible enough, and yet somehow I could not follow it. It is certainly a worldly-wise and safe course to follow, that of never enquiring into the fates of your unfortunate fellow-voyagers across the tempestuous sea of life; it saves trouble, it prevents your own feelings from being harrowed, and it is altogether a comfortable doctrine. But the sweet plaintive voice of the "Zéphyr" haunted my ears, the serious child-face, with its frame of golden curls, got into my dreams at night, and at last I made up my mind to go, accompanied by a friend, to that questionable street in a still more questionable neighbourhood, and make enquiries after the "Zéphyr's" health. After some trouble, I found the dirty lodging-house to which I had been directed, and stumbling up a very dark rickety flight of stairs, I knocked at a door, and asked if "Miss M—" was at home. The door was flung suddenly wide open, and a pretty girl of some seventeen years of age, with a quantity of fair hair falling loosely over her shoulders, and large blue eyes that looked heavy and tear-swollen, demanded in a somewhat hardened tone of voice, "Well; what do you want?" My companion answered, "A lady has come to know how your little sister is, the one that acts at the theatre." I then stepped forward and added as gently as I could, "I heard from Mr. — , the manager, that the child was ill — is she better?"

The girl looked at me steadily without replying. Then suddenly, and as if with an effort, she said, "Come in." We passed into a dark and dirty room, ill-smelling, ill-ventilated, and scarcely furnished at all, and while I was trying to distinguish the objects in it, I heard the sound of a feeble singing. Could it be the "Zéphyr's" voice that sounded so far away, so faint and gasping? I listened, and my eyes filled unconsciously with tears. I recognized the tune and the refrain —

> "Follow me, fairies! follow me soon
> Back to my palace behind the moon,
> Where I reign for ever and ever!"

"Where is she?" I asked, turning to the fairhaired girl, who stood still regarding me, half-wistfully, half-defiantly. She nodded her head towards a corner of the room, a corner which, though very dark, was still sheltered from any draught from either window or door, and there, on a miserable pallet bed, lay the poor little "Fairy Queen," tossing from side to side restlessly, her azure eyes wide open and glittering with feverish trouble, her lovely silken hair tangled and lustreless, and her tiny hands clenching and unclenching themselves mechanically and almost fiercely. But as she tossed about on her miserable pillow, she sang unceasingly, if such a feeble wailing might be called singing. I turned from the heartrending sight to the elder girl, who, without waiting to be asked, said abruptly, "She has got brain-fever. The doctor says she cannot live over to-morrow. It's all been brought on through overwork, and excitement and bad food. I can't help it. I know she has never had enough to eat. I am often half-starved myself. Father drinks up every penny that we earn. It's a good thing, I think, that Winnie will get out of it all soon. I wish I were dead myself, that I do!" And here the hardened look on the pretty face suddenly melted, the defiant flash in the eyes softened, and, flinging herself down by the little pallet, she broke into a passion of sobs and tears, crying out, "Poor Winnie — poor little Winnie!"

I prefer to pass over the remainder of this scene in silence. Suffice it to say that I did what I could to alleviate the physical sufferings of poor little "Zéphyr" and her unfortunate sister; and before leaving I earnestly entreated the now quite softened and still sobbing elder girl to let me know whether her sister grew better or worse. This she promised to do, and leaving my name and address, I kissed the hot little forehead of the fallen "Fairy Queen," and took my departure. The next morning I heard that the child was dead. She had died in the night, and with her last fluttering breath she had tried to sing her little fairy song. And so the human "Zéphyr" had floated away from the stage of this life, where fairy-land is only the dream of poets, to the unknown country — to the

"Island valley of Avilion,
Where never wind blows loudly."

Thinking of her as I write, I almost fancy I see a delicate sprite on rainbow pinions flitting past me; I almost hear the sweet child-voice rendered powerful and pure by the breath of immortality, singing softly —

> *"Follow me soon*
> *Back to my place behind the moon,*
> *Where I reign for ever and ever!"*

And who shall assert that she does not reign in some distant glorified region — the little queen of a chosen court of child-angels for whom this present world was too hard and sorrowful?

TINY TRAMPS

The idea of childhood is generally associated in our minds with mirth, grace, and beauty. The fair-haired, blue-eyed treasures of proud and tender mothers, the plump, rosy little ones whose fresh young hearts know no sorrow save the sometimes ungratified longing for a new toy or new game — these are the fairy blossoms of our lives, for whom childhood really exists, and for whose dear sakes we think no sacrifice too great, no pain too wearisome, no work too heavy, so long as we can keep them in health, strength, and happiness, and ward off from their lives every shadow of suffering. And as we caress our own dimpled darlings, and listen to their merry prattling voices and their delightful laughter, we find it difficult to realise that there are other children in the world, born of the same great Mother Nature, who live on without even knowing that they *are* children, and who have "begun life" in the bitterest manner at a time when they can scarcely toddle; children to whom toys are inexplicable mysteries, and for whom the bright regions of fairyland have never been unclosed.

These poor little waifs and strays, no matter how young they are in years, are old — one might almost say they were born old — they are familiar with the dark and crooked paths of life, and the broad, shining, golden road of love, duty, wisdom, and peace has never been pointed out to their straying little feet.

Homes for destitute children may and do exist, refuges and charities of all kinds are open to those who seek them, and yet, in spite of all that is done, or is doing, poor child-wanderers walk the earth, and meet us in streets and country roads, clothed in rags, their pinched faces begrimed with dirt and tears, and their tiny voices attuned to the beggar's whine, while too often, alas! their young hearts are already withered by the corroding influences of deceit and cunning.

The other day one of these tiny tramps came to my door, and implored in piteous accents for a crust of bread. He was a pretty little fellow of some seven or eight years old, and his blue eyes looked bright with innocence and trust. His tiny naked feet were cracked and sore, and covered with mud, and his clothes were in so dirty and ragged a condition that it seemed a miracle how they could hang together at all. Through the large holes in these wretched garments, however, might be seen many pretty glimpses of soft pink and white skin, and his face was as plump, and fair, and rosy as the fondest mother could desire it to be. Nevertheless, he assured me in the most mournful manner that he was very cold and hungry, and that his feet were so very sore he could scarcely stand; so, without more ado, we took him into the kitchen, bathed his feet for him in refreshing warm water, and provided him with a warm pair of stockings and a strong pair of boots. Then we put him on a chair by the fire, and feasted him with a large bowl of barley-broth, which he appeared to enjoy exceedingly. A piece of cake was then given to him as a concluding relish, and when he had quite finished his meal, I asked him where he was going.

My small tramp screwed his knuckles into his eyes, and mournfully replied, "Home."

"Where is home?" I inquired.

"With mother."

"And where does mother live?"

"Please, 'm, she lives on the road."

"Lives on the road!" I exclaimed; "but where does she sleep?"

"On the road, 'm, please, 'm."

I looked at the small waif in silence. He met my glance with a weird upraising of his eyes and eyebrows, which gave him an expression that was half-plaintive, half-cunning.

"What road does she live on?" I asked.

"Please, 'm, any road as comes 'andy."

I sighed involuntarily. He was such a pretty child; and what a life seemed in store for him!

"What does your mother do?" I continued.

"Please, 'm, she sells *buttings*."

"Buttings?"

"Yes, 'm, buttings, an' 'ooks an' 'ise."

Buttons, and hooks and eyes. I knew the kind of woman she must be — bold, slovenly, and dirty, most likely, wearing a flashy bonnet on one side of her head, and brass rings on her fingers. A woman with a carneying voice, with which she insinuated herself into the good graces of servants, and persuaded them to purchase her trumpery goods.

"Have you a father?" I asked.

"Yes, 'm. He gits drunk, 'm."

Dismissing the idea of the father at once, I continued my catechising.

"Why doesn't your mother send you to school?"

"I dunno, 'm." Here the small knuckles were screwed into the eyes more violently than ever.

"Where is your mother now?"

"I dunno, 'm."

"Well, then, how are you going to find her?"

"I dunno, 'm. I kin try."

"Do you know where to try?"

"Yes, 'm. I knows her pub."

"Do you mean the public-house?"

"Yes, 'm, please, 'm." And as if the recollection of the "pub" had suddenly aroused him to action, the little forlorn wanderer slipped off his chair by the fire, and prepared to start. I fastened an old warm cloth jacket round him, and turning his little rosy face up that I might survey it closely, I said —

"Now, suppose you cannot find your mother, will you come back here? I'll take care of you till we can find her for you, and you shall have some more cake. Do you understand?"

"Yes, 'm."

"Stop a minute," I said; and seizing a scrap of paper, I hastily wrote the words—" Should you wish this child taken care of, put to school, and brought up to earn an honest livelihood, you can call at this house any day during the next three weeks and adding my name and address, I sealed the paper carefully. Then putting it in the pocket of the jacket I had just given him, I again addressed my small tramp —

"Will you give that letter to your mother when you find her?"

He looked decidedly astonished, and somewhat doubtful about the propriety of acceding to this request; but after a moment of consideration, he gave me his invariable reply —

"Yes, 'm, please, 'm."

Raising the child in my arms, I kissed his rosy intelligent face, my heart swelling with pity for his hard fate, and then I led him to the front door. He made a kind of attempt at a salute, by pulling one of his chestnut curls into his eyes, and then scrambled down the steps and ran away, while I rushed to my window, which commands an entire view of the street, and watched him. He looked round now and then to see if any one were near, and finding the road pretty well deserted, he finally seated himself on a doorstep, and I was able to observe the whole of his proceedings, which filled me with the greatest surprise and dismay.

The first thing he did was to take off the boots and stockings with which he had been provided, and to tie them in a bunch together. He then deliberately walked into a heap of the thickest black mud he could find, and tramped and splashed about therein till the feet, which had been so nicely washed, were as black and grimy as they could well be. This done, he took off the warm jacket, and rolling it up in as small a bundle as he could manage to make, he tucked it under his arm, then giving himself two or three dexterous shakes which had the effect of displaying the large holes in his own tattered garments to the best advantage, he uttered a sort of wild whoop or yell, and scampering up the street as fast as he could go, he disappeared from my sight. I knew his destination as well as if it had been told to me then and there. He was going to convert that jacket and those boots and stockings into money at the nearest old-clothes shop, and then he would no doubt hasten to his mother's "pub," and detail to her his successful morning's adventure. She would take the money he had obtained for the clothes, and, perhaps, give the child twopence for himself as reward for his smartness and there would be an end, while certainly the letter I had prepared would never be thought of or even discovered unless by some old Jew salesman, who would not comprehend its meaning. Yet could I blame the poor little tramp for his behaviour? No, indeed, I only pitied the unfortunate child more than ever.

Trained to deceive as thoroughly as we train our children to speak the truth, could anything else have been reasonably expected of him? It would have been a real matter for surprise had he acted differently. Still, I was foolish enough to feel somewhat disappointed, for the boy's face had attracted me. It is curious, too, to observe how very many attractive child-faces there are among the little vagrants of the London streets. Children with beautiful eyes and hair — children whose flesh is a perfect marvel of softness and fair delicacy, in spite of the dirt that grimes them from top to toe — and children whose limbs are so gracefully and finely formed, and whose whole manner and bearing are so indescribably lofty, that one would 'almost deem them to have been born in the purple. An excellent type of the tramp aristocracy came to me one morning in the shape of an Italian boy of about ten or eleven years of age, who strolled under my window, twanging prettily enough the chords of a much-used, far-travelled, but still sweet-toned, mandoline. I have always an extra soft heart for these straying minstrels from my own sunny land of song, and I immediately called him, and entered into conversation with him. He told me he had travelled far and earned little, and that he seldom had enough to eat, but he was merry. "Oh, yes," he said, smiling his bright southern smile, "he was always hopeful and lighthearted."

Some peculiarity in his accent impelled me to ask him if he were not from Lombardy, and never shall I forget the superb gesture of head and the proud flash of his eyes, as he drew himself up, and replied, with dignity, "No, signorina, *io son Romano*" ("I am a Roman").

If he had declared himself an emperor, he could not have asserted himself with more dignity. Many a languid dandy, dawdling through the saloons of fashion, might have envied his grace of figure and princely bearing.

There was a very interesting account once in the *Telegraph*, concerning two baby tramps known as "Sally and her Bloke." Sally was eight, and her boy companion, the "Bloke," was nine. No matter how great the distances each had to traverse during the day in obedience to the will of the tyrannical parents or masters who employed them to beg, or sell matches in the streets, as surely as the evening fell these two mites were always found together. Some irresistible attraction, some inexplicable sympathy, drew them together, and the poor little things entertained for each other so harmless, and withal so true, an affection, that even the coarse companions with whom their lot was cast were touched by their behaviour, and spoke with rough good-nature akin to respect of "Sally and her Bloke," and forbore to interfere with their pretty and pathetic little romance. I wondered at the time if anything would be done for this forlorn little couple, but the matter seems to have died out in mere sentiment, and "Sally and her Bloke" will no doubt be left to grow up as such children do grow up — in vice and misery.

A great step in advance has been made since the great English author, Charles Mackay, wrote his famous poem, "The Souls of the Children," which so powerfully impressed the late Prince Consort that he had thousands of copies printed at his own personal expense, and circulated them freely all over the land. This poem helped largely to influence the minds of English philanthropists and statesmen in favour of universal popular education; but, surely, there yet remains much to be done! True, the question may be justly asked, can anything more be done? It is, indeed, terrible to think that we must always be doomed to see sorrow, ignorance, and vice imprinted on the tender, flowerlike faces of the very young, and that there must always be, in spite of the efforts of the wisest and best men, a large majority of babes and children for whom there is and can be no hope of good. Must there be a perpetual sacrifice of the innocents to the god of all evil? One of the saddest sights to me, among all the sad sights of London, are the neglected children who have somehow eluded the kindly-meant, though occasionally stern, grasp of the Government officials, and who have literally nothing to hope for, nothing to render their lives of value to the nation; and who, as far as their wretched parents are concerned, might be better out of the world than in it. The streets swarm with such helpless little ones, and yet it seems impossible to do more than is being done every day. English men and women have tender hearts full of pitiful gentleness for the helplessness of infancy, and the charities that are instituted for poor and neglected children are, I believe, most generously supported; yet, amid such a mass of distress and evil, how futile seems all the best work of statesmen and philosophers! We must, however, continue to hope for better times, when every child that is born into the land may be recognised as the child of the Government no less than of its parents, and may be brought to realise its own responsible position and value as a servant of the state. This was the condition of things in Sparta, — and, though the Spartans carried their ideas rather too far, still it must be admitted that their system had its foundation in very excellent common sense. Whatever mistakes and shortcomings Lycurgus may have had to answer for, it is certain that he never would have tolerated baby tramps.

THE LADY WITH
THE CARNATIONS

A DREAM OR A DELUSION?

It was in the Louvre that I first saw her — or rather her picture. Greuze painted her — so I was told; but the name of the artist scarcely affected me — I was absorbed in the woman herself, who looked at me from the dumb canvas with that still smile on her face, and that burning cluster of carnations clasped to her breast. I felt that I knew her. Moreover, there was a strange attraction in her eyes that held mine fascinated. It was as though she said "Stay till I have told thee all!" A faint blush tinged her cheek — one loose tress of fair hair fell caressingly on her half-uncovered bosom. And, surely, was I dreaming? — or did I smell the odour of carnations on the air? I started from my reverie — a slight tremor shook my nerves. I turned to go. An artist carrying a large easel and painting materials just then approached, and placing himself opposite the picture, began to copy it. I watched him at work for a few moments — his strokes were firm, and his eye accurate; but I knew, without waiting to observe his further progress, that there was an indefinable something in that pictured face that he with all his skill would never be able to delineate as Greuze had done — if Greuze indeed were the painter, of which I did not then, and do not now, feel sure. I walked slowly away. On the threshold of the room I looked back. Yes! there it was — that fleeting, strange, appealing expression that seemed mutely to call to *me*; that half-wild yet sweet smile that had a world of unuttered pathos in it. A kind of misgiving troubled me — a presentiment of evil that I could not understand — and, vexed with myself for my own foolish imaginings, I hastened down the broad staircase that led from the picture-galleries, and began to make my way out through that noble hall of ancient sculpture in which stands the defiantly beautiful *Apollo Belvedere* and the world-famous *Artemis*. The sun shone brilliantly; numbers of people were passing and repassing. Suddenly my heart gave a violent throb, and I stopped short in my walk, amazed and incredulous. Who was that seated on the bench close to the *Artemis*, reading? Who, if not "the Lady with the Carnations," clad in white, her head slightly bent, and her hand clasping a bunch of her own symbolic flowers! Nervously I approached her. As my steps echoed on the marble pavement she looked up; her grey-green eyes met mine in that slow wistful smile that was so indescribably sad. Confused as my thoughts were, I observed her pallor, and the ethereal delicacy of her face and form — she had no hat on, and her neck and shoulders were uncovered. Struck by this peculiarity, I wondered if the other people who were passing through the hall noticed her *deshabille*. I looked around me enquiringly — not one passer-by turned a glance in our direction! Yet surely the lady's costume was strange enough to attract attention? A chill of horror quivered through me — was *I* the only one who saw her sitting there? This idea was so alarming that I uttered an involuntary exclamation; the next moment the seat before me was empty, the strange lady had gone, and nothing remained of her but — the strong sweet odour of the carnations she had carried! With a sort of sickness at my heart I hurried out of the Louvre, and was glad when I found myself in the bright Paris streets filled with eager, pressing people, all bent on their different errands of business or pleasure. I entered a carriage and was driven rapidly to the Grand Hotel, where I was staying with a party of friends. I refrained from speaking of the curious sensations that had overcome me — I did not even mention the picture that had exercised so weird an influence upon me. The brilliancy of the life we led, the constant change and activity of our movements, soon dispersed the nervous emotion I had undergone; and though sometimes the remembrance of it returned to me, I avoided dwelling on the subject. Ten or twelve days passed, and one night we all went to the Théâtre Français — it was the first evening of my life that I ever was in the strange position of being witness to a play without either knowing its name or understanding its meaning. I could only realise one thing — namely, that "the Lady with the Carnations" sat in the box opposite to me, regarding me fixedly. She was alone; her costume was unchanged. I addressed one of our party in a low voice —

"Do you see that girl opposite, in white, with the shaded crimson carnations in her dress?"

My friend looked, shook her head, and rejoined —

"No; where is she sitting?"

"Right opposite!" I repeated in a more excited tone. "Surely you can see her! She is alone in that large box *en face*."

My friend turned to me in wonder. "You must be dreaming, my dear! That large box is perfectly empty!"

Empty — I knew better! But I endeavoured to smile; I said I had made a mistake — that the lady I spoke of had moved — and so changed the subject. But throughout the evening, though I feigned to watch the stage, my eyes were continually turning to the place where SHE sat so quietly, with her stedfast, mournful gaze fixed upon me. One addition to her costume she had — a fan — which from the distance at which I beheld it seemed to be made of very old yellow lace, mounted on sticks of filigree silver. She used this occasionally, waving it slowly to and fro in a sort of dreamy, meditative fashion; and ever and again she smiled that pained, patient smile which, though it hinted much, betrayed nothing. When we rose to leave the theatre "the Lady with the Carnations" rose also, and drawing a lace wrap about her head, she disappeared. Afterwards I saw her gliding through one of the outer lobbies; she looked so slight and frail and childlike, alone in the pushing, brilliant crowd, that my heart went out to her in a sort of fantastic tenderness.

"Whether she be a disembodied spirit," I mused, "or an illusion called up by some disorder of my own imagination, I do not know; but she seems so sad, that even were she a Dream, I pity her!" This thought passed through my brain as in company with my friends I reached the outer door of the theatre. A touch on my arm startled me — a little white hand clasping a cluster of carnations rested there for a second — then vanished. I was somewhat overcome by this new experience; but my sensations this time were not those of fear. I became certain that this haunting image followed me for some reason; and I determined not to give way to any foolish terror concerning it, but to calmly await the course of events, that would in time, I felt convinced, explain everything. I stayed a fortnight longer in Paris without seeing anything more of "the Lady with the Carnations," except photographs of her picture in the Louvre, one of which I bought — though it gave but a feeble idea of the original masterpiece — and then I left for Brittany. Some English friends of mine, Mr and Mrs. Fairleigh, had taken up their abode in a quaint old rambling chateau near Quimperlé on the coast of Finisterre, and they had pressed me cordially to stay with them for a fortnight — an invitation which I gladly accepted. The house was built on a lofty rock overlooking the sea; the surrounding coast was eminently wild and picturesque; and on the day I arrived, there was a boisterous wind which lifted high the crests of the billows and dashed them against the jutting crags with grand and terrific uproar. Mrs. Fairleigh, a bright, practical woman, whose life was entirely absorbed in household management, welcomed me with effusion — she and her two handsome boys, Rupert and Frank, were full of enthusiasm for the glories and advantages of their holiday resort.

"Such a beach!" cried Rupert, executing a sort of Indian war-dance beside me on the path.

"And such jolly walks and drives!" chorussed his brother.

"Yes, really!" warbled my hostess in her clear gay voice, "I'm delighted we came here. And the château is such a funny old place, full of odd nooks and corners. The country people, you know, are dreadfully superstitious, and they say it is haunted; but of course that's all nonsense! Though if there *were* a ghost, we should send you to interrogate it, my dear!"

This with a smile of good-natured irony at me. I laughed. Mrs. Fairleigh was one of those eminently sensible persons who had seriously lectured me on a book known as "A Romance of Two Worlds," as inculcating spiritualistic theories, and therefore deserving condemnation.

I turned the subject.

"How long have you been here?" I asked.

"Three weeks — and we haven't explored half the neighbourhood yet. There are parts of the house itself we don't know. Once upon a time — so the villagers say — a great painter lived here. Well, his studio runs the whole length of the chateau, and that and some other rooms are locked up. It seems they are never let to strangers. Not that we want them — the place is too big for us as it is."

"What was the painter's name?" I enquired, pausing as I ascended the terrace to admire the grand sweep of the sea.

"Oh, I forget! His pictures were so like those of Greuze that few can tell the difference between them — and —— —— —"

I interrupted her. "Tell me," I said, with a faint smile, "have you any carnations growing here?"

"Carnations! I should think so! The place is full of them. Isn't the odour delicious?" And as we reached the highest terrace in front of the château I saw that the garden was ablaze with these brilliant scented blossoms, of every shade, varying from the palest salmon pink to the deepest, darkest scarlet. This time that subtle fragrance was not my fancy, and I gathered a few of the flowers to wear in my dress at dinner. Mr. Fairleigh now came out to receive us, and the conversation became general.

I was delighted with the interior of the house; it was so quaint, and old, and suggestive. There was a dark oaken staircase, with a most curiously carved and twisted balustrade — some ancient tapestry still hung on the walls — and there were faded portraits of stiff ladies in ruffs, and maliciously smiling knights in armour, that depressed rather than decorated the dining-room. The chamber assigned to me upstairs was rather bright than otherwise — it fronted the sea, and was cheerfully and prettily furnished. I noticed, however, that it was next door to the shut-up and long-deserted studio. The garden was, as Mrs. Fairleigh had declared, full of carnations. I never saw so many of these flowers growing in one spot. They seemed to spring up everywhere, like weeds, even in the most deserted and shady corners. I had been at the château some three or four days, when one morning I happened to be walking alone in a sort of shrubbery at the back of the house, when I perceived in the long dank grass at my feet a large grey stone, that had evidently once stood upright, but had now fallen flat, burying itself partly in the earth. There was something carved upon it. I stooped down, and clearing away the grass and weeds, made out the words

"MANON

Cœur perfide!"

Surely this was a strange inscription! I told my discovery to the Fairleighs, and we all examined and re-examined the mysterious slab, without being able to arrive at any satisfactory explanation of its pictures. Even enquiries made among the villagers failed to elicit anything save shakes of the head, and such remarks as "Ah, Madame! si on savait!..." or "Je crois bien qu'il y a une histoire là!"

One evening we all returned to the château at rather a later hour than usual, after a long and delightful walk on the beach in the mellow radiance of a glorious moon. When I went to my room I had no inclination to go to bed — I was wide awake, and moreover in a sort of expectant frame of mind; expectant, though I knew not what I expected.

I threw my window open, leaning out and looking at the moon-enchanted sea, and inhaling the exquisite fragrance of the carnations wafted to me on every breath of the night wind. I thought of many things — the glory of life; the large benevolence of Nature; the mystery of death; the beauty and certainty of immortality, and then, though my back was turned to the interior of my room, I knew — I felt, I was no longer alone. I forced myself to move round from the window; slowly but determinedly I brought myself to confront whoever it was that had thus entered through my locked door; and I was scarcely surprised when I saw "the Lady with the Carnations" standing at a little distance from me, with a most woebegone, appealing expression on her shadowy lovely face. I looked at her, resolved not to fear her; and then brought all my will to bear on unravelling the mystery of my strange visitant. As I met her gaze unflinchingly she made a sort of timid gesture with her hands, as though she besought something.

"Why are you here?" I asked, in a low, clear tone. "Why do you follow me?"

Again she made that little appealing movement. Her answer, soft as a child's whisper, floated through the room —

"You pitied me!"

"Are you unhappy?"

"Very!" And here she clasped her wan white fingers together in a sort of agony. I was growing nervous, but I continued —

"Tell me, then, what you wish me to do?"

She raised her eyes in passionate supplication.

"Pray for me! No one has prayed for me ever since I died — no one has pitied me for a hundred years!"

"How did you die?" I asked, trying to control the rapid beating of my heart. The "Lady with the Carnations" smiled most mournfully, and slowly unfastened the cluster of flowers from her breast — there her white robe was darkly stained with blood. She pointed to the stain, and then replaced the flowers. I understood.

"Murdered!" I whispered, more to myself than to my pale visitor—" murdered!"

"No one knows, and no one prays for me!" wailed the faint sweet spirit voice—" and though I am dead I cannot rest. Pray for me — I am tired!" And her slender head drooped wearily — she seemed about to vanish. I conquered my rising terrors by a strong effort, and said —

"Tell me — you *must* tell me" — here she raised her head, and her large pensive eyes met mine obediently— "who was your murderer?"

"He did not mean it," she answered. "He loved me. It was here" — and she raised one hand and motioned towards the adjacent studio—" here he drew my picture. He thought me false — but I was true. 'Manon, cœur perfide!' Oh, no, no, no! It should be 'Manon, cœur fidèle!'"

She paused and looked at me appealingly. Again she pointed to the studio.

"Go and see!" she sighed. "Then you will pray — and I will never come again. Promise you will pray for me — it was here he killed me — and I died without a prayer."

"Where were you buried?" I asked, in a hushed voice.

"In the waves," she murmured; "thrown in the wild cold waves; and no one knew — no one ever found poor Manon; alone and sad for a hundred years, with no word said to God for her!"

Her face was so full of plaintive pathos, that I could have wept. Watching her as she stood, I knelt at the quaint old prie-Dieu just within my reach, and prayed as she desired. Slowly, slowly, slowly a rapturous light came into her eyes; she smiled and waved her hands towards me in farewell. She glided backwards towards the door — and her figure grew dim and indistinct. For the last time she turned her now radiant countenance upon me, and said in thrilling accents —

"Write, 'Manon cœur fidèle!'"

I cannot remember how the rest of the night passed; but I know that with the early morning, rousing myself from the stupor of sleep into which I had fallen, I hurried to the door of the closed studio. It was ajar! I pushed it boldly open and entered. The room was long and lofty, but destitute of all furniture save a battered-looking, worm-eaten easel that leaned up against the damp stained wall. I approached this relic of the painter's art, and examining it closely, perceived the name "Manon" cut roughly yet deeply upon it. Looking curiously about, I saw what had nearly escaped my notice — a sort of hanging cupboard, on the left-hand side of the large central bay window. I tried its handle — it was unlocked, and opened easily. Within it lay three things — a palette, on which the blurring marks of long obliterated pigments were still faintly visible; a dagger, unsheathed, with its blade almost black with rust; and — the silver filigree sticks of a fan, to which clung some mouldy shreds of yellow lace. I remembered the fan the "Lady with the Carnations" had carried at the Théâtre Français; and I pieced together her broken story. She had been slain by her artist lover — slain in a sudden fit of jealousy ere the soft colours on his picture of her were yet dry — murdered in this very studio; and no doubt that hidden dagger was the weapon used. Poor Manon! Her frail body had been cast from the high rock on which the château stood "into the wild cold waves," as she or her spirit had said; and her cruel lover had carried his wrath against her so far as to perpetuate a slander against her by writing "Cœur perfide" on that imperishable block of stone! Full of pitying thoughts I shut the cupboard, and slowly left the studio, closing the door noiselessly after me.

That morning as soon as I could get Mrs. Fairleigh alone I told her my adventure, beginning with the very first experience I had had of the picture in the Louvre. Needless to say, she heard me with the utmost incredulity.

"I know you, my dear!" she said, shaking her head at me wisely; "you are full of fancies, and always dreaming about the next world, as if this one wasn't good enough for you. The whole thing is a delusion."

"But," I persisted, "you know the studio was shut and locked; how is it that it is open now?"

"It isn't open!" declared Mrs. Fairleigh—" though I am quite willing to believe you dreamt it *was*."

"Come and see!" I exclaimed eagerly; and I took her upstairs, though she was somewhat reluctant to follow me. As I had said, the studio *was* open. I led her in, and showed her the name cut on the easel, and the hanging cupboard with its contents. As these convincing proofs of my story met her eyes, she shivered a little, and grew rather pale.

"Come away," she said nervously—" you are really *too* horrid! I can't bear this sort of thing! For goodness' sake, keep your ghosts to yourself!" I saw she was vexed and pettish, and I readily followed her out of the barren, forlorn-looking room. Scarcely were we well outside the door when it shut to with a sharp click. I tried it — it was fast locked! This was too much for Mrs. Fairleigh. She rushed downstairs in a perfect paroxysm of terror; and when I found her in the breakfast-room she declared she would not stop another day in the house. I managed to calm her fears, however; but she insisted on my remaining with her to brave out whatever else might happen at what she persisted now in calling the "haunted" château, in spite of her practical theories. And so I stayed on. And when we left Brittany, we left all together, without having had our peace disturbed by any more manifestations of am unearthly nature. One thing alone troubled me a little — I should have liked to obliterate the word "*perfide*" from that stone, and to have had "*fidèle*" carved on it instead; but it was too deeply engraved for this. However, I have seen no more of "the Lady with the Carnations." But I know the dead need praying for — and that they often suffer for lack of such prayers — though I cannot pretend to explain the reason why. And I know that the picture in the Louvre is not a Greuze, though it is called one — it is the portrait of a faithful woman deeply wronged; and her name is here written as she told me to write it —

"MANON

Cœur fidèle!"

MY WONDERFUL WIFE

CHAPTER I

She was really a wonderful woman! — I always said so! She captivated me with a smile; she subjugated my frail and trembling soul with a glance. She took such utter possession of me from the very moment I set eyes on her that I had no longer any will of my own; in fact, to this day I don't know how I came to marry her. I have a hazy idea that *she* married me. I think it is very likely, knowing, as I know now, what a powerful, sweeping-away-of-all-obstacles sort of intellect she has. But when I first saw her she was a glorious girl! One of those "fine" girls, don't you know? — with plump shoulders, round arms, ample bosom, full cheeks, good teeth and quantities of hair — a girl with "go," and "pluck," and plenty of "style just the kind of creature for a small, mild, rather nervous man like me. She had just come back from the Highlands, where she had "brought down" a superb stag with a single unerring shot from her gun; and all the blowsy glow of the Scotch breeze was about her, and all the scent of the gorse and heather seemed to come out in whiffs from her cropped and frizzy "fringe." She talked — ye gods! how amazingly she talked — she laughed, till the superabundant excess of her immense vitality made me positively envious! She danced with the vigour and swing of a stalwart amazon — danced till my brain swung round and round in wild gyrations to the delirious excitement of her ceaseless twirl. For *she* never tired, never felt faint, never got giddy — not she! She was in sound health, mark you; sound and splendid physical condition, and had appetite enough for two ordinary men of middle size; moreover, she ate a mixture of things that *no* ordinary man could possibly eat without future spasms. I watched her that night we met (we were at one of those "at homes" with a small "dancing" in the corner of the card which help to make up the melancholy pleasures of London social life) — I watched her, I say, in breathless surprise and admiration, as between every couple of dances she ate three ices and a plateful of lobster-salad — I stared at her in unfeigned ecstasy and awe when at supper she made such short work of the mayonnaise, the salmon and cucumber, the veal and ham pie, the cream puffs, the red jelly, the cheese and sardines, the champagne and tipsy-cake, and then *more* ice cream! I hastened to provide her with two cups of coffee, one after the other, and a thrill of wonder and delight ran through me when, in reply to my interested query, "Does not coffee keep you awake at night?" she gave a loud and cheerful laugh at my simplicity and replied —

"Me? Why, I sleep like a top, and wake as fresh as a daisy."

Fresh as a daisy! How suggestively beautiful! I believed her thoroughly. Such a physique as she had, such a clear skin, such a bright, full, almost wild eye! Health radiated from her; her very aspect was invigorating as well as commanding, and I was completely overpowered and taken captive by her superb masterfulness and self-assertion. She was so utterly unlike the women in Walter Scott's novels, you know — the women our great-grandfathers used to admire — those gentle, dignified, retiring, blushing personages, who always wanted men to fight for them and protect them — poor, wretched weaklings *they* were, to be sure! Of course, all that sort of thing was very pretty and made a man think himself of some consequence and use in the world; but it was great nonsense when you come to consider it. Why should men be at the bother of looking after women? They can look after themselves, and pretty sharply, too; they have proved it over and over again. And as to business, they beat a man hollow in their keen aptitude for money transactions.

Well, as I was saying, this splendid girl, Honoria Maggs — that was her name — bowled me over completely—" knocked me into a cocked hat," as I heard the Duke of Havilands remark the other day at a race-meeting, and as he is a royal and exalted individual I suppose it is the most aristocratic expression in vogue. One must always strive to imitate one's betters; and he is unquestionably my better by several thousands of pounds, for nowadays, as we are all aware, we only rank superiority in mind by superfluity of cash. I recognised in this same Honoria Maggs my fate, from whom there was no escaping; I followed her from "at home" to "at home," from ball to ball, from concert to concert, from race-course to racecourse, with an unflagging pertinacity that bordered on mania — a pertinacity which surprised everybody, myself included. I don't know why I did it, I'm sure. If it will gratify the "spiritualists," I am quite willing to set it down to "astral influence." On the other hand, if it will oblige the celebrated Dr. Charcot, of Paris, I am ready to believe it was hypnotism. She "drew" me — yes, that is the correct term. Honoria Maggs "drew" me on, and I allowed myself to be "drawn," regardless of future consequences. At last things came to the usual crisis. I proposed. I made a full and frank statement of the extent of my financial resources, carefully explained how much I had to my credit in the bank, and how much was invested in Consols, all with an agreeably satisfactory result. I was accepted, and for the next month or two went about receiving the congratulations of my friends, and inanely believing myself to be the happiest of men. During our courtship Honoria was not in the least bit sentimental; she was far too sensible for that. She never wanted a kiss in a dark passage; she would have been justly enraged had I suggestively trodden on her toes under the table. She never wished to stop and look at the moon on her way home from any neighbour's house or place of amusement; not a bit of it! She was a thoroughly practical, capable, healthy female, utterly devoid of romance. I was glad of this, because I had been lately reading in the magazines and newspapers that romance of any kind was unwholesome, and I did not want an unwholesome wife. And she was tremendously healthy; there was no sickly mawkishness or die-away languor about *her!* She wrote a novel — yes, and published it too; but it was not rubbish, you understand. By rubbish, I mean it was not full of silly sentiments, like Byron's verses or Shakespeare's plays; it had no idyllic-sublime stuff in it. It was a sporting novel, full of slap-dash vigour and stable slang; a really jolly, go-ahead, over-hill-and-dale, crosscountry sort of book, with just a thread of a plot in it, which didn't matter, and an abrupt wind-up that left you in the lurch, wondering what it was all about; in short, the kind of reading that doesn't bother a fellow's brain. It was a great success, partly because she, Honoria Maggs, found out the names of all the critics and "beat them up," as she frankly said, in her own irresistibly dominant way, and partly because the Duke of Havilands (I mentioned him just now) swore it was "the most doosid clever thing he had ever clapped eyes on in print." Her name was in everybody's mouth for a short time, and in the full flush of her glory she went off to the moors partridge-shooting, and "bagged" such a quantity of game that the fact was chronicled in all the society journals; particularly that smart paper that always abuses our venerable Queen in its delightful columns. She rose higher than ever in popular estimation. Redfern implored her to let him "build" her gowns; all the rival tailors sent her their circulars and estimates free of charge; the various makers of soap entreated her to use their different specimens regularly every morning; the photographers offered her "sittings" gratis, and she was very nearly becoming a "professional beauty," as well as a crack shot and literary genius. Yes, I know "*genius*" is a big word; but if Honoria Maggs did *not* have genius, then, I ask, what *did* she have? What active demon or legion of demons possessed her? But I anticipate. I have just remarked that she was at this time nearly becoming a "professional beauty," and in that character might possibly have gone on the stage, there to get rid of some of that amazing energy of which she had such a superabundance, but that I stepped in and cut matters short by marrying her. Yes; I suppose I *did* marry her. I must have done so, though, as I before hinted, it seems to me that she was the imperative, and I the passive party in the arrangement. I know my responses in church at the marriage service were very inaudible, and that hers were so distinctly uttered that they echoed through the chancel and almost frightened me by their decisive resonance. But she always had a resonant voice; good lungs, you know — not a touch of consumption *there!*

It was a pretty wedding, people said. It may have been. I know nobody looked at or thought of *me.* I was the least part of the ceremony — the bride was everything; the bride always *is* everything. And yet the bridegroom is an absolute necessity; he is wanted, is he not? The affair would not go on well without him? Then *why* is he, as a rule, so obstinately ignored and despised by his friends and relatives at his own wedding? This is one of the perplexing problems of social life that I shall never, never understand!

We had a great number of presents. My wife, of course, had the most; and one among her numerous marriage gifts struck me as singularly inappropriate. It was a cigar and ash tray, in oak and silver, very prettily engraved with her monogram, and it came from the friend she had been staying with in the Highlands, when she had brought down the stag with the six-branched antlers; antlers which now, tipped with silver, were destined to adorn the entrance-hall of our new house. When we were driving away from the scene of our bridal festivities, and endeavouring to shield ourselves from the shower of rice that was being pelted through the carriage-windows by our over-zealous well-wishers, I remarked playfully —

"That was a singular gift for you, my darling, from Mrs. Stirling of Glen Ruach — she must have meant it for *me!*"

"Which?" demanded Honoria abruptly. (She never wasted words.)

"The cigar and ash tray," I replied.

"Singular?" and the newly-made partner of my joys and sorrows turned upon me with a brilliant smile in her fine eyes. "Not singular at all. She knows I smoke."

Smoke! A feeble gurgle or gasp of astonishment came from my lips and I fell back a little in the carriage.

"Smoke? *You* smoke, Honoria? — You — you—"

She laughed aloud. "Smoke? I should think so! Why, you silly old boy, didn't you know that? Haven't you smelt my tobacco before now? Real Turkish! — here you are!"

And she produced from her pocket a mannish-looking leather case embossed with silver, full of the finest "golden-hair" brand so approved by connoisseurs, and having at one side the usual supply of rice-paper wherewith to make cigarettes. She rolled up one very deftly as she spoke, and held it out to me.

"Have it?" she asked carelessly; but I made a sign of protest and she put it back in the case with another laugh.

"Very rude you are!" she declared. "Very! You refuse the first cigarette made for you by your wife!"

This was a stab, and I felt it keenly.

"I will take it presently, Honoria," I stammered nervously; "but — but — my darling, my sweetest girl, I do not like you to smoke!"

"Don't you?" and she surveyed me with the utmost nonchalance. "Sorry for that! But it can't be helped now! *You* smoke — I've seen you at it."

"Yes, yes, I do; but I am a man, and — and—"

"And I am a woman!" finished Honoria composedly. "And we twain have just been made *one!* So I have as much right to smoke as you, old boy, being part and parcel of you; and we'll enjoy our cigars together after dinner."

"Cigars!"

"Yes; or cigarettes — which you please. It doesn't matter in the least to me; I'm accustomed to both!"

I sat dumb and bewildered. I could not realise the position. I stared at my bride, and suddenly observed a masculine imperviousness in her countenance that surprised me; a determination of chin that I wondered I had not noticed before. A vague feeling of alarm ran through me like a cold shiver. Had I made a mistake after all in my choice of a wife? And was this fine bouncing creature — this splendidly-developed, vigorously healthy specimen of womanhood going to prove too much for me? I recoiled from my own painful thoughts. I had always laughed to scorn those weak-spirited men who allowed themselves to be mastered by their wives. Now, was *I* also destined to become a laughing-stock for others? And should *I* also be ruled with the female rod of iron? Never, never, *never!* I would rebel — I would protest! But in the mean time — well, I was just married, and, as a perfectly natural consequence, I dared not speak my mind!

CHAPTER II

That evening — the evening of my marriage day — I beheld a strange and remarkable spectacle. It was after dinner in our private sitting-room (we had engaged apartments at a very charming hotel down at Tenby, where we meant to pass the honeymoon), and my wife had just left me, saying she would return in an instant. I drew a chair up to the window and gazed at the sea; and, after a little while, I felt in my pocket and pulled out my cigar-case. I looked at it affectionately, but I resisted the temptation to smoke. I made up my mind that I would not be the first to suggest the idea to Honoria. For if she *had* fallen into such an unwomanly vice, then it was clearly my duty as her husband to get her out of it. Here some captious readers may say, "Well, if you didn't mind her going about with a gun, you ought to have been prepared for her having other masculine accomplishments as well." Now, just allow me to explain. I *did* mind her going about with a gun; I minded it very much; but, then, I was always an old-fashioned sort of fellow with old-fashioned notions (I am trying to break myself of them by degrees), and one of these notions was a deep respect and chivalrous homage for the ladies of the English aristocracy. I believed them to be the *ne plus ultra* of everything noble and grand in woman, and I felt that whatever *they* did *must* be right, and not only right, but perfectly well-bred, since it is their business and prerogative to furnish models of excellent behaviour to all their sex. And when Honoria was still Miss Maggs, and made her mark as a sportswoman, she was only imitating the example (for I read it in the society papers) of three of the most exalted ladies of title in the land. Moreover, I thought that after all it was merely a high-spirited girl's freak, just to show that she could, on occasion, shoot as well as a man. I felt quite sure that when Miss Maggs became Mrs. Hatwell-Tribkin (William Hatwell-Tribkin is my name) she would, to speak poetically, lay aside the gun for the needle, and the game-bag for the household linen. Such was my limited conception of the female temperament and intelligence. But I know better now! And since I have learned that the "highest ladies in the land" *smoke* as well as shoot — well, I will not say openly what I think! I will merely assure those who may be interested in my feelings on the subject, that I have now no old-fashioned partiality whatever for *such* aristocratic personages; let them do as they like and sink to whatever level they choose, only for Heaven's sake let them *not* be taken as the best examples we can show of England's wives and mothers! Several persons who have recently aired their opinions in the roomy columns of the *Daily Telegraph* (all honour to that blessed journal, which provides so wide and liberal a pasture land *gratis* for sheep-like souls to graze upon!) have advocated smoking for women as a perfectly harmless and innocent enjoyment, tending to promote pleasant good-fellowship between the sexes. All I can say is, let one of these special pleaders marry an inveterate woman-smoker, and try it!

The evening of one's marriage day is not exactly an evening to quarrel upon, and so I could not quarrel with Honoria, when she treated me to the amazing spectacle alluded to at the commencement of this chapter — the spectacle of herself, transformed. She came back into the sitting-room with that cheerful, wholesome laugh of hers (Oscar Wilde and others might think it a trifle too loud, still it was lively), and said —

"*Now* I'm comfortable! Got a chair for me? That's right! Push it up in that corner, and let's be chummy!"

I gazed at her as she spoke, and my voice died away in my throat; I could almost feel my hair rising slowly from my scalp in amazement and horror. What — *what* did my Honoria — my bride, whom I had lately seen a rustling vision of white silk and lace and orange-blossoms, what did she look like? Like a *man!* Ye gods! yes, though she had petticoats on — like a *man!* She had changed her pretty travelling dress for a short and extremely scanty brown tweed skirt; with this she wore a very racy-looking jacket of coarse flannel, patterned all over with large horse-shoes on a blue ground. On her head she had perched a red smoking-cap with a long tassel that bobbed over her left eyebrow, and she surveyed me as she sat down with an air of bland unconsciousness, as though her costume were the most natural thing in the world. I said nothing; she did not expect me to say anything, I suppose. She glanced at the sea, shining with a lovely purple in the evening light, and said briefly —

"Looks dull rather, doesn't it? Wants a few racers about. Fancy! I had no yachting this year — all the boys went away to Ireland instead."

"What boys?" I murmured faintly, still staring at her with dazed, bewildered eyes. She was a boy herself, or very like one!

Again that cheerful laugh vibrated in my ears.

"What boys? Good gracious, Willie, if I were to run over all their names, it would be like an hotel visitors' list! I mean *the* boys. All the men who used to take me about, don't you know?"

A kind of resolution fired my blood at this.

"They will hardly take you about *now*," I said, with, I hope, a gentle severity. "You are married now, Honoria, and it will be *my* proud privilege to take you about, so that we shall be able to dispense with the *boys*."

"Oh, certainly, if you like," she replied, smiling unconcernedly; "only you'll soon get tired of it, I expect! We can't always hunt in couples — Darby and Joan sort of thing — awfully bad form; must go different ways sometimes. You'll get sick to death of always doing the different seasons with me.

"Never, Honoria!" I said firmly. "I shall be perfectly happy with you for ever at my side; perfectly contented to be seen always in your company!"

"Really!" and she raised her eyebrows a little, then laughed again, and added coaxingly, "Don't be spooney, Will, there's a good fellow! I do hate being spooned upon — *you* know! Let us be as jolly as you like; but though we *are* just married, don't let people take us for a pair of fools!"

"I fail to understand your meaning, Honoria," I said rather vexedly. "Why *should* we be taken for fools? I really cannot see—"

"Oh, *you* know," laughed my boyish-looking wife, diving into one of her capacious jacket-pockets in search of a *something* — I instinctively knew what it was. Yes, there, out it came! No cigarette-case this time, but one full of *cigars*, and I at once rose to the occasion with a manly fortitude that, I trust, did not ill become me.

"Honoria," I said, "Honoria, my dear, my darling! *Do* oblige me by *not* smoking; not this evening, at any rate! I shall not be able to bear the sight of a cigar in *your* sweet mouth; I shall not indeed. I *am* a 'spooney' fellow, perhaps, but I love you and admire you, my dear, too much to let you appear even before *my* eyes at a disadvantage. It is not good for your health, I assure you! It will spoil your pretty teeth and play havoc with your nerves; and, besides this, Honoria, it is *not* a nice thing for a woman, especially an English woman. It is all very well for ugly Russian matrons and withered old Spanish gipsies, but for a young, bonnie, fresh creature like you, Honoria, it is not the thing, believe me! Moreover, it gives you a masculine appearance, which is not at all becoming. I am in earnest, my dear! I want my wife to be above all things womanly, and now we are married I can tell you frankly that I hope you will never take a *gun* in your hands again. It was very plucky of you to show that you *could* shoot, you know, Honoria. I admired your spirit, but, of course, I always knew you only did it for fun. A woman can never be an actual follower of sport, any more than she can become a practised smoker, without losing the beautiful prestige of modesty and dignity with which Nature has endowed her."

Thus far Honoria had listened to me in absolute silence, a smile on her lips and her cigar-case still open in her hand. Now, however, she gave way to unfeigned and irrepressible laughter.

"Upon my word," she exclaimed, "I never heard a better bit of sentimental palaver than that! Willie, you *are* a goose! For pity's sake, don't talk such old-fashioned nonsense to me. I'm past it. Georgie might like that sort of thing" (Georgie was my wife's youngest sister, a timid little morsel of a woman I had always despised), "but I thought you knew *me* better. Come, you're longing to have a smoke yourself, you know you are! Here!" and she held out her cigar-case with the most brilliant smile in the world. "You won't? Don't be a mule, now!" and she whipped out of her side-pocket a tiny silver match-box, lit a cigar, and again proffered it to me. I took it mechanically. I should have been a brute to refuse her on *that* evening of all evenings; but I still remonstrated feebly.

"Honoria, I don't like it—"

"Don't like what?" she inquired mirthfully. "The cigar? Then you don't know the flavour of good tobacco!"

"No, no, I don't mean the cigar," I said, puffing at it slowly as I spoke; "it is an exceedingly choice cigar, in fact, remarkably so; but I don't like *your* smoking one."

And I watched her in melancholy amaze as she placed a similar cigar to my own between her rosy lips and began to puff away in evident delight. "I don't like your smoking," I repeated earnestly. "No, Honoria, I do *not*! I shall never like it!"

"Then you're very selfish," she returned, with perfect good-humour. "You wish to deprive your wife of a pleasure you indulge in yourself."

Now, *there* was a way of putting it!

"But, Honoria," I urged, "surely, surely men are permitted to do may things which, pardon me, are hardly fitted for the finer susceptibilities of women?"

She flicked off the ash from her "weed" with her little finger, settled her smoking-cap, and smiled a superior smile.

"Not a bit of it!" she replied. "Once, in those detestable 'good old times' some people are always talking about, men *were* permitted to keep women out of every sort of enjoyment, and nice tyrants they were! But now, *nous avons change tout cela*" — she had a very charming French accent by the way—" and we are no longer the drudges, housekeepers, general servants and nurses that adorned that bygone age of darkness! We are the equals of man. What he can do, we can do as well, and often better; we are his companions now, not his slaves. For instance, here am I — your wife — am I not?"

"Just so, Honoria," I murmured. What an excellent cigar she had given me, to be sure!

"You are indeed my wife, my very dearly beloved wife—"

"Don't!" she interrupted. "It sounds like an epitaph!"

I laughed — it was impossible to help laughing. She was such a whimsical creature, such an extraordinary girl! She laughed too, and went on —

"Suppose I had lived and suppose *you* had lived in the 'good old times,' Willie, do you know what we should have done?"

I shook my head drowsily in the negative, and blinked my eyes at her in bland admiration. (That cigar was really first-class, and it was gradually having a softening influence on my brain.)

"We should have *died* of dulness," she declared emphatically. "Just *died* of it! We could never have borne it. Fancy! I should have been shut up nearly all day in the house, with a huge apron on, sorting jams and pickles, and counting over the sheets and pillow-cases like a silly old noodle, and *you* would have tumbled home drunk regularly every afternoon, and gone to bed under the table every evening!"

She nodded her head decisively and the tassel of her smoking-cap came down over her nose. She cast it off defiantly and looked at me with such a twinkling mischief in her eyes that I fairly roared.

"That last part of the daily entertainment would have been lively, Honoria" — I giggled convulsively—" lively for *me* at any rate!"

"No, it wouldn't," she said. "You've no idea how tired you'd have got of being continually drunk! It might be all very well for a time, but you would have wanted a change. And in that period there was *no* change possible! A man and his wife had to jog on together for ever and a day — Amen to it! — without a single distraction to mar the domestic bliss of the awful years! Domestic bliss — ugh! it makes me shudder!"

I grew suddenly serious. "Why, surely, Honoria," I said, "you believe in domestic bliss, don't you?"

"Certainly not! Good gracious, no! What on earth is domestic bliss all about? I've studied it, I assure you. I'll tell you what it is. In winter, the united members of a large family sit solemnly round the fire and roast chestnuts to the tune of 'Home, sweet Home,' played by the youngest boy on the old harmonium (harmonium that belonged to darling dear grandmamma, you know!); in summer they all go down to the sea-side (still fondly united) and sit in a ring on the hot sand, reading antediluvian novels, quite happy! and *so* good, and *so* devoted to one another, and *so* ugly, most of them; no wonder they can never get any other company than their own!"

She puffed away at her cigar quite fiercely, and her eyes twinkled again. As for me, I was off once more in an uncontrollable fit of laughter.

"Honoria, Honoria!" I gasped, "what a droll girl you are; where *do* you get your ideas from?"

"Can't imagine," she replied smilingly. "They come. Inspiration, I suppose, as the towzle-haired 'geniuses' say. But I *am* jolly — I believe there's no denying *that*. You'll find me quite a good fellow, don't you know, when you've once got accustomed to my ways. But I may as well tell you at once that it's no use your expecting me to give up my smoke. It's possible I may get tired of shooting; when I do I'll let you know. And one word more, old boy — don't preach at me again, will you? Can't bear being preached at; never could. Say right out what you mean without sentiment, and we'll see how we can settle it. I never lose temper — waste of time. Much better to come to a calm understanding about everything — think so?"

I agreed heartily, and would have kissed her, but that vile cigar stuck out of her mouth and prevented me. Besides, I was smoking my own particular "vile" and it was no use disturbing myself or her just then. Moreover, did she not evince a wholesome dislike of sentiment? And is not kissing a sentimental business, totally unsuited to the advanced intelligence of the advanced woman of our advancing day?

CHAPTER III

Honeymoons are generally supposed to be the briefest of all moons, and mine was particularly so, as it only lasted a fortnight. I will not here attempt to describe the chronic state of wonder, doubt, affection, dismay, admiration, and vague alarm in which I passed it. It seemed to me that I was all the time in the company of a very cheerful, good-tempered lad just home from his college for the holidays. I knew this "lad" was a woman and my wife, but somehow, as the Americans say, I couldn't "fix" it. At the end of our recognised "spooney" season, we returned to our own house in Kensington, a comfortable dwelling, luxuriously furnished, and provided with all the modern improvements, electric light included, and settled down to the serious realisation of our married existence. We had hosts of friends; too many friends, I thought. We certainly could not boast of a "quiet" home, neither could we be accused of indulging in the guilty tameness of "domestic bliss." All "the boys" fraternized with me; those "boys" who before Honoria's marriage had been, she assured me, like so many brothers to her. They were most of them young men, none of them above thirty, and I was approaching my fortieth birthday. Moreover, I had the sundry cares of the business of living upon me; the "Battle of Life" (I have to thank the noble *Daily Telegraph* for this admirable and entirely new expression) had to be fought by me single-handed, and this gave me the appearance of being older than I actually was. In fact "the boys" seemed to consider me a sort of harmless *paterfamilias;* but I myself often wondered whether I was not more like the meek proprietor of an exceptionally convenient hotel, where bachelors under thirty might find board, lodging, and good entertainment free of charge. At first, I did not feel my position so keenly, because really "the boys" were not bad fellows. They were like young colts, frisky and full of fun. They were fools undoubtedly, but they were not knaves, and to this day I don't think there was an ounce of wit among them, so that they lacked the means to be seriously mischievous; in fact there was no malice about them, they were too absolutely silly for that — more like Brobdingnagian babies than men. They had a great many old associations with Honoria. Many of them had known her long before I did, and one of these declared to me joyously that "it was no end of a lark, dontcherknow, to think she was married!" I would have sought an explanation from this vivacious and muscular youth (he was over six feet high) as to his reasons for considering it "no end of a lark" but that he was such an utterly brainless "boy," such a cheerfully-confessed and openly-advertised donkey, that I saw at once it would be no use asking him any questions that did not lead up somehow or other to a discussion on lawn-tennis, which was the only subject in earth or heaven that appealed to his minute fragment of intellect. There was just one other individual who surpassed him in fatuous foolishness; this was a "boy" with heavy moustaches, whose sole delight in life was to "scull." Sculling up and down the river, sculling here, sculling there (with a very useless skull of his own, Heaven knows! — excuse the unintentional pun), his pride and joy were concentrated in the steady work of strengthening his muscles and reducing his brain by swift degrees from the little to the infinitely less. He had fine eyes, this "boy," and his moustaches, "long, silky and sweeping" (vide "Ouida"), threw all little school-girls and inexperienced housemaids into ecstasies of admiration. He looked very well in his white boating flannels; so well, that he was, by some rash persons who did not know him, judged intelligent, but, to speak with exactitude, a more hopeless idiot never existed. He was such an overpoweringly polite idiot too, exceedingly deferential to me, and automatically courteous to everyone, though he always maintained that delightfully funny air of coy reserve which very good-looking young men sometimes assume, that air which is meant as a mild touch-me-not or warner-off to over-susceptible ladies — for these sort of absurd fellows generally flatter themselves that every woman who sees them is bound to fall in love with them on the spot. This particular "boy" was constantly in and out of our house; he liked Honoria because she made such game of him and his stand-offish manner. I suppose the poor devil was so flattered everywhere else (on account of those moustaches) that he found some comfort in being ridiculed now and then. And my wife had a great talent for ridicule, an immense and ever-developing talent; she "chaffed" people unmercifully; in fact, after the novelty of our marriage had worn off a bit, she began to "chaff" me. I am bound to confess I did not quite like this, but I forbore to complain — she had such high spirits, I thought, and she did not really mean to wound my feelings.

However, taking it all in all, home was not the home I had hoped for. There was no repose in it — no relief from the business fatigues and worries of the day. And the whole place was always horribly redolent of tobacco — tobacco-smoke permeated every room in it, including even the big dining-room — and the smell of cigars was in my nostrils morning, noon and night. All those "boys" smoked, of course; they were very friendly, and used to sit chatting away with me after dinner till long past midnight (Honoria being of the party). I could scarcely turn them out without being rude, and naturally I did not wish to be rude to my wife's old friends. I had my own friends also, but they were men of a different stamp. They were older, more serious, more settled in their modes of life; they liked to talk on the politics, progress and science of the age; and though they admired Honoria (for she could converse well on any subject) they could not get on with the "boys," no, not with any of them. So one by one they dropped off, and by and by a sort of desolate shutout feeling began to steal over me — and I wondered ruefully if I should be obliged to go on living like this for the rest of my days. I sat down in my arm-chair one evening and seriously considered my position. Honoria was out; she had gone to supper with her friend Mrs. Stirling, of Glen Ruach (the misguided woman who had presented her with that wedding-gift of the cigar and ash tray), who was staying in London for a couple of weeks, and I knew they and their "set" would make a night of it. I had not been asked to join the party — I was evidently not wanted. I sat, as I said, in my chair, and looked at the fire; it was cold weather, and the wind whistled drearily outside the windows, and I took to hard and earnest *thinking*. Was I happy in my married life? No! most emphatically *not*. But why? I asked myself. What prevented my happiness? Honoria was a bright woman, a clever woman, handsome, good-tempered and cheerful as the day, never ill, never dull, never cross. What on earth was my complaint? I sighed heavily; I felt I was unreasonable; and yet, I had certainly missed something out of my life — something I felt the want of now. Was it the frequent visitations of "the boys" that fretted my mind? No, not exactly; for, as I said before, they were thoroughly harmless fellows. And as for Honoria herself, whatever her faults (or what I considered her faults) might be, she was good as gold, with a frank, almost blunt straight-forwardness and honesty about her that was really admirable — in fact, she was the kind of woman to knock down a man who would have dared to offer her any insult; and thus far her "mannishness" set her above all suspicion of deceit or infidelity. It was impossible to doubt her word — she never told a lie — and she had a sort of military-disciplined idea of honour, rare to find in the feminine nature. Yes, her sterling virtue was unquestionable. What qualities, then, did she lack? Why did I feel that she was in a way removed from me, and that instead of having a woman by my side, I had a sort of hybrid human growth which was neither man nor woman — which confused and perplexed me instead of helping and comforting me, and which filled me with surprise rather than respect? Again I sighed, and stirring the smouldering fire into a blaze watched its flickering flashes on the wall of the room. It was a large room — we called it the library, because there were books in it. Not rare volumes by any means, still what there were I liked; in fact they were mostly mine. My wife read nothing but the newspapers; she devoured the *Referee* on Sundays, and she took the *Sporting Times* because she always had certain bets on certain racing events. Needless to say I objected to her betting, but with no result beyond the usual laugh, and the usual, "Don't be a goose, Willie; it's all right! I never bet with *your* money!" Which was true enough. She had turned out another sporting novel at a "dead heat," as she herself expressed it; the publisher had paid her well for it, and she certainly had every right to do as she liked with her own earnings. Moreover, she generally won her bets, that was the odd part of it; she seemed to have an instinctive faculty for winning. Her losses were always small, her gains always large. In fact, as I have already remarked, she was a wonderful woman!

Apropos of this last novel of hers, I reflected uneasily that I had not yet read a word of it. It was only just published, I had seen no reviews of it, and she seemed to attach no importance to it herself. She had no real love for literature; she called all the ancient classic writers "old bores," and all the works of the after-giants, such as Shakespeare, Byron, Shelley, Walter Scott, Dickens, or Thackeray, "stuff and rubbish." *She* wrote a novel as she wrote a letter — almost without taking thought, and certainly without correction. She would hand the proofs over to one of "the boys" who knew all about sporting terms, that he might see whether her slang was correct, and when his hall-mark said (as it did once, for I saw it pencilled on the margin of a chapter), "Bully for you!" off the whole thing went to the publisher without further anxiety or trouble on her part. And when people said to me, sweetly, "Your wife is quite a literary genius?" in the usual humbugging way of polite society, I was very well aware that they didn't mean it; I knew in my very heart of hearts that Honoria, judged strictly from an art and letters point of view, was a *fraud* — positively a *fraud!* The thought stabbed me to the soul, but still I had to think it if I would be at peace with my own conscience. I am not a clever man myself, yet I know very well what female literary "genius" is. We have it in the poems of Elizabeth Barrett and the romances of Georges Sand, and when we consider the imperishable work of such women as these, the sporting novels of even a Honoria Hatwell-Tribkin sink into shadowy insignificance! And I am a great believer in woman's literary capability. I think that, given a woman with a keen instinct, close observation and large sympathies, she ought to be able to produce greater masterpieces of literature than a man. But there is no necessity for her to part with her womanly gentleness because she writes. No, for it is just that subtle charm of her finer sex that should give the superiority to her work — not the stripping herself of all those delicate and sensitive qualities bestowed on her by Nature, and the striving to ape that masculine roughness which is precisely what we want eliminated from all high ideals of art. But, as I have hinted, it was absurd to call *my* wife "literary she was a mere scribbler of sporting platitudes, and I have only been led on to speak of her entering the ranks of pen and ink at all, because (on referring to some back numbers of the *Daily Telegraph)* I understand that there are a few uninstructed persons about, in the shape of "London clergymen" and others, who think that women who write books are *therefore* rendered unwomanly. Never was there a greater mistake. One of the sweetest and most womanly women I ever met is rapidly coming to the front as a most gifted and brilliant writer. She neither smokes nor keeps late hours; she does not hunt, or fish, or shoot; she dresses exquisitely; her voice is "low and sweet" as "Annie Laurie's," and the roughest man of her particular circle — one who has been called the "Ursa Major" of literature — becomes the softest and most courtly *preux chevalier* in her presence, much to the relief and satisfaction of all his and her friends. To my idea the "mannish" woman should be altogether debarred from entering into the profession of literature, inasmuch as she can do no good whatever in it. She takes a wrong view of life; her theories are all at sixes and sevens; she mixes up her rights and privileges with those of the coarser sex till she does not know which is which; she has wilfully blunted all her finer susceptibilities, and is therefore practically useless as a thinker-out of high problems, or a consoler to her fellow-creatures. Literature of itself does not unsex a woman; its proper influence is a softening, dignifying and ennobling one; therefore if, in that calling, a woman proves herself unwomanly in her speech, manners and customs, you may be sure the unsexing process was pretty well completed before she ever took up the pen.

I was still sitting before the fire in melancholy mood, musing over what, reasonably or unreasonably, I felt to be the desolation of my wedded existence, when I heard a latch-key turn in the lock of the street door — another instant, and a firm step marching along the outer passage assured me of my wife's return. I glanced at the clock — it was close upon midnight. I had been alone since dinner-time, alone and melancholy, and I felt more injured and irritated than I cared to admit to myself. A strong whiff of tobacco heralded Honoria's approach; she entered, clad in a long buttoned-up ulster and cloth jockey cap, her eyes brilliant, her cheeks flushed, and a half-smoked-out cigar in her mouth. A sudden anger possessed me. I looked up, but did not speak. She threw off her cloak and cap, and stood before me in evening dress — a clinging gown of grey velvet, touched here and there with silver embroidery.

"Well!" she said cheerfully, removing her cigar from her lips to puff out a volume of smoke, and then sticking it in again.

"Well," I responded somewhat sullenly.

Her bright eyes opened wide.

"Hullo! All down in the mouth and low in the dumps — eh, old boy?" and she poked the fire into a blaze. "What's up? Stocks queer? Bank broken? Shares gone down? You look like an unfortunate publisher!"

"Do I?" and I averted my gaze from hers and stared gloomily into the fire.

"Yes," and she gave that ringing laugh that somehow had latterly begun to jar my nerves. "*You* know the man! — bad-times-no-sale-out-of-season-no-demand-in-the-provinces sort of fellow! Awful! — and all the while he's pocketing profits on the sly. Funny expression he gets after long practice. *You've* got it exactly just now!"

"Thanks!" I said curtly.

She surveyed me wonderingly.

"Got the toothache?" she asked with some commiseration in her voice.

"No."

"Headache?"

"No."

She gave me a meditative side-glance, still smoking, then nodded in a wise and confidential manner.

"*I* know — indigestion!"

This was too much; I jumped up from my chair and faced her.

"No, Honoria," I said, in accents that trembled with suppressed excitement—" it is *not* indigestion! It is nothing of the kind, madam! You see before you a broken, dispirited man — a miserable, homeless wretch who hasn't a moment's peace of his life — who is disgusted — yes, *disgusted*, Mrs. Tribkin — at the way you go on! You are out every day, more often with others than with me; and if you are not out, the house is full of gorging, lounging, grinning young fools, who no doubt laugh at me (and at you too, for that matter) in their sleeves. You smoke like — like — a *dragoon!* Yes!" — I spluttered this word out desperately, determined to bring her to book somehow—" and behave yourself altogether in a fashion that *I* consider indecorous and unbecoming to a lady in your position. I will not have it, Honoria! I will NOT have it! I have borne it as long as I *can* bear it, and my patience is quite exhausted! I tell you I am sick of the smell of tobacco — I loathe the very sight of a cigar! Smoking is a detestable, vulgar, and unwholesome vice, and as far as I am concerned I have done with it for ever! I *used* to like a quiet smoke in the evening" — here my voice took on a plaintive, almost tearful, wail—" but now — now, Honoria, I *hate* it! *You* have worked this change in me! I have seen you smoking, morning, noon and night, till my very soul has been nauseated by such an unnatural and unfeminine spectacle! You have robbed me of what was once my own peculiar enjoyment — and I can endure it no longer! I cannot, Honoria! I will NOT...!"

I gasped for breath, and sinking back again in my chair, glared steadily at the wall. I was afraid to encounter the whimsical look of my wife's eye, lest I should give way to convulsions of wild laughter — laughter which really would not have been far off the verge of tears, I was so thoroughly shaken from my usual self-control.

"Whe-e-e-e-w!" — and the long and dismally drawn-out whistle she gave made me glance at her for a second. She had taken her cigar from her mouth, and was regarding me fixedly. "Good gracious, Willie! I never did! Look here, you know this won't do at all! I never lose temper — it's no use your trying to make me. I see what it is. You've got the fidgets, and you want to quarrel and make me cry and go off into a fit of hysterics, and then pet me and bring me round again. But it isn't the least bit of good attempting it. I *can't* do it — I *can't* work hysterics anyhow! I never could since I grew up. I might manage to scream once, if that would oblige you, but I *know* it would scare the people next door! Now, don't rant and rave like Wilson Barrett when he's got his red Chatterton wig on, but be calm and sensible, and tell us what's the matter."

She spoke like a friendly young man, and I peered at her doubtfully.

"Honoria," I began, then my feelings got the better of me again, and I muttered, "No, no! it is too much! I will NOT — I *cannot* be calm!"

"Then go to bed," she said soothingly, laying one hand on my shoulder, and looking quite benignantly at me, in spite of my endeavour to bestow upon *her* a lordly scowl. "Something's upset you; your liver's wrong, that I can see in the twinkling of an eye. I haven't studied medicine for nothing!

You should have taken a cooling draught and gone to bye-bye" (gone to *bye-bye!* Silly minx! did she take me for a baby!) "hours ago. Why did you sit up for me?"

I fixed my reproachful gaze upon her, solemnly, penetratingly, and — *quailed!* She looked so handsome, especially now that she had thrown away the end of that horrible cigar. She had such a commanding presence — that clinging grey velvet gown became her so admirably, and round her full white throat she wore the diamond pendant I had given her on our wedding-day — a pendant containing a miniature portrait of myself. *My* portrait! She wore it — she, this stately, beautiful young woman wore my miserable physiognomy on her bosom! My wrath melted into sudden maudlin sentiment.

"Honoria," I said feebly, slipping my arm round her waist—" oh, Honoria! if you only *loved* me!"

She bent her head towards mine, lower and lower till her lips almost touched my ear.

"Look here, old boy," she then whispered confidentially, "you may as well make a clean breast of it! Have you — *have you been at that brandy I left out on the sideboard?*"

CHAPTER IV

It will now, I think, be readily understood that Honoria was a difficult woman to argue with. There was no imaginativeness about her, no romance, no sentiment. If a man gave way to his feelings (as I did on the occasion just related), she set his natural emotion down either to indigestion or insobriety. The "tide of passion" — the "overflowing of the human heart," and all that sort of thing — belonged, she considered, to the "stuff and rubbish" books written by Scott, Thackeray, and Dickens, or, worse still, suggested poetry. And if there was anything in the world Honoria positively hated, it was poetry. She didn't mind the "Ingoldsby Legends" or the "Biglow Papers," but poetry, real poetry, was her favourite abomination. She always went to sleep over a play of Shakespeare's. The only time I ever saw her laugh at any performance of the kind was during Irving's representation of "Macbeth." *Then* she was in silent convulsions of mirth. Whenever the celebrated Henry gasped a gasp, or wriggled a wriggle, she seemed to be seized with spasms. But the play itself didn't move her one iota; she dozed off comfortably in the carriage going home, and waking up suddenly just as we reached our own door, she demanded —

"I say, Willie, what became of the old man who went to stop with Irving in his cardboard castle? Never saw *him* again? Wasn't it funny? Must have left out a bit of the play by mistake!"

I realised then that she had never comprehended the leading *motif* of the sublime tragedy — namely, the murder of King Duncan — and with anxious care and laboured precision I explained it to her as best I could. She listened amiably enough, and, when I had finished, yawned capaciously.

"Good gracious! So *that* was what it was all about! Well, it didn't seem clear to *me*! *I* thought Irving had stuck the *blue* man — the old blue thing with a patch over his eye that came up through a trap-door at dinner-time." (She meant Banquo's ghost!)— "*He* was funny — awfully funny! He was just the colour of a damp lucifer match — *you* know, one of those things that *won't* strike, but only fizzle and smell! Anyhow it was a muddle, couldn't tell who was killed and who wasn't. Lovely last sprawl that of Irving — looked as if he were coming out of his skin! *He* was done for — *he* was killed in the play, wasn't he?"

"He was," I assented gravely.

"*Thats* all right! Hope he ate a good supper afterwards! Must make a man peckish to work about a big sword like that — all for nothing too! Poking at the air — just fancy! Dreadfully exhausting!"

And off she went to bed with no more notion of the grandeur and terror and pathos of Shakespeare's most awe-inspiring production than if she had been a woman of wood! So I *knew* she had no sentiment in her, and of course I was a fool to expect any sympathy from her in my hours of irritation or despondency. And those hours were getting pretty frequent, but for various reasons I held my peace and made no further complaints. I would wait, I resolved, and patiently watch the course of events.

Events progressed onward as they are prone to do, and my wife continued her independently masculine mode of living without any fresh remonstrances from me just then. The time I had anticipated came at last, and a boy was born to us; a remarkably fine child — (yes, I know! the most weazened infant, if it be the first-born, is always "remarkably fine" in the opinion of its parents; but this one was *not* a humbug — he was really and truly a good specimen), and with his birth I became happy and hopeful. Surely *now*, I thought, with a swelling heart — *now* my Honoria will realise her true position, and will grow ashamed of those "mannish" habits, which rob a woman of the refined grace and sweetness that should attach to the dignity of motherhood. My spirits rose. I pictured my wife as a different and more lovable creature, retaining all her bright humour and frank vivacity, but gradually becoming more softened in character, and more chastened in disposition; I saw her, in my mind's eye, carrying her child in her arms, and murmuring all that pretty baby nonsense which men pretend they despise, but which in their hearts they secretly love to hear, and I built up a veritable *château en Espagne* of home-happiness as I had never yet known it, but which I now sincerely believed I was destined to enjoy.

Need I say that my hopes were doomed to disappointment, and that I cursed myself for being such a sentimental ass as to imagine they could ever be realised? Honoria was up and about again in no time, and seemed almost, if not quite, cheerfully unconscious of our boy's existence. He, poor mite, was consigned to the care of two nurses — large, beer-consuming women both, and ungrammatical of speech — and when his screams announced that all was not going well with his infant career — that pins were being put in the wrong places, or that windy spasms were the result of over-feeding, Honoria would smile at me and remark blandly —

"*There's* a savage little brute! Doesn't he *roar!* Never mind! Perhaps he'll scare away the organ-grinders!"

On one of these occasions, when my son's complaints were so heartrending that they threatened to lift the very roof off the house by sheer volume of sound, I said —

"Don't you think you'd better go and see what's the matter, Honoria? It's not quite fair to leave him entirely at the mercy of the nurses!"

"Why not?" she responded composedly. "*They* understand him — I don't. He's a perfect mystery to *me.* He screams if I touch him, and rolls right over on his back and makes the most horrible faces at me when I look at him. Nurse says I hold him wrong — it seems to me impossible to hold him *right.* He's as soft as putty, and bruises everywhere. Can't lay a finger on him without bruising him black and blue. *You* try it! I wanted to amuse him yesterday — blew the cab whistle for him as loud as I could, and I thought he would have burst with howling. We don't take to each other a bit — isn't it funny? He doesn't want me, and I don't want him — we're better apart, really!"

"Honoria," I said (we were at breakfast, and I rose from the table with an angry movement), "you are heartless! You speak cruelly and slightingly of the poor child. You don't deserve to be a mother!"

She laughed good-humouredly.

"You're right, Willie; that's one for you! I don't deserve to be, and I didn't want to be. Oh, what a bear you look! Be off to the City, for goodness' sake; don't stop scowling there! Would *you* like to take baby out for once? I'll fetch him for you — he'll be *such* a nice quiet companion for you down-town!"

I beat a hasty retreat; I had no words wherewith to answer her, but I released my pent-up wrath by banging the street door as I went out with a violence that I freely admit was femininely pettish and unworthy of a man. And I went down to my office in a very angry mood, and my anger was not lessened when, turning sharp round a corner, I ran up against the "boy" with the moustaches.

"So glad to meet you," he said with his gentlemanly drawl and elegant air. "Hope you're coming to the moors this year with Mrs. Tribkin?"

I stared at him — he looked provokingly cool and comfortable in his white flannels (always white flannels! However, it was a fact that August had just begun) — and then I replied with some frigidity —

"I am not aware that Mrs. Tribkin is going to the moors at all. I believe — indeed I am sure — our — er — *my* intention is to spend a quiet holiday at the seaside for the benefit of the child's health."

"Oh," murmured the "boy" languidly. "Then I suppose I have made a mistake. Some one told me she had taken a share in the grouse-shootings this season — gone halves with Mrs. Stirling, of Glen Ruach, dontcherknow. Quite a big party expected down there on the Twelfth."

"Really," I snarled, for I was getting angrier every minute. "Are *you* going?"

He looked fatuously surprised.

"*Me?* Oh, dear, no! I'm on the river."

"You're always on the river now, I suppose, aren't you?" I enquired, with a sarcastic grin.

"Always," he replied placidly. "Won't you and Mrs. Tribkin come and see me in my little house-boat? Awfully snug, dontcherknow — moored in capital position. Delighted to see you any time!"

"Thanks, thanks!" and here I strove to snigger at him politely in the usual "society" way. "But we are very much tied at home just now — my son is rather too young to appreciate the pleasures of river-life!"

"Oh, of course!" And for once the "boy" appeared really startled. "It would never do for a — for a little kid, you know. How is he?" This with an air of hypocritical anxiety.

"He is very well and flourishing," I answered proudly. "As fine a child as—"

"Yes — er — no doubt," interrupted Moustaches hurriedly. "And Honoria — Mrs. Tribkin — is awfully devoted, I suppose?"

"Awfully!" I said, fixing my eyes full and sternly upon his inanely handsome countenance.

"She is *absorbed* in him — absorbed, heart and soul!"

"Curious — I mean delightful!" stammered the hateful young humbug. "Well — er — give my kind regards, please, and just mention that I'm on the river!"

As well mention that Queen Anne was dead, I thought, scornfully, as I watched him dash over a crossing under the very nose of a plunging cab-horse and disappear on the opposite side. He was a fish, I declared to myself — a fish, not a man! Scrape his gills and cook him for dinner, I muttered deliriously as I went along — scrape his gills and cook him for dinner! This idiotic phrase became fixed in my mind, and repeated itself over and over again in my ears with the most tiresome monotony, whereby it will be easily comprehended that my nerves were very much unstrung and my system upset generally by the feverish mental worry and domestic vexation I was undergoing.

On reaching home that afternoon I found Honoria in high glee. She was lounging in one of those long, comfortable "deck" chairs, which, when properly cushioned, are the most luxurious seats in the world, smoking a cigarette and reading *Truth*.

"I say!" she exclaimed, turning round as I entered. "Here's a lark! Georgie's going to marry the Earl of Richmoor!"

I confess I was rather surprised.

"What, *Georgie?*" I echoed incredulously.

"Yes, *Georgie!*" repeated my wife with emphasis. "Little sly, coaxy-woaxy Georgie, who can't say be! to a goose. Going to be a real live countess — think of it! Good gracious, what a fool Richmoor is — he might have had *me!*"

"Might he, indeed, Honoria?" I enquired coldly, drawing off my gloves, and thinking for the thousandth time what a thorough *man* she looked. "Did he know that such a chance of supreme happiness was to be had for the asking?"

"Of course he didn't." Here she tossed away *Truth*, and catching up a horrible fat pug she adored, she kissed its nasty wet nose with effusion. "And he never tried to find out. He's an awful swell, you know — the kind of fellow that coolly 'cuts' the fresh-dollars American, and won't have anything to do with trade. Writes books and sculpts."

"Is that a new word, *sculpts?*" I asked satirically.

"Don't know, I'm sure. It means that he carves out busts and things in marble — not for money, you know, just for his own amusement. Oh, he's a queer card! But fancy his proposing to *Georgie*, of all people in the world — such a little scrub of a woman!"

I reflected on this description. My wife's youngest sister was little, certainly, but she could scarcely, in justice, be called a "scrub." She had beautiful eyes — not so beautiful in colour as in their dreamy expression of tenderness; she had a sweet, soft, kissable face, a charming fairy-like figure, and a very gentle, yet fascinating, manner. There was nothing decidedly "striking" about her, and yet she was about to make a more brilliant match than could have been possibly hoped for an entirely portionless girl in her position. Honoria went on meditatively —

"Yes, he might have had *me*, and just think of the difference! Look at me, and look at Georgie! One would scarcely take us for sisters."

"Scarcely, indeed!" I assented, with a muffled sigh. "Your ways are rather opposed to hers, Honoria. For instance, *she* does not smoke!"

"No, poor little thing!" and Honoria threw away the end of her cigarette and immediately lit another. "She thinks it horrid."

"So do I," I said with marked emphasis—" Honoria, so do I think it horrid!"

She glanced at me, smiling.

"I know you do," she cheerfully admitted; "you've said so often enough." She smoked a little in silence, and then resumed, "Now look here, Willie, listen to me! I've been thinking over things lately, and I've come to the conclusion that we must talk it out! That's the term — talk it out."

"Talk *what* out, Honoria?" I stammered nervously.

"The marriage question," she replied. "There's no doubt whatever that it has been, and that it *is*, a ghastly mistake!"

"*Our* marriage a mistake, dear?" I began anxiously. "Surely you—"

But she checked me with a slight gesture of her hand.

"I don't wish to say that I think ours a greater mistake than anybody else's," she went on. "Not a bit of it. I think *all* marriages are mistakes — the institution itself is a mistake."

I gazed at her blankly. My mind recoiled upon itself and wandered drearily back through long vistas of back numbers of the *Daily Telegraph* (that glorious and ever-to-be-praised journal is everybody's discussion-ground), and there beheld, set forth in large capitals, "Is Marriage a Failure?" attended by masses of correspondence from strong-minded ladies and woeful-spirited men. Was Honoria of the former class, as I most assuredly was of the latter?

"The institution of marriage is itself a mistake," repeated Honoria firmly. "It ties a man to a woman, and a woman to a man, for the rest of their mortal lives, regardless of future consequences. And it doesn't work. The poor wretches get tired of always trotting along cheek by jowl in the same old road, and there's no way of breaking loose unless one or the other elects to become a scamp. There's not change enough. Now, take us two, for example. *You* want a change, and I want a change — that's plain!"

The time had come for me to speak my mind out manfully, and I did so.

"I *do* want a change, Honoria," I said gently, and with all the earnestness I felt, "but not the sort of change you hint at. I want a change, not *away* from you, my dear, but *in* you. I want to see the *womanly* side of your nature — the gentleness, softness and sweetness that are all in your heart, I am sure, if you would only let these lovely qualities have their way, instead of covering them up under the cloak of an assumed masculine behaviour, which, as I have often said to you before, is highly unbecoming to you, and distresses me greatly. I suffer, Honoria, I really suffer, when I see and hear *you,* my wife, aping the manners, customs, and slang-parlance of men. It is surely no disgrace to a woman to be womanly; her weakness is stronger than all strength; her mildness checks anger and engenders peace. In her right position, she is the saving-grace of men; her virtues make them ashamed of their vices, her simplicity disarms their cunning, her faith and truth inspire them with the highest, noblest good. Honoria, dear Honoria! I know there are many women now-a-days who act as you do, and think no shame or harm of it — who hunt and fish and shoot and smoke and play billiards, and who are the declared comrades of men in all their rough sports and pastimes — but, believe me, no good can come of this throwing down of the barriers between the sexes; no advantage can possibly accrue to a great nation like ours from allowing the women to deliberately sacrifice their delicacy and reserve, and the men to resign their ancient code of chivalry and reverence! No, Honoria, it is not in keeping with the law of nature, and whatever is opposed to the law of nature must in time be proved wrong. It will be a bad, a woeful day for England when women as a class assert themselves altogether as the equals of men — for men, even at their best, have vile animal passions, low desires, and vulgar vices that most of them would be bitterly sorry to see reflected in the women whom they instinctively wish to respect. Believe me, dear, I speak from my heart! Give me a little of that self-abnegation which so gloriously distinguishes your sex in times of sickness and trouble! Be a true woman, Honoria; leave off smoking and betting, and let me find in you the sweet wife I need to encourage and cheer me on my way through the world! You are precious to me, Honoria; I want to see you at your best — I want—"

Here my voice failed me. I was sincerely moved; a foolish lump rose in my throat, and I could not go on. Honoria, too, was serious. She had listened with admirable patience, and now, taking her cigarette from her lips, she flicked the ash off and looked at it reflectively.

"It's a bad job," she said at last with a short sigh— "a regular bad job! I'm — I'm *awfully* sorry for you, old boy!"

And she held out her hand to me with a sort of manly candour that was simply indescribable.„ I clasped that hand, I kissed it, whereupon she hastily withdrew it.

"Don't do that," she laughed. "It gives me the creeps! Fact, really! can't bear it! Now listen, Willie! The case is as clear as daylight. You've married the wrong sister!"

"Married the wrong sister!" I echoed bewilderedly.

"Of course you have, you dear old dunderhead! You should have taken Georgie while you had the chance of a choice. She would have sat on your knee, cuddled in your arms, curled your hair with her fingers, and kissed you on the tip of your nose! That's Georgie all over! Turtle-dove and 'Mary's lamb' in one! That's what you wanted, and that's what you haven't got, poor dear! I'm not a dove, and I'm certainly not a lamb. I'm — I'm a fair specimen" — she smiled candidly—" a fair specimen of the woman of the future, and you, old *boy, you* want a woman of the past. Now haven't I hit it off exactly?"

I leaned back in my chair with a half groan, and she continued —

"You see, Willie, you want me to change my nature and become a big transformation scene like they have in those pantomimes, when the old witch of the piece turns into a fairy perched on the edge of a rainbow. Those things are all very well on the stage, but they can't be done in real life. You know I was at school at Brighton?"

I assented, wondering what was coming next.

"Well, there, among other accomplishments, we learnt how to ride, and our riding-master (a dashing sort of fellow, full of fun) taught us how to smoke, lessons *gratis*. Fact! We all learnt it — on the sly, of course, just as he flirted with us all on the sly; but we became proficients in both arts. We were fifty girls at that place, and we all smoked whenever we had the chance, and got to like it. We ate loads of scented bonbons afterwards to kill the smell, and we were never found out. Brighton schools are not celebrated for strictness, you know; the young women do pretty much as they like in every way, and get into no end of scrapes often. But that's wide of the mark.

The point is, that I learnt to smoke at school, and when I came home I met lots of women who smoked also, and naturally I went on with it till the habit became second nature. Why, you might as well ask a washerwoman to give up her tea as ask me to give up my cigar!"

"Is it so bad as that?" I stammered weakly. "Yes, it *is* 'so bad as that' — or so good!" she laughed amiably. "You used not to have such violent prejudices, Willie! You've smoked enough yourself, I'm sure!"

"But, Honoria, I am different—" I began.

"Pardon me," she interposed smilingly; "that is just what I cannot see! I do not understand why there should be any difference between the customs of men and the customs of women."

"Good God!" I exclaimed, sitting bolt upright and speaking with some excitement. "Do you mean to say that women are capable of doing *everything* that men do? Can you contemplate a battle being fought by women? Could they undertake a naval engagement? Are women fit to lay down railways, build bridges and construct canals? Will they break stones on the road and drive hansom-cabs and omnibuses? Will they become stokers and porters? Will they dig wells and put up telegraph wires? I tell you, Honoria, this craze, this mania for striving to make women the equals of men, is as wicked as it is unnatural, and can engender nothing but misery to the nation as well as to the individual!"

"In what rank, then, would you propose to place woman," demanded Honoria calmly, "if she is *not* (as *I* hold she *is*) the equal of man? Is she his inferior or superior?"

"She is his inferior in physical strength," I answered warmly; "his inferior in brute force and plodding power of endurance; his inferior too in consecutive far-planning and carrying out of plans; her brain is too quick, too subtle, too fine, to hold much of the useful quality of that dogged and determined patience which distinguishes so many of our greatest inventors and explorers. But, Honoria, she is (if she is true to herself) infinitely his superior in delicate tact, sweet sympathy, grand unselfishness and divinely-awful purity. I say divinely-awful, because if she be indeed 'chaste as ice and pure as snow,' though she may not escape the calumny of the wicked, she commands and retains the passionate reverence of men who know the worst, side of the world well enough to appreciate such angelic and queenly qualities. Compared with man, woman is therefore his inferior and superior both in one — a complex and beautiful problem, a delicious riddle which the best men never wish to have completely guessed; they prefer to leave something behind the veil — something mysterious and forever sanctified, and shut out from the vulgar gaze of the curious crowd!" Thus far I had proceeded in eloquence when Honoria interrupted me.

"That sounds all very nice and pretty," she said, "but to speak bluntly, it won't wash! Don't talk of your sex, my dear boy, as though they were all romantic knights-errant of the olden time, because they're not! They're nasty fellows, most of them, and if women are nasty too, why, then they help to make them so! Look at them! Talk of smoke, why they're always smoking — dirty pipes, too, full of beastly tobacco — cheap tobacco; and as for their admiration of all those womanly qualities you describe, they don't care a bit for them! They'll run after a ballet-dancer much more readily than they'll say a civil word to a lady, and they'll crowd round a woman whose name has been bandied about in a horrid divorce case, and neglect the good girl who has never made herself notorious."

"Not always," I interposed quickly. "You've got an example in your own sister, and *she* is to marry the Earl of Richmoor."

"True enough," and my wife rose from her chair, shook her skirts, and flung away the last fragment of her cigarette. "But he's an exception — a very rare exception — to the rule. And all the same, Willie, *I* can't change myself any more than the leopard can change his spots, as the Bible says. I'm a result of the age we live in, and you don't quite like me!"

"I *do* like you, Honoria—" I began earnestly.

"No, you don't — not quite!" she insisted, her eyes twinkling satirically. "And I promise you. I'll think over the position very carefully and see what I can do. Meanwhile, you needn't have the *boys* any more if they're disagreeable to you."

"They're not disagreeable," I faltered; "but—"

"Yes, I understand — want the house to yourself. All right! I'll give them the straight tip!

I can see them elsewhere, you know; they're not bound to come here often."

"Elsewhere?" I questioned in some bewilderment. "Where, Honoria, if not here?"

"Oh, all sorts of places," she answered laughingly. "On the river, at the Grosvenor, Hurlingham — heaps of old haunts we used to go to."

"But suppose I object, Honoria," I said with warmth. "Suppose I do not approve of your meeting the 'boys' at these different haunts, what then?"

"Oh, you won't be such an old goose," she replied cheerfully. "You know there's no harm, no real mean *lowness* about *me*, don't you?"

Her clear eyes met mine straightly and truthfully as star-beams.

"Yes, I know, Honoria," I said gently but seriously; "I'm perfectly aware of your goodness and honour, my dear — but there *is* such a thing as gossip; and that you should go about at all with these young men seems to me like a rash laying of yourself open to society backbiting and scandal."

"Not a bit of it," she averred. "Lots of women do it — in fact, *I*'ve not yet come across a married woman who wants to set up for a prude in *these* days! And I couldn't drop the boys altogether, you know — poor chaps, they'd feel it awfully! Now don't be so down in the mouth, Willie. Cheer up! As I told you, I'm going to think over the position and see what I can do for you."

Just at that moment a wild screech from the nursery announced more sufferings on the part of Master Hatwell-Tribkin.

"Doesn't he just *yell!*" remarked Honaria serenely. "Lungs of seasoned leather he must have! Ta-ta!"

And with a light wave of her hand she left me to my own reflections, which were very far indeed from being consolatory. What a strange difficulty I was in! There was not a tinge of wickedness, not the least savour of deceit, about Honoria. She was as honest and true as steel, and yet — yet I was never more dismally conscious of anything in my life than that the time was approaching when I might find it no longer possible to endure her company!

CHAPTER V

The next day, having business in that particular neighbourhood, I lunched at the Criterion. I had scarcely sat down to my modest chop and potatoes when two gentlemen entered and took the table just behind me, and glancing round in a casual sort of way I recognised in one of them the Earl of Richmoor. He was a good-looking fellow, with rather a thoughtful yet kindly face, and a very "winning" smile. I had only met him on one occasion at a large "at home" given by Honoria's mother, and it was not likely he would have any very distinct recollection of me; so I kept my back carefully turned, not wishing to obtrude myself upon his notice. Presently, however, something he was saying to his friend attracted my attention. With my knife and fork suspended in air I listened anxiously.

"It's a thousand pities," he remarked. "She's a handsome creature, wonderfully clever and spirited. I was half inclined to fall in love with her myself at one time, but, by Jove! I wanted a *woman,* you know, not a semi-man in petticoats!"

"She won't wear petticoats long, I should say," returned the other man with a laugh. "If report knows anything about her, she'll be in trousers before she's many years older."

"Heaven forbid!" exclaimed Richmoor, and I heard him pouring out wine into his glass. "If she does, I shall have to cut her, though she *is* Georgie's sister!"

Down clattered my knife and fork, and I drank a large gulp of water to cool my feverish agitation. It was *my wife* they were talking of! and my ears tingled with shame and anger. *My* wife! *My* Honoria!

"She's a *good* woman, you know," added Richmoor presently. "Never plays a double game — couldn't be false if she tried. In fact her only fault is that horrible masculinity of hers; she thinks it's 'the thing,' unfortunately; she fancies men admire it. Poor soul! if she only knew! Of course there *are* some young asses who like to see women smoking and who encourage them to do it, and a few despicable snobs who urge them to shoot and go deer-stalking; but these sort of gaby fellows are in the minority, after all. It's a most pitiable thing to see otherwise nice women wilfully going out of their natural sphere."

"It is — exceedingly so," agreed his friend energetically. "I can't think why they do it; they only get laughed at in the long run. That woman Stirling, of Glen Ruach, helped to spoil Honoria Maggs; she's a regular cad. Have you ever met her?"

"No."

"Oh, *she* dresses as nearly like a man as is compatible with the present *convenances*; cuts her hair quite short, wears shirt-fronts and men's ties, shoots, bags her game, goes after salmon (she landed two the other day weighing twelve pounds each), rides a tricycle, has a perfect mania for foxhunting (always in at the death), and *smokes* — ye gods, how she *does* smoke! She's got a regular Turkish pipe in her boudoir, and is always at it."

"Disgusting!" said Richmoor. "Where's her husband?" —

"Where?" and the other laughed. "Not with *her,* you may depend upon it! Couldn't stand *her* for long! He's in India, beating up tigers in the jungle, I believe; most probably he thinks it better to be torn to pieces by tigers than live with such a wife."

"Talking of husbands, I wonder how poor Hatwell-Tribkin gets on," said Richmoor meditatively. "He must have an awful time of it, I expect!"

I could stand this no longer. Rising abruptly from my seat I seized my hat and umbrella and grasped them convulsively in one hand; then, approaching the next table, I forced a politely awful smile and laid my visiting card solemnly down beside Richmoor's plate without a word!

He started violently and his face flushed deeply, the colour spreading to the very roots of his hair. "Tribkin!" he exclaimed. "My dear fellow, I — I — I really — Upon my word, I — I"

He broke off confused, and exchanged uneasy glances with his friend. I watched his discomfort keenly, in that special way that the snake, according to novelists, watches the fascinated sparrow.

"I overheard your remarks, my lord," I said in a sort of stage whisper, accentuated by much stuttering severity. "I overheard — unintentionally and with pain — your remarks concerning my — my wife! I need scarcely say that they were not agreeable to me. I consider — I most emphatically consider, sir, that you owe me an apology!"

"My dear Tribkin," and the young man eagerly extended his hand, "pray let me make it at once! I apologise most sincerely, most penitently. I am awfully sorry, really! My friend here, Mr. Herbert Vaughan, is as sorry as I am, I'm sure, aren't you, Vaughan?" The gentleman appealed to, who had been diligently sorting crumbs on the table-cloth, looked up with a burning blush, bowed low, and acquiesced. "It's very foolish to get talking about — about people, you know; one can never be certain that they are not close at hand.

I *hope* you forgive me! I really didn't mean—"

Here I cut him short; he was evidently so sincerely grieved and vexed that my anger cooled down completely, and I pressed his proffered hand.

"That's enough," I said dismally, but gently too. "I know people *will* talk, and I suppose Mrs. Tribkin" — here I brightened up a bit—" is handsome enough and clever enough to *be* talked about!"

"Exactly," and the young earl looked immensely relieved at this way of putting it. "That's what Georgie always says. You know I'm going to marry Georgie?"

"I know," I replied, "and I congratulate you!"

"Thanks! Now do have a glass of wine, won't you? Here, waiter, bring another bottle of Beaune."

I was half disposed to decline this invitation, but he pressed me so cordially that I could not very well refuse. I therefore sat down, and we all, including the young gentleman named Vaughan, conversed for some time on the subject of Woman generally — woman judged from two points of view, namely, the high and dignified position which Nature evidently intended her to occupy, and the exceedingly cheap and low level at which she, in these modern days, seems inclined to place herself. It may and it will no doubt surprise many fair readers of these unpretending pages to learn that, taken the majority of opinion held by the best and bravest men of England (and by the best and bravest I mean those who have their country's good at heart, who revere their Queen, and who have not yet trampled chivalry in the dust and made a jest of honour), it will be found that they are unanimous in wishing to keep sweet woman in her proper sphere; a sphere, I may add, which is by no means narrow, but, on the contrary, wide enough to admit all things gracious, becoming and beautiful; inspiring things both in art and loftiest literature; things that tend to refine, but not to degrade and vulgarize. Men have no sort of objection to make when women, gifted with a rare and subtle power of intellect, take to the study of high philosophy and glorious science; if, like Mary Somerville, they can turn their bright eyes undismayed on the giddy wonders of the firmament and expound in musical phrase the glittering riddles of astronomy, we hear them with as much reverence and honour as though they were wise angels speaking. If, like Elizabeth Barrett, they pour from a full sweet heart such poetry as is found in the "Sonnets from the Portuguese," we listen entranced and moved to the lovely music that "Gentlier on the spirit lies, Than tired eyelids upon tired eyes." Who does not admire and revere the woman who wrote the following exquisite lines which, with all their passion, are still true womanly:

"How do I love thee? Let me count the ways:
I love thee to the depth and breadth and height
My son can reach, when feeling out of sight
For the ends of Being and Ideal Grace;
I love thee to the level of every day's
Most quiet need, by sun and candlelight;
I love thee freely, as men strive for Right,
I love thee purely, as they turn from Praise;
I love thee with the passion put to use
In my old griefs, and with my childhood's faith;
I love thee with a love I seemed to lose
With my lost saints — I love thee with the breath,
Smiles, tears of all my life! — and, if God choose,
I shall but love thee better after death!"

In fine, we — I speak for the men — we do not want to shut out woman from what she can becomingly do without destroying the indefinable soft attraction of her womanhood. But when she wishes to vulgarize herself; when instead of a queen she elects to be a street scavenger or the driver of a dust-cart, we object. We object for her sake quite as much as for our own; because we know what the direful result of such a state of topsy-turvy-dom must infallibly be. When women voluntarily resign their position as the silent monitors and models of grace and purity, down will go all the pillars of society, and we shall scarcely differ in our manners and customs from the nations we call "barbaric," because as yet they have not adopted Christ's exalted idea of the value and sanctity of female influence on the higher development of the human race.

But I am getting serious — too serious to be borne with by the impatient readers of to-day. All the same, we *must* be serious sometimes; we cannot always be grinning about like apes among cocoa-nut trees. There's too much grinning now-a-days — false grinning, I mean. We grin at our friends, grin straight through the length and breadth of an "at home," grin in church and out of church, grin at scandals, grin at suicides, grin at everything, everywhere. We might as well be death's heads at once and have done with it. We shall be some day; but I fancy we are rather anticipating the pleasure!

When I got home that evening I did not fail to report to my wife the faithful account of my meeting with the Earl of Richmoor and his friend Mr. Vaughan, and what *they* had said, and what *I* had said about *her* and about her sex generally. She heard me with that admirable equanimity which always distinguished her, but it made no effect upon her.

"Richmoor's a prig," she said curtly. "He always was, you know. One of those dreadfully stuck-up, blue-blood, long-lineage fellows. Bobbie is nothing to him." ("Bobbie" was the "boy" with the moustaches; scrape his gills and cook him for dinner, I mused dreamily.) "And so you said I was handsome and clever enough to be talked about, did you?"

"I did."

"Well now, old boy, that was awfully nice of you," and she gave me a bright smile. "Husbands are not always so complimentary behind their wives' backs. You deserve a reward, and I'm going to give it to you! You shall get rid of me for a whole six weeks: there!"

"Get rid of you, Honoria?" I faltered amazed. "What do you—"

"Look here," she went on rapidly, "I've arranged it all. Mother will take baby — she's quite agreeable — and you can shut up the house and go where you like and do what you like, and have a real jolly good time. I sha'n't ask what you've been up to! This is the fourth of August; well, say we meet again here about the twentieth of September, or later if you like; that'll give us a good long swing apart."

"But, Honoria," I exclaimed in utter bewilderment, "what do you mean? Where are you going? What do you propose to do?"

"Shoot," she replied promptly. "I'm booked to Trottie Stirling for the Twelfth, and mean to bag more game than any of the male duffers she's asked down to Glen Ruach this season. She's invited *you!* — Poor dear! it would never suit yoil to see me blazing away over the heather and tramping across the moors in leggings; but it's awful fun though!"

"No, you are right! It would *not* suit me!" I vociferated, giving way to the wrath I could no longer restrain. "It would not, and it *will* not suit me! Honoria, I am master in my own house; you are my wife, and I expect you to obey me. I have never exacted my right of obedience from you till now, Honoria; but now, now I *do* exact it! You will *not* go to this horrible woman at Glen Ruach (wretch! she ought to be ashamed of herself),you will *not*, Honoria! You will remain with me and the child, as it is your duty to do. I will not permit you to indulge in these unladylike sports any longer; you will become the laughing-stock of the town and make me a laughing-stock too! And no wonder; *no* man with any spirit would allow you to make such a fool of yourself — yes, a *fool*, Honoria, whether you like the expression or not; you *must* look a fool with a gun in your hand, 'blazing away,' as you call it; and in leggings too — good God!"

And I laughed bitterly, and flung myself into a chair, trembling with excitement. She surveyed me quite coolly, showing no sign of temper.

"Thanks!" she said. "Thanks awfully! You *are* polite, upon my word! *You* don't want a six-penny handbook on etiquette, evidently! But you're old-fashioned, Willie — frightfully old-fashioned! Behind the time altogether — miles and miles behind! You don't suppose I'm going to disappoint all my 'set' down at Glen Ruach just to gratify your middle-ages prejudices, do you? Not a bit of it! I advise you to run across Channel for a while — take the waters at Homburg or something — you'll feel twenty per cent, better afterwards. I've arranged to leave here on the tenth, so you can make your plans accordingly." She was imperturbable, and I flared round upon her once more.

"Honoria, I shall speak to your mother!"

"What for?" she calmly enquired.

"I shall tell her of your unwomanly — your unwifely — your *impossible* conduct!"

"Good gracious! That *will* be funny! Poor old Mammy! She knows all about me, and so did *you* know all about me before you married me — what in the world are you grumbling at?"

"I did not know," I gasped, wrenching my handkerchief round and round in my hand as a sort of physical relief to my feelings. "I did not know you went to — to such lengths, Honoria!"

"As the leggings?" she demanded. "Well, they *are* long, there's no doubt about that!"

And with a ringing burst of laughter she left me — left me to consume myself in as silent and impotent a fury as ever racked a long-enduring spirit of married man!

CHAPTER VI

I kept my word. I *did* speak to Honoria's mother, and a very dreary conversation we had of it. Mrs. Maggs was a thin, sheep-faced, flabby old lady, who impressed people at first sight as being "*so* sweet!" on account of the feebly-smiling chronic amiability of her expression; but those who came to know her well, as I did, grew rapidly sick of her smile, and passionately yearned to shake her into some semblance of actual vivacity. She was the most helpless, tame old woman I ever met with, watery blue eyes, and tremulous hands that were for ever busy smoothing down the folds of her black silk dress, or settling the lace she always wore about her shoulders, or playing with the loosely-flying strings of her cap. Those hands used to worry me — they were never still. When she made tea (which she did frequently and always badly) they hovered above the tray like bleached birds' claws, shaking over the sugar and wobbling about with the cream-jug, till any enjoyment of the "cup that cheers" became impossible to me. I spoke to her, however, because I had threatened Honoria I *would* do so (and it is very foolish to threaten and not perform — even children find *that* out and despise you for it). I called on her for the express purpose of speaking to her, as I explained in a note marked "*Confidential*," which I sent round to her house (three squares off from us) by my manservant. Time was going on, and Honoria was going on too, or rather she was going off. Her portmanteau was packed and labelled for Scotland; her gun-case and sporting equipments stood prepared in the hall; she herself had been absent from home for three or four days, staying with a Mrs. Netcalf on the river — a place quite close to the spot where "Bobbie" with the moustaches had got his "little house-boat" moored. She had written to me briefly explaining that they were all having a "high old time," and asking me (for mere form's sake, of course) whether I would not leave my "prejudices" behind and join them? To this letter, which I thought impertinent, considering the seething state of our domestic affairs, I vouchsafed no reply; my mind was too full of my own increasing grievances. The baby — my helpless son — had already been packed off to his grandmother's, nurses and all. He was sent away during one of my daily absences in the city, and a nice row we had about him, poor innocent, when his screams no longer cheered the silence of our dwelling. I learned then that Honoria, after all, *had* a temper; not precisely the sort of temper we generally credit woman with, which may be described as a swift summer hurricane — eyes flashing lightning and pouring tears at once, followed by brilliant sunshine. No! Honoria's temper merely developed itself into a remarkable facility for saying very nasty and sarcastic things — things that riled a fellow horribly and rubbed him up entirely the wrong way. Witty, cold-blooded, "smart" remarks she threw at me; epigrammatic sentences that were about as clever as they could well be — and I *knew* they were clever, and was all the more hurt by them. Because, as far as her intelligence went, she was (I must really repeat it) a *wonderful* woman — simply wonderful! She leaped across country, metaphorically speaking, and seized a galloping idea by the mane, as though it were a horse, while others were peeping doubtfully at it under cover and round the corner — that was *her* way of mastering information. Men can't do that sort of thing; they have to coax knowledge into their slow brains by degrees; clever women absorb it like sponges, without any apparent trouble. So that we had once or twice what I should freely describe as a devil of a row. *I* got red in the face, and *she* never changed colour — *I* swore, and *she* dropped me a mocking curtsey — I held on to a chair to save myself from getting lifted bodily off the ground by the honest warmth of my indignation, and *she* lounged on a sofa, smoked, and grinned at me. Yes! I say *grinned!* I would no longer call that white glistening tooth-display of hers a *smile;* it had a cold and snarly look that I could not conscientiously admire. And yet I was fond of her too, and I knew she was a good woman — none better, so far as honesty and straight principles were concerned. And thus it was that, torn by conflicting emotions, fagged and worn out by the constant fret of my own domestic wretchedness, I determined to appeal to Mrs, Maggs, though I instinctively felt, before I made the attempt, that it was an act of mere desperation, and that it would result in no sort of advantage or help to me in the unfortunate position I occupied.

The old lady was in a more than usually nervous state when I arrived, and came fluttering to meet me at the drawing-room door with that anxious propitiatory smile I abhorred, more pronounced than ever.

"My *dear* William!" she murmured, her hands waving about me like the hands of a very stagey mesmerist. "It is so nice of you to come and see me, so *very* nice and kind of you!" Here she caught her breath and sighed. She was fond of doing that — her pet idea was that she had heart-disease. "Dear baby is doing *so* well, and is quite happy upstairs! Georgie goes and sits on the floor and lets him play with her back hair, and he *does* tear it so" — her pale eyes watered visibly at this—" I tell her she'll have none left on her scalp to be married with. Dear girl! You've heard about Richmoor? Yes, such a *brilliant* match, and he's such a *nice* man; not very communicative, but very gentlemanly. And *he* plays with baby too; isn't it pretty of him? He goes upstairs with Georgie constantly, and I hear them laughing together, dear things! It is *so* nice of him, you know, being a man, to like stopping up in the nursery, which must be dull — no newspapers or anything — and he can't smoke, or he *won't*, on account of Georgie's being there; he's very particular about that sort of thing; besides smoke would be bad for baby's eyes." Here she stopped for breath again, pressing her hand on her side, while I gazed at her and forced a politely-soothing smile. (I was obliged to smile, because she thought everybody who didn't smile at her was cross or ill, and I did not wish to pose as either one or the other.) "Yes, baby is quite a boon," she went on in plaintively cheerful tones. "A positive boon! keeps everybody employed, and is such a *darling!* I'm so glad you'll let us take care of him while Honoria is away."

"It is just about Honoria that I came to speak to you," I said, clearing my throat and edging past those ghostly fingers of hers that seemed to give me Honoria's favourite malady, "the creeps."

"I am sorry to say we've had a little difference—"

"Oh, dear!" faltered Mrs. Maggs, gliding nervously to the tea-tray, which stood ready as usual, and beginning to make a feeble noise with the cups and saucers, "Oh, dear me, William! don't say so! One cannot have all sunshine, you know, dear William, in one's married life. I'm sure when Mr. Maggs was alive — ah! it seems only the other day he died, poor darling! (Lord bless the woman, he had been mouldering in his grave for eighteen years!) — we used often to have a little quarrel about things, especially about blue ties! I never could bear blue neckties, and he always *would* wear one on Sundays! It was really very tiresome, because we used to find the Sundays so disagreeable, you know — so — so unchristian! Of course it was my fault as much as it was his; both were to blame, and that is the way always with married people, dear William; both are to blame, it is never all on one side — it *can't* be — you must bear and forbear—"

Here she let fall the sugar-tongs with a clatter, and trailed off into unintelligible nothings.

"Yes, I know — I know all about that," I said, making a desperate effort to be patient with this trembling, pale jelly of a woman, who always seemed on the point of dissolving into tears. "But the present matter is very serious, and it is becoming more and more serious every day. You see, when a man marries he wants a *home*—"

"Oh, my dear William, I'm sure you've *got* a home," moaned Mrs. Maggs, turning her weak eyes reproachfully upon me. "You can't say you haven't — you really *can't*, William! A *beautiful* home! Why, the carpets alone in it cost a small fortune, and as for the drawing-room curtains, they're good enough to make court-trains of — they positively *are*, William! Every bit pure silk, and all the flower-pattern raised! I can't imagine what you *can* want better! And I remember when that overmantel was bought at Salviati's, all Venetian glass! I couldn't sleep a wink for nights and nights, thinking of it, and I went myself to see the men put it up, for I was *so* afraid they would break it, and it *was* so expensive! Why, you've got lovely things everywhere, William, and how *can* you say you want a home?"

By this time I was beginning to lose my equanimity.

"Dear me, madam," I snapped out testily, "you surely don't suppose it's the *furniture* that makes a home, do you! The drawing-room curtains won't cure me of misery; the Venetian mirror won't help me out of a difficulty!" My voice rose agitatedly. "I can't exist on the tables and chairs, can I? I can't make a friend and confidant of the carpet! I repeat, that when a man marries, he wants a home; and when I married your daughter Honoria, I wanted a home, and I haven't got it!"

"You haven't got it, William?" stammered Mrs. Maggs, approaching me, with a cup of that weak, over-sweetened tea she always made in her shaking hand. "You haven't got it, dear? Why, how is it that Honoria—"

I motioned the tea away with a tragic gesture, and my pent-up passion burst forth.

"Honoria is not a woman!" I exclaimed wildly—" not a whole woman by any means! She is half a man! She is a mistake; she is a freak of nature" — here I broke into a delirious laugh. "She should be exhibited as an eccentricity in some museum!"

This time I had achieved a feat not common to man — I had scared my mother-in-law! The poor feeble thing tottered back to the tea-tray and set down the cup I had just rejected; then nervously drawing her lace scarf round her shoulders, she quavered —

"Don't, William, don't. Oh! *don't* be so — so *dreadful!* You frighten me! You don't know what you say, William, you really don't. You've been taking something in the city, haven't you? There now, don't be offended, William! Will you have some soda water?"

I have said there were times when those who knew Mrs. Maggs well, yearned to shake her. One of those times had come now. It was with the greatest difficulty that I refrained from pouncing on her frail form and rendering her suddenly breathless. But I controlled myself; I made a desperate effort to be calm, and succeeded in merely surveying her with a proper manly scorn.

"You are very like your daughter in some respects," I said. "When you see a fellow as wretched as he can be, suffering mental tortures more acutely than he can describe, you think him drunk! Very sympathetic, I'm sure!"

She smoothed her grey hair tremulously and produced her chronic smile.

"I'm sorry you are suffering, William, very sorry; but you needn't be so *rough,* dear! Tell me what's the matter. Has Honoria been flirting with Bobbie?"

"No," I answered proudly. "That is one thing I cannot accuse her of; she does *not* flirt. She has — I *will* say that for her — too great a sense of honour. She is guiltless of all feminine coquetries and petty vanities. She puts on no airs, and though she's handsome, she's not a bit conceited. She's good and honest — but — but she should never have married; she's not fit for it.'

"Not fit for it," whimpered Mrs. Maggs. "Oh, William! how cruel you are! Not fit for it! How *can* you say so?"

"I can *say* so because I've *proved* so," I replied bluntly. "I repeat — she's not fit for it. She should have lived in the world apart, alone, and worn her no-sex as best she could. She would have no doubt worn it admirably! As a wife she's out of her element; as a mother she's still further out of her element. A smoking, betting, crack shot is scarcely the person to undertake the commonplace care of an infant; a notable female deerstalker is not precisely suited to the *degradation* (and I emphasised the word bitterly) of marriage. In fact, it is because I feel the position of affairs as so extremely serious — serious even to the degree of possible mutual separation — that I have come to *you*, Mrs. Maggs, to ask you to speak to Honoria quietly, to reason with her, and point out how little her behaviour conduces to my happiness, and also how much she exposes herself to the ridicule and slanderous judgment of those who do not understand her as well as you and I do. A mother's arguments may win the day where those of a husband fail."

I had spoken with so much gravity that my mother-in-law's eyes now watered in real earnest, and she pulled out a filmy bit of a lace handkerchief and wiped away the tears effusively.

"It's no use, William," she snivelled weakly; "no use whatever *my* speaking to Honoria! She wouldn't listen to me for a minute; she never would when she was a child, and now she is married she'd only tell me I had no business to interfere. I used to say I thought it was very wrong for her to smoke and go shooting with that Mrs. Stirling — really a very vulgar woman — but she only laughed at me. She's got a great way of laughing at everything, has Honoria. But she's very clever, William; you *know* she is! Professor Muddlecums, who was here the other evening, said that she was simply the most *wonderful* woman he ever met! Such a grasp of things, and such a memory! You mustn't mind, William, you really mustn't mind her smoking, and all that. I don't believe she could do without it; you know some of the papers say it's very soothing to the nerves. Don't *you* like smoking, dear?"

"I *used* to like it," I answered gloomily. "I don't now; Honoria has *sickened* me of it!"

"Dear, dear, that *is* a pity," and Mrs. Maggs's hovering hands went to work again in the usual style. "But perhaps you'll take to it again after a bit. Anyway, *don't* ask me to speak to Honoria, William! I *couldn't*, you know! My heart is very weak, and I should be almost dead with nervousness. You must arrange your little matrimonial differences" — chronic smile once more—" between you; it never does any good to interfere. What! are you going?" For I had risen dispiritedly and was now making my weary way towards the door. "Won't you see baby before you go? He is such a dear *darling, do* see him!" I hesitated, but there was a certain parental tugging at my heart-strings. After all, he was *my* child, and I wanted him to know me a little.

"Yes, I'll see him," I said briefly.

Whereupon Mrs. Maggs became mildly fluttered and pleased, and, opening the drawing-room door, she called up the stairs —

"Georgie! Georgie!"

"Yes," answered a clear girlish voice.

"Bring baby down; William's here, and wants to see him."

Another couple of minutes, and Georgie entered, carrying my young hopeful in her arms, clean and fresh as a rose, *not* screaming, *not* angry, as was his wont, but with a fat smile puckering up his small features into countless little wrinkles, and a fearless confidence shining in his round, big, honest blue eyes. The child was evidently perfectly happy, and I knew at once who had made him so.

"Thank you, Georgie," I said simply, as I shook hands with her.

"For what?" she asked, laughing.

"For taking such care of him."

"Nonsense!" And she set her burden down on the hearth-rug, where he immediately pulled off his woollen shoe and began eating it. "He wants scarcely any care, he's so good. Do you know I don't think we need more than one nurse; would you mind if we sent away the other?"

"Not at all," I replied. "Do as you like."

She seated herself in a chair and looked at her mother, smiling.

"Give me some tea, mammy dear," she said. "Haven't you had any, William?"

"No."

"Have some now, and keep me company," and, springing up, she peered doubtfully into the fresh cup Mrs. Maggs poured out, then shook her head in playful remonstrance.

"Too weak, mammy; William likes it rather strong. May I put some more tea in the pot?"

"I'm sure Georgie," began her mother plaintively, "there's plenty in, only it doesn't seem to draw properly. I don't know how it is, the tea isn't half so good now it gets advertised on the walls so much; in *my* young days it was a luxury!"

"Yes, mother," laughed Georgie, who during this feeble chatter had been quietly manipulating the teapot, and now handed me a delicious cup, aromatic in odour and tempting to look at, "and now it's a positive necessity! All the worse, say the wise men, for us and our poor nerves. Oh, baby!" This as Master Tribkin uttered a sound something between a chuckle and a coo, expressive of his ecstasy at having found on the carpet a large tin-tack which he was laboriously striving to put in his eye. "Oh, what an ugly thing for baby to play with! Auntie doesn't like it. See!" and she made the most comical little face of disgust and threw the objectionable nail out of the window; whereupon my infant became imitatively disgusted also, and in turn made eloquent signs of deep repulsion for the vanished thing he had lately deemed a treasure; signs which were so excessively flabby and funny that Georgie laughed, and I, catching the infection from her, laughed also, heartily, and a trifle nervously too, for there was something very queer about my feelings just then. I tell you, let the "practical" period say what it will, a man *has* a heart; he is not a mere machine of wood and iron; and I was conscious of a soft and sudden sense of rest in Georgie's presence — little Georgie, whom I once had scarcely noticed, the "scrub of a woman" looking just now the very picture of sweet maidenhood and modesty in her pretty white cotton gown, with a "fetching" little bunch of pansies and mignonette carelessly slipped into her waistband. I drank my tea in slow sips and surveyed her, while Mrs. Maggs sank languidly down in an arm-chair and heaved her heart-disease sigh.

"William is vexed," she began, glancing at me with a gently distrustful melancholy. "Georgie, William is vexed about Honoria."

"Yes?" and Georgie looked up quickly. "You do not want her to go to Mrs. Stirling's, I suppose?"

"No, I do *not*," I said emphatically. "Georgie, I'm sure *you* can understand—"

Georgie nodded. "Yes, I understand," she replied instantly. "But I'm *afraid* it's no use arguing about it, William. She *will* go; nothing will dissuade her. *I've* spoken to her about it."

"You have? That was kind of you," I said. Then, after a pause I added, "You always were a kind little soul, Georgie. Richmoor's a lucky man!"

She smiled, and a warm blush swept over her cheeks.

"*I'm* lucky too," she answered softly. "You can't imagine, William, what a nice fellow *he* is!"

"I'm sure of that—" I hesitated, then went on desperately, "So you think it's best to let Honoria have her own way then this time, Georgie?"

"I'm *afraid* so," and she looked at me very sympathetically. "You see when she's away she may take a better view of things — she may even get tired of all those vulgar sporting men and women, and begin to long for home, and — and for you, and the baby — and that would be *such* a good thing, you know!"

"Yes, it would," I answered despondently, "if it ever happened; but it *won't* happen!"

"Wait and see," said Georgie confidently. "Honoria's got a good heart after all; she can be very sweet if she likes, and if you don't thwart her just now she may completely alter her ideas. I think it's quite possible — it would be natural — for she's certain to give up sporting and hunting *some* day; it *can't* last—"

"Can't last? Of course it can't last!" declared Mrs. Maggs, unclosing her eyes, which had been shut till now in placid resignation. "No woman can go on shooting for ever, William dear; why, she'll get old, you know, and she'll want to be quiet!"

"And I must wait till she *gets* old, I suppose; that's what you mean to imply?" I said with a haggard attempt at smiling. "All right; but age will not cure her of smoking, I fear! However, I won't bore you any more with my worries. Good-bye, Georgie!"

"Good-bye!" and she held out her hand; then, as I took it, she whispered, "I'm so sorry about it all, William — so sorry, I mean, for *you!*"

"I know you are," I answered in the same low tone, and I pressed her kindly-clinging little fingers. "Never mind; every one has got troubles; why should I be an exception? Goodbye, youngster!"

This to my small son, who was now busy dragging all the music out of the music-stand in a cheerfully absorbed silence. "I suppose he'd scream if I took him up?"

"Oh, no," said Georgie; "he's not a bit shy; try him!"

Whereupon I lifted him gingerly in my arms, and he stared at me with deliberate and inquisitorial sternness. Suddenly, however, he burst into a wild war-whoop of delight, and patted my cheeks violently and condescendingly; and when I set him down again he was convulsed with laughter. I don't know why, I'm sure. I cannot pretend to enter into an infant's sense of humour. I only realised that he was a very good-natured baby, and that his good-nature had never been apparent under the maternal roof. Mrs. Maggs bade me farewell very effusively.

"*Do* come and sit with us, dear William, in the evening whenever you feel lonely," she entreated mournfully; "and perhaps you can arrange to come down to Cromer with us also. We are going there for a little change of air; it will do baby so much good. We shall be quite pleased to have you, you know. Indeed, it is to be expected you will want to see your own baby sometimes, especially when you cannot see your own wife! You *will* come, won't you, William?"

I said I would think of it, and with a few more hurried words I departed. No good had come of my visit *there* I thought, as I shut the street door behind me; no good whatever, except the sight of Georgie. *She* was a refreshing glimpse of woman hood at any rate, and I dwelt on her pretty image in my mind with pleasure. I reached my own house and let myself in as usual with the latchkey; the place had a vacant and deserted air; the rooms smelt of stale tobacco, and a sense of despondency, loss, and failure crept over me as I stood for a moment looking in at the semi-darkened library, where I had passed so many solitary evenings. It was no good stopping at home I decided; the very word "home" was a mockery to one in my position. I therefore did what every man does who finds his wife unwifely and his domestic surroundings uncomfortable; went down to my club to dinner, and returned no more till I returned to bed.

CHAPTER VII

August was past and gone. September was drawing near its close; my wife had won fresh distinction as a sportswoman of the highest rank down at Glen Ruach, and I had spent a very quiet holiday at Cromer with Mrs. Maggs and all her family (seven boys and girls, without counting Honoria), passing the time in making friends with my own infant son. And now the summer vacation was over; people were returning to town in straggling batches, and I returned amongst others. My wife had written to me now and then, chiefly on post-cards, and I had replied by the same cheap and convenient method of correspondence, which leaves no room for romance. *She* was not romande, and if I had a vein of sentiment anywhere in my composidon, I was determined not to make a display of it to *her* again. She was coming home; she had announced her intention of arriving on a particular evening which she named, and she had requested me not to bother about meeting her at the station. So I *didn't* bother about it. Georgie had been busy at our house — Mrs. Maggs also; preparing it and putting it in order for the return of its mistress, and all was in readiness — all except the baby, who still remained with his young aunts and uncles and grandmother. The time fixed upon had come, and I sat at the library window looking out on the square and awaiting my wife's arrival. I had made up my mind to welcome her as an affectionate husband should; I had resolved that we would talk about our differences in a quiet and perfectly amicable manner, and that if she could not or would not resign her mannish habits out of love or respect for me, why, then I would in all gentleness suggest a mutually-agreed-upon separation. I hoped it would not come to this; but I was positively determined I would stand her masculine behaviour no longer. It had sickened me to the soul to read the various accounts of her that appeared from time to time in the "Society" papers. I had longed to thrash the insolent little paragraphists who wrote of her as the "Amazonian Mrs. Hatwell-Tribkin,"

"the stalwart Mrs. Hatwell-Tribkin," et cetera, especially when they finished off their descriptions with satirical exclamations, such as "Bravo, Honoria!" or "Well done for Mrs. H.-T.!" I had felt every drop of blood in my body tingle with vexation whenever I saw her name bandied about in company with all the theatrical and "fast" notorieties of the day, but how could I complain? She had laid herself open to it; her conduct invited it, and if her gowns *were* described, and her good looks discussed and her "points" criticised as though she were some fine mare for sale at Tattersall's, it was *her* fault — it was certainly not mine. I was tired of the whole business, and I had firmly and finally resolved that I would not consent to be known *merely* as the matrimonial appendage of Mrs. Hatwell-Tribkin. I would have a distinct personality of my own. There are too many weak, good-natured husbands about in society, who, rather than have continual rows with their wives, consent to be overshadowed and put to shame by their feminine arrogance and assumption of superiority. I tell these wretched beings once for all that they are making a woeful mistake. Let them assert themselves, no matter with how much difficulty and unpleasantness, and it will be better for them in the long run. The world will never blame any fellow for steadily refusing to live with a woman who, in mind and character, is more than half a man.

I waited, as I said, at the library window — waited and watched for Honoria's return, glancing from time to time at the evening papers and listening intently to every distant sound of cab wheels. At last I saw a hansom (one of those dangerously silent things, with tinkling bells which scarcely suffice to warn aside the unwary foot passenger) whirl round the corner of the square, with the well-known gun-case and portmanteau on top; in one minute it had stopped at the door; in another Honoria was out of it and in the hall.

"How do?" she exclaimed loudly as I went forth to greet her. (Naturally, I made no foolish attempt to kiss her.) "You look fairly fit! Here, Simmons!" — this to the man-servant—" take all my traps out and send them upstairs — half-a-crown fare — here you are!"

And she tossed him the coin and marched into the library with a firm, rather heavy tread, I following her in a deeply hurt and vexed silence, for I noticed at the first glance that she had cut her hair quite short. All those beautiful bright nut-brown tresses I had admired when I courted her were gone, and I had some ado to speak with any sort of gentleness.

"I see you have cut your hair, Honoria," I said, looking at her as she stood before me, tall and commanding as a grenadier guard, clad in her buttoned tweed ulster and deer-stalking cap. "I think you've spoilt yourself."

"Do you? I don't!" she retorted, taking off the cap and displaying a mass of short boy's curls all over her head. "It's ever so much cooler, and ever so much less troublesome. Excuse me, don't be shocked!"

And unfastening her ulster, she threw it off Great heavens! what — what extraordinary sort of clothes had she got into! I mistrusted my own eyesight; were those — those nether garments *knickerbockers?* positively *knickerbockers?* Yes! by everything amazing and unfeminine they *were!* and over them came a loose blouse and short — very short — frilled petticoat, something like the "Bloomer" costume, only several degrees more "mannish" in make. I stared at her open-mouthed and utterly dismayed; so much so that I was speechless for the moment.

"My shooting costume," she explained cheerfully. "It's such a comfort to travel in, and no one sees under my ulster!"

"Would you care if any one *did* see, Honoria?" I inquired coldly.

"No, I don't suppose I should," she answered gaily, ruffling up her curls with one hand. "Well, Willie, as I said before, you look *fit!* Had a good time at Cromer? and are you glad to see me back again?"

"Of course, Honoria," I replied in the same quietly unmoved tone; "of course I am glad to see you, but — well, we will talk over things presently. Supper is ready, I believe; will you not change your — your—"

And I pointed to the knickerbockers with, I think, rather a sarcastical expression on my countenance. She flushed just a little; it must have been my glance that confused her for an instant; then, I suppose, a devil of mischief entered into her and made her obstinate.

"No, what's the good of changing; such a bother!" she answered. "Besides, I'm as hungry as a hunter; I'll sit down to supper as I am. Awfully comfortable, you know!"

"Honoria!" I said with a sort of desperate politeness, "you must really pardon me! I refuse — I utterly refuse to sit at table with you in that costume! Do you want the very servants to giggle at you all through the meal?"

"They may giggle if they like," she replied imperturbably; "their giggles won't hurt *me*, I assure you!"

"Honoria!" and I spoke with deliberate gentleness and gravity. "Will you oblige *me* by changing those masculine habiliments of yours, and dressing like a *lady?*"

She looked at me, laughed, and her eyes flashed.

"No, I won't!" she said curtly.

I bowed; then quietly turned round and left the room, and not only the room but the house. I went to my club and supped there, needless to say, with no enjoyment whatever, and with no heart to enter into conversation with any of my friends. I think most of them must have seen I was seriously put out, for they left me pretty much alone, and I was able to take counsel with myself as to what I should do next. I returned home late, and retired to a separate apartment, so that I saw no more of Honoria till the next morning, when she came down to breakfast in her smoking-suit — *i.e.*, the same sort of skirt and large-patterned man's jacket she had surprised me with on the evening of our marriage day. I studied her attentively. Her skin, which had recently been exposed so ruthlessly to the sun and wind on the grouse moors, was beginning to look rough and coarse; her eyes had a bold, hard, indifferent expression; her very hand, as she poured out the tea, was red and veiny, like that of a man accustomed to rough weather, and I realised with immense regret that her beauty would soon be a thing of the past; that it was even possible she might become positively ugly in an incredibly short time if she continued (as it was pretty evident she *would* continue) her masculine mode of life. It was she who first began the conversation that morning.

"Got over your temper, Willie? Do you know you're becoming a perfect demon?"

"Am I?" I said patiently. "I'm sorry, Honoria; I used to be considered a good-natured fool enough, but I've had a great deal to vex me lately, and I fancy you know the cause of my vexation."

"Yes," she answered indifferently, helping both me and herself to toast as she spoke; "I know, but I've settled all that. I never take long making up *my* mind! We must part — that's about the long and the short of the matter. We can't work together — it's no use, oars won't pull evenly — we shall only upset the boat. It's easily done — have an agreement drawn up as they do for house leases, sign it before witnesses, and we split — quite amicably — no fuss. And that will leave me free and comfortable for my lecturing tour."

"Your lecturing tour!" I echoed, forgetting for a moment my own annoyances in the fresh surprise of this announcement. "Are you going a-lecturing, Honoria?" and despite my wish to be gentle, I am aware my voice was decidedly sarcastic in its inflection. "What on, pray? Politics or temperance? Do you like the idea of becoming a platform woman?"

"As well be a platform woman as a platform man," she replied with a touch of defiance. "I've got a good voice — better than most men's — and I've heaps to say. I met a Mr. Sharp down at Glen Ruach; he's an agent for that sort of thing — farmed out lots of lecturers both here and in the States; he's agreed to farm out *me*. Good terms too; he says he knows I'll 'draw' immensely. All expenses paid — in fact, you needn't bother about making me any allowance unless you want to for form's sake — I can earn my own living comfortably."

"Has he heard you lecture?" I inquired, ignoring this independent latter part of her speech. "Is he acquainted with your capabilities in that line?"

She smiled — a wide hard smile.

"Rather; I gave them all a taste of my quality down at Glen Ruach — lectured on Man — and I thought Sharp would have split with laughing! Awfully funny fellow, Sharp — Sharp by name and Sharp by nature. But he's first-class — awfully first-class! I signed the agreement with him before leaving."

"Without consulting *me*," I observed frigidly. "Very wifely and kind on your part, Honoria!"

"Oh, bother!" she said rapidly; "wives don't consult their husbands now-a-days — that sort of thing's exploded. Each party manages his or her own affairs. Besides, I knew you'd make all manner of objections."

"Oh, you *did* know that!" and I looked at her steadfastly. "Well, Honoria, in that case perhaps it *will* be best to do as you say — mutually agree to separate, for a time at least; though you have not thought of the child in the matter; is he to be my care or yours?"

"Good gracious! Yours, of course," she replied very emphatically. "I can't go touring about the country with a shrieking brat! Has he roared old Mammy into deafness yet?"

"No, he has not," I said. "He has not indulged much in 'roaring,' as you call it, since he left your tender maternal care, Honoria!"

I pronounced the words "tender maternal care" with marked and slightly scornful emphasis. She glanced at me, and her full lips curled disdainfully.

"Look here, Mr. William Tribkin!" she announced. "You're a slow coach! that's what you are — a slow coach of very mediæval pattern! Your wheels want greasing; you take too long a time getting over the road! And you talk a vast deal of old sentimental rubbish, and I never could put up with sentimental rubbish. I hate it! I hate fads too, and you are a faddist! You want me — *me* — to be a docile, thank-you-for-nothing-humbleservant-yours-faithfully sort of woman, dragging about the house with a child pulling at her skirts and worrying her all day long; you want to play the male tyrant and oppressor, don't you? but you *won't!* not with *me*, at any rate! You've got a free woman in me, *I* tell you, not a sixteenth-century slave! My constitution is as good as yours; my brain is several degrees better; I'm capable of making a brilliant career for myself in any profession I choose to follow, and you are and always will be a mere useful nonentity! You are—"

"Stop! that is enough, Honoria," I said decisively, rising from the table. "You need not go out of your way to insult me — pray spare yourself! Mere 'useful nonentity' as I am, I am man enough to despise vulgar notoriety; and you, though your conduct is *unwomanly,* are still woman enough to court and eagerly accept that questionable distinction. As you so elegantly express it, I am a slow coach;' my ideas of womanhood are sadly old-fashioned indeed! I do not wish to play the 'male tyrant,' but I want to *feel* the part of the true lover and loyal husband, and this is an honour unhappily denied to me! Our marriage has been an error; it only remains to us now to make the best of our position. You wish to go your way, and your way is distinctly not mine. As *you* will not submit to me, and *I* have not so completely ignored my manhood as to submit to *you*, why, then it follows that we must separate; let us hope — let *me* hope, Honoria, that it may only be for a short time. You may rely on my pursuing the honourable fidelity I swore to you on our marriage day, and!" I paused, then continued earnestly:

"I would not insult you by presuming to question yours." Again I waited; she was quite silent, but she drew from her side-pocket her case of cigarettes, and lighting one, puffed away at it in a meditative fashion. "This is a fast age, Honoria," I went on regretfully, "and it breeds an unconscionable number of 'fast' women and men; but I want you to believe, if you can, that chivalry is not altogether extinct — that there are a few gentlemen left, of which class I hope I may humbly call myself one — a very poor-spirited, dull gentleman, no doubt, but who still would rather lead a lonely and uncheered life in the world than interfere with your happiness, or spoil what you imagine to be the brilliant promise of your independent career. You have never deemed yourself under any sort of authority to me — that would be too 'old-fashioned' a notion for an advanced feminine intelligence like yours" — here she puffed out the smoke from her lips in little artistic rings—" so that there is no need to say to you, 'Be at liberty!' You *are* at liberty; you always have been — no doubt you always will be. But there are various sorts of liberty; one is the non-restraint and licence riskily enjoyed by young men about town, whose families are utterly indifferent to their fate (and this is what you seem to desire); another is that gentle latitude controlled by the affectionate solicitude and protection of those who love you better than themselves; another (and here we find the truest liberty of woman) is the freedom a wife possesses to guide and comfort and inspire to greatest ends her husband's life and career. Through woman's love, man performs his noblest labours. Believe it! Through woman's love, I say, not through woman's opposition! But I must apologise to you for talking sentimental rubbish again. It is understood that we agree to separate for the present; and I will call on my lawyer about the matter this afternoon. Half of every penny I have or earn shall be yours as is your just due; this house, which I shall vacate as soon as possible, is also at your service. And I hope, Honoria" — here I cleared my throat from an uncomfortable huskiness—" I hope this arrangement, though it seems necessary now, may not be of long continuance — I shall be a proud and happy man when the day dawns on which my wife and I can meet again and live together in that absolute sympathy I so earnestly desire!"

I ceased. She looked up through the cloud of tobacco-smoke that encircled her head, and there was just a little softness about her eyes which made them prettier for the moment. Taking her cigarette from her mouth, she flicked off the ash into her breakfast plate.

"You're a capital fellow, Will," she said; "regular first-class, only a *leetle* slow!" and she extended one hand, which I took and pressed earnestly in my own. "Look here, I tell you what! I'll get through my lecturing tour, and if you want me back after that, why, I'll come — honour bright!"

I sighed; released her hand gently and left her. I dared not enquire so far into the future; I hesitated to speculate as to whether I should indeed want her back *then!* However, our minds were unanimously made up on one point — namely, the advisability of separation for the present; and within the next few days the affair was quietly arranged, much to the distress of old Mrs. Maggs, who wept copiously when she heard of it, and for some mysterious reason, known only to herself, persisted in calling my child a "poor orphan." Georgie said little, but no doubt thought the more, and was sweetly, silently sympathetic. My wife started for some big manufacturing town in the provinces, where she was to begin her lecturing campaign; our house was let for twelve months (Honoria's management — she was a wonderful business woman); the baby remained in the charge of his grandmother, and I took a set of chambers near Pall Mall and resumed a hum-drum bachelor life.

CHAPTER VIII

The cynical philosopher and the self-sufficient epicurean may now perhaps feel disposed to congratulate me on having easily and conveniently got rid of my wife; the modern Diogenes of the literary clubs may growl "Lucky man!" and the nineteenth-century Solomon of Hyde Park and Piccadilly may murmur over these pages: "There is nothing, under the circumstances, better for a fellow to do than to eat, drink and be merry all the days of his life, for whatever cometh *not* of these is vanity!" But, truth to tell, I was not in an enviable condition at all. The resumption of a solitary existence in chambers was far from agreeable to me; for I had passed the age when going to the theatre seemed the chief glory of life, and I had not yet arrived at that matured paunchiness when to dine well and drink good wine till the nose becomes rosy and lustrous, is the acme of every sensible man's ambition. So that I was very lonely, and very conscious of my loneliness. The gaunt, pious and respectable female who attended to my rooms was not exactly the sort of person one would choose to provide a drooping spirit with mental cheer; the hall porter at my club — an exceedingly friendly fellow — seemed sorry for me now and then, but refrained from inviting me to weep out my woes upon his brassbuttoned breast. True, I visited my mother-inlaw's house frequently — saw the fair little Georgie and her betrothed earl, and looked on mournfully at their demurely graceful love-making; and I danced my infant son on my knee to Banbury Cross and back again with much satisfaction, finding that every time I did it his soft chuckles became more and more confidential, and that though at present his language was unintelligible, he evidently meant it kindly. Still I had the feeling upon me of being a desolate and deserted man, and though I absorbed myself as much as possible in books and made the best of my position, I could not deem myself happy. Life, which I had fancied rounded into completion when I married, seemed now broken off in some strange and uncouth way — it was like one of those odd-looking roses that through blight or disease bloom half-petalled, and never get shaped into the perfect flower.

Honoria had been a long time absent in the provinces; fully five months had passed since our parting, and the February of the new year was now just at an end. I had never heard from her all that time, neither had she written to any member of her own family. Her allowance had been paid to her regularly through her bankers, and so far as I knew she was well and flourishing. Now and again I heard far-off rumours of Mrs. Tribkin's ability as a lecturer, but I rather avoided all those newspapers in which her doings were likely to be mentioned. I shrank from the penny-worths of scandal, called by courtesy *journals*, lest I should find her name figuring ridiculously in a set of vulgarly worded paragraphs such as are sometimes strung together for the sake of gratuitously insulting our good and noble Queen in her old age (I wonder what British officers are about, by-the-by, that they let this sort of thing go on without a single soldierly and manful protest?), and thus it happened that to me it was almost as if my wife were dead, or at any rate gone on some exceedingly far journey from which it seemed highly probable she would never return. So that I received, a positive shock of surprise one afternoon when, on arriving at my club, I found a letter addressed to me in the big bold handwriting which was like nobody's in the world, so thoroughly characteristic was it of Honoria, and of Honoria alone. I opened it with a sort of eager trepidation. Was she regretting the step she had taken, and was this to propose a friendly meeting with a view to partnership in joy and sorrow once more? A thick card dropped out of the envelope; — I picked it up without looking at it; my eyes were fixed on the letter itself — my wife's letter to me — which ran as follows:

"DEAR WILLIE:
"I've done the provinces, and am coming to London to give a lecture in Prince's Hall, Piccadilly. As you've never heard me hold forth, I enclose a Ticket — Five Shilling Fauteuil — so I hope you'll be comfortable! It's a good seat, where you'll have a straight view of me any way. How are you?

First-class, I hope. *I* never was better in my life. Am leaving for the States in the middle of March, they're 'booming' me there now. I'm beating all the 'Whistling Ladies' hollow! Would you like to dine with me at the Grosvenor before I start? If so, come behind the platform after the lecture and let me know.

"Yours ever,

"HONORIA HATWELL-TRIBKIN."

Dine with her at the Grosvenor! She seemed to entirely forget that I was her *husband* — her separated, deserted husband! It was the letter of a man to a man, yet she was my *wife* — parted from me — but still my wife. Dine with her at the Grosvenor! Never — never! I put the letter back in its envelope with trembling fingers, and then looked at the ticket — the "Five Shilling Fauteuil." Good heavens! I thought I should have tumbled in a swooning heap on the carpet, so great was my astonishment and dismay! This is what I read:

PRINCE'S HALL. PICCADILLY. LECTURE

BY

MRS. HONORIA HATWELL-TRIBKIN.

SUBJECT:

"ON THE ADVISABILITY OF MEN'S APPAREL FOR WOMEN."

HEADINGS: x. The Inconvenience of Women's Dress Generally.
2. The Superior Comfort Enjoyed by Men.
3. Cheapness, Quality, and Durability of Men's Clothing.
4. The Advantages of Social Uniformity.

N.B. — The Lecturer will give from time to time Practical Illustrations of her theory.

TO COMMENCE AT 8 P.M. PRECISELY.

FAUTEUIL, 5s. — ADMIT ONE.

Men's apparel for women! Social uniformity! Practical illustrations of the theory! Ye gods! I gasped for breath, and staggered to an arm-chair, wherein I sank exhausted by the excess of my wonder! The idea of the "practical illustrations" was what worried me. I tried to imagine their nature, but failed in the effort. I could not conceive any "practical illustrations" on such a subject possible — in public! Would she have an assorted pile of men's garments on a table beside her, and taking them up one by one, point out their various attractions? Would she discourse eloquently on the simplicity of the shirt; the rapid sliding-on of the trousers; the easy charm of the waistcoat, and the graceful gaiety of the "monkey-jacket"? Would she attempt to describe the proper setting of a stiff collar, for instance? No! let her not *dare* such a task as this! Let her not presume to touch on that supremest point of sublime masculine agony! My own collar became suddenly ill-fitting as I thought of it, and hitched up against my ear. Full of that wild rage which convulses a man when his linen worries him, I flew to the looking-glass and busied myself for some minutes setting it straight, my countenance darkening into an apoplectic red as I strained at the starchy button-hole and refractory button. D — n it! There! it was all right now; and heaving a sigh of relief, I sat down again and fell into a melancholy reverie. I would *not* go and dine at the Grosvenor with that wonderful wife of mine (everybody said she was wonderful, and I don't deny it); no, I would *not!* But should I go and hear her lecture? This was the question that now tormented me. Perhaps it would be wise on my part; perhaps my very presence would arouse in her mind some touch of remorse, some tinge of regret, for days that once had been; ah! days that once had been! That sounded like poetry, and I knew where I had heard it. A sweet maid of about fifty had sung it at Mrs. Maggs's the other evening in a voice that sounded rather like a penny whistle which had got a drop of water into it by mistake. I hummed it under my breath sentimentally —

"We wandered by the little rill
That sparkled o'er the green,
And oh! we lov'd the mem'ry still
Of days that once, o-once ha-ad been!"

Ah! rills might "sparkle" over any amount of "green," but Honoria would never wander by them more; never — never! She never *had* wandered, and she never *would* wander; the wandering business was reserved for me! Here I recognised that my thoughts were becoming confused, and rising, I thrust my wife's letter and the five-shilling ticket into my pocket, determining to think no more about it.

As a matter of fact, however, I *did* think more about it. I thought about it so much that at last I could not get it out of my head. The "subject" of that threatened dissertation "On the Advisability of Men's Apparel for Women" wrote itself on the air before me. I found myself looking into tailors' shops with a morbid curiosity, and wondering how such and such a check or striped pattern would suit pretty little Georgie, who in the June of that year was to be made Countess of Richmoor; and then I took to fancying how I, a specimen of despised and wretched man, should figure in one of those lustrous silk brocades and dainty gossamer stuffs that filled the drapers' plate-glass windows; for if women liked men's apparel so much as to wear it, why then, if only for the sake of trade, apart from the question of contrast, men would have to go into trains and tight bodices. Everything was going to be turned topsy-turvy, I dismally decided; this planet had surely got an awkward tilt from some mischievous demon of misrule, and we were all going mad or eccentric in consequence. *My* brain was in a whirl anyway, and that wretched "Bobbie" with the moustaches seemed to know it. I met him one day by chance; he was still "on the river," though it was wintertime; he was painting and decorating the interior of his "little house-boat" with Wonderall's Enamel or something of that kind. He looked more like a "penny novelette" hero than ever, and of course *he* was fully aware of Honoria's lecturing powers.

"Oh, I should go and hear her if I were you," he said, with a languid lifting of his eyelids, which was a trick of his, practised in order to display the length of his dark lashes and the feminine softness of his big brown eyes.

"She's *awfully* clever, you know; regular A One! Her 'subject' too will 'draw' immensely. If I were not on the river just now I'd go too, I really would! It's sure to be capital fun!"

Thoughtless young brute!— "Capital fun!" for *me?* Did he actually think so? I suppose he did; he was a perfect idiot on all "subjects" save boating — a mere fish! Scrape his gills and cook him for dinner! That meaningless absurdity of a phrase came ringing back on my ears with all the delirious pertinacity of its first suggestion, and I parted from him abruptly in no very friendly mood. He told me I looked "seedy" as he went on his way, and I fancied I saw a smile of amused compassion under those long moustaches of his — a smile for which I loftily despised him.

Finally, after much painful hesitation, I resolved to be present at my wife's lecture, and having once made up my mind, felt a little more at ease. I tried to get into that cynical don't-carish mood that some fellows are able to adopt very quickly when their wives prove disappointing, but I am (unfortunately) rather a soft-hearted booby, and it will take a good while to turn me into a downright hard-as-nails business curmudgeon. I've made several efforts in that direction; efforts which my podgy and dimpled son invariably causes to come to naught with one blow of his chubby fist, and one chuckle of his remarkably abstruse language. However, let that pass; I know there are a good many men like me, so I'm not alone in my folly!

The evening — the fated, fatal evening — came at last, and by half-past seven I was so much excited that I found it would be impossible to walk calmly to Prince's Hall without attracting attention by my erratic behaviour. I felt that I should grin convulsively, gesticulate and talk to myself on the way, in exactly the same fashion that old Bowser of the Stock Exchange does when he's annoyed, much to the surprise and amusement of staring street passengers. So to avoid unpleasantness I took a hansom. I must not omit to mention that I had told Mrs. Maggs and all her household about it. Mrs. Maggs had wept, Georgie had sighed, and the other members of the family had exchanged comical glances one with the other, but none of them would accompany me to hear Honoria's eloquence. Her "subject" seemed to them rather more alarming than attractive. I told Richmoor and he shrugged his shoulders, looked amiable as was his wont, and pressed my hand with particular warmth and sympathy, but he made no remark, nor did *he* volunteer to support me in the trial I had resolved to undergo. For it *was* a trial — it *is* a trial to any true man to see his wife made vulgarly notorious. I can pity from my soul the set-aside husbands of "professional" beauties and "society" actresses; I can sympathise with them — I *do* sympathise with them! And I would advise young fellows who have not yet made up their minds where to choose a wife, to avoid taking one from any public exhibit. Don't marry a "beauty" out of a prize-show; don't take a Dulcinea of the bottle and tap; don't select a smoking, betting, "crack-shot" and sportswoman, as I, in blind ignorance, did; don't give any preference to a female anatomist and surgeon, who knows the names of every bone and muscle in your body; in fact, don't take any "celebrity" at all, unless her celebrity be worn with that grand unconscious simplicity which marks a sweet woman's nature as well as a great genius's career. But I mustn't stop to moralize — the married clergymen who run away with young girls will do that much better than I can. My business is to relate the sufferings I underwent at that never-to-be-forgotten discourse "On the Advisability of Men's Apparel for Women." As I said, I took a hansom, and was driven up to the door of Prince's Hall in a stylish, plunging manner, that did considerable credit to the guiding Jehu of the course, and found a large number of people filing in, men and women. Among the latter I noticed several of the "fine" bouncing type of girl, such as Honoria had been when I first made her acquaintance. There was a good deal of sniggering and laughing, I thought uncomfortably, especially on the part of some carelessly attired gentlemen with rather rough hair, whom I afterwards discovered to be reporters for the different newspapers. Was — was the *Daily Telegraph* represented? I really don't know, but I should say it was. I cannot imagine any corner of the earth, air or ocean where that sublimely sonorous organ of the Press is *not* represented!

I could not find my *fauteuil,* and a shabby gentleman in a threadbare dress suit, with a much-worn pair of lavender kid gloves, came to my assistance, took my ticket, and beckoned me in a ghostly manner to follow him, I obeyed, with a deep sense of confusion upon me. Did he guess I was the lecturer's despised husband, I wondered? and was that the reason why he smiled so spaciously, displaying a set of extremely yellow teeth, as I stumbled with a muttered "Thanks!" into the middle of the very front row of *fauteuils*, right opposite the platform? It was very warm, I thought; excessively so for March! and furtively wiping my heated brow, I looked about me. The hall was filling fast, and the suppressed sniggering and laughter continued. Two of the gentlemen with the disorderly hair before mentioned were ushered respectively into the seats on each side of me. They were stout and I was thin, so that I -seemed to be thrown in casually between them, like the small piece of meat in a station sandwich. They were old acquaintances evidently, and conversed now and then with each other behind my back; one scattering odours of recent ale from his beard, the other dispensing a warm onion breath down my neck. But I was always a timid man and a patient one. I did not like to move from the seat Honoria had specially chosen for me, and I never was successful in the art of casting indignant glances out of the corner of my eye, so I sat very quiet, fumbling nervously with the printed "Synopsis of Lecture," which was a mere repetition of what had already been announced on the ticket of admission, and waiting, in really dreadful suspense, for my wife's appearance.

The hall was now pretty full, a good many stragglers occupying the balcony as well; they were admitted, I afterwards heard, for the modest sum of threepence. Eight o'clock struck, and punctual to the minute there stepped briskly on the platform a young fellow who was greeted with quite a burst of tumultuous shouting and applause. I gazed at him doubtingly. I supposed he had come to say that Mrs. Tribkin was not quite ready, but that she would appear immediately; when he suddenly smiled and gave me a friendly nod of recognition. Good heavens! "the young fellow" was Honoria herself! I turned faint and giddy with surprise — *Honoria?* Yes! it *was* Honoria, dressed precisely like a man, in an ordinary lounge suit of rough tweed, the only difference being that the coat was rather more ample in its skirts and was made to come slightly below the knee. I stared and stared and stared, till I thought my eyes would have dropped out of my head on the floor! Shirt-front, high collar, necktie, waistcoat, trousers, everything complete, there she was all ready; ready and willing to — *to make a fool of herself!* Yes, it was nothing more or less than this; and I realised it with smarting indignation and shame! Had I not occupied such a prominent seat I should then and there have left the hall; indeed I was almost on the point of doing so, when her voice struck through the air with that resonant vibration it always possessed, — the subdued murmur and giggling of the audience ceased, and there was an expectant silence.

"Ladies and gentlemen," said the lecturer, "you are very welcome!" Here she raised her hat and smiled benignly. (I forgot to mention that she wore a regular "deerstalker" when she first came on, for the sole reason, as it now appeared, of "practically illustrating" the careless mode of a man's salutation.) "You see *how* I greet you, easily and without affectation! I do not curtsey to you like a milkmaid receiving an unexpected shilling, nor do I perform a back-sweeping smirking reverence like a fashionable prima donna who desires her audience to mentally calculate the cost of her gown before testing the value of her voice. I raise my hat to you; I put it down altogether — a simple action which signifies that I am at home with you for the present, so perfectly at home that I have no intention of taking an abrupt leave!" Another smile, and the "deerstalker" was placed on a chair beside her, and a violent clapping of hands, mingled with some faint "bravoes," rewarded these first sentences. She ruffled up her short hair, and bringing the lecturing desk more into position turned over the pages of a manuscript thereon with a considering air, thus giving the audience time to study her through their opera-glasses, and the reporters to take notes. —

"Fine woman, isn't she?" whispered the aleodorous man behind me to his press comrade.

"Can't tell," replied this other imperturbably. "Wants her own clothes on to show her off. She may have a shape, or she may not; that coat defies detection."

They laughed silently, and went to work scribbling in their note-books; while I wondered drearily how long I should be able to endure my horrible martyrdom. I pictured myself as suddenly rising in my *fauteuil* with hands uplifted in frantic protest at the whole performance; or perhaps, and this seemed more probable in my overwrought condition, I should *laugh* — laugh so loudly and so long, that I should be taken for a lunatic, and led out of the hall by the gentleman with the yellow teeth and lavender kids, who would straightway confide me to the care of a policeman. If I could only get away from those two reporters! But I could not; I was the sandwich of Fate — the meat between the bread — and bit by bit Misery was devouring me!

And in another minute Honoria began, and I listened like one who hears awful nothings in a bad dream. Against the "inconvenience of women's dress generally" she poured the most violent denunciations; of heavy skirts, that clog the movements of the nether limbs (she said "legs" openly, but I have too much respect for the scruples of my dead grandmother to transgress so far), of numerous and unnecessary petticoats; of corsets, of "busks" (what are "busks" of "bustles," of "pads," of "cushions," of "steels," of low necks and short sleeves (here let me put in a word and say frankly that I like these; — I think a pretty neck, when not indecently exposed, and a pretty pair of rounded white arms, are most fascinating studies to the eye of miserable man, who has few pleasures, Heaven knows, and who will have fewer still if the women are all going to be strong-minded); of long hair pinned up in heavy brain-stupefying coils with diamond pins that drag, and tortoise-shell pins that break; of bodices that button in all manner of odd places where fastening them becomes a difficulty — at the side, at the back, under the arm, and on the shoulder; of court trains, their length, their weight, their costliness, and their absurdity (they give splendour to the Queen's Drawing-room, though, and are a boon and an encouragement to the silk trade); of jewels and other useless adornments; of bouquets made at great expense and carried with infinite trouble; of fans, and the affectation the use of them implies; ay, down to the long glove with its innumerable tiny buttons, which take some people nearly half an hour to fasten (I remembered Richmoor was never so happy as when he was gingerly at work putting all Georgie's little glove-buttons through their respective holes; he was such a time about it, and he could talk such a lot of nonsense while thus employed) — of all these mystic things, and more than these, Honoria discoursed volubly and dictatorially, showering scorn on the vanity, frivolity, and total want of intelligence displayed by the feminine mind that could continue to countenance such follies in the way of clothing. "Simplicity," she said, or rather shouted, thumping her manuscript as she spoke— "simplicity and comfort are the two main principles to be observed in the garmenting of human beings. From the earliest ages of history down to our own time the race has shown a barbaric tendency towards a superabundance of adornment, which is most pernicious, and fatal to true intellectual progress. From the traditional fig-leaf, man came, according to the Bible, to the wearing of coats of skins; then followed in sequence the absurd trinkets such as beads, belts and head-ornaments, which to this day render the appearance of a mere savage ridiculous! It is against these useless parts of costume that women should open their campaign, and so make a wider advance upon that glorious land of freedom of which they have only just crossed the border!"

Here she drew herself up with an air of defiance, and directed a glance of supreme contempt at *me!* Yes, I'm positive it was meant chiefly for me, though it swept over and encompassed with its withering light the two reporters, who bent over their note-books and went into noiseless spasms of mirth.

"When I come to consider," she resumed in tragic tones, "the second division of my lecture, namely, the superior comfort enjoyed by men, my whole soul rises up in arms against the *odious* contrast!" (Voice from the balcony, "Hear, hear! Go it, young feller!") "Why, in Heaven's name — *why*, I ask, *should* men enjoy superior comfort? They boast of their physical strength! How long, I should like to know, would their physical strength endure if they were weighted down with the heavy skirts worn by women? Could they walk twenty-five miles a day in women's boots? Could they play cricket or football in women's corsets? *No!* Thus it is plainly evident that they enjoy superior physical strength *only* because they are properly clothed; they have the free use of their limbs; they are not hampered in any movement; they can go out in all weathers and not suffer in consequence. There is no reason either in law or nature why they *should* possess this advantage. Women, by adopting their style, of dress, will secure to a great extent much of their muscular and powerful physique — a condition of things which is greatly to be desired. It is acknowledged by all impartial and advanced thinkers that men and women are, viewed as human beings merely, absolute *equals;* therefore it is necessary to equalize everything that seems to set a false dividing distinction between them, and the question of clothing is one of the most important to be considered. Now I will ask you, ladies and gentlemen, to look at *me*," and she advanced unblushingly to the edge of the platform. "Is there anything incongruous in *my* appearance?" — ("Rather so," cried the irrepressible person in the balcony; but, whoever he was, his voice was promptly stifled.) "I am perfectly comfortable; I walk with ease" — here she strode up and down manfully, while I leaned back in my *fauteuil* and shut my eyes. "Here" — I opened them again—" here are the various convenient pockets which hold so many things without confusion." (I realised that this was a "practical illustration," and observed her with melancholy attention.) "And I would remind you, ladies and gentlemen, that women, as a rule, are only provided with *one* pocket." ("Oh, oh, Honoria," shouted a man in some far corner, "what of their husbands' pockets?") He — she — my wife — paid no attention to this interruption, and went on composedly. "Only *one* pocket, which scarcely suffices to contain the purse, handkerchief and card-case. Now, in this," here she felt in the left-hand slit of her jacket, "I have my cigarettes, for I smoke, of course; in this," another illustrative gesture, "my cards and handkerchief; in this my keys; in this my purse, and so on. There is a place for everything, and everything is *in* its place! The waistcoat I wear is soft and yielding to the figure; it is warm without being oppressive, and no woman who has not yet worn them can properly estimate the comfort of *trousers*!"

Here the decorous gravity of the audience entirely gave way, and the whole place rang with laughter. The gentleman in the balcony became wildly obstreperous and exclaimed spasmodically, "Hooray! True for you, my boy. Go it, go it!" till he was smothered once more into silence. The laughter lasted some seconds, and the reporter on my left hand, the man with the beery beard, wiping away the moisture of merriment from his eyes, bent towards me in the openness of his heart and whispered confidentially, "What a game, isn't it?"

I looked at him with a sad and frozen stare — I was too wretched to be indignant — and managed to force a smile and stiff nod of assent. He seemed rather taken aback by my expression, for the mirth passed off his face, leaving only a whimsical surprise. He mused within himself for a while, and again the ale-scented beard approached my ear.

"Know her, perhaps, do you?"

"I — I knew her once!" I replied sombrely.

He glanced at me more curiously than before.

"I wonder where her husband is?" was his next remark.

"Can't imagine," I said with curt and desperate sternness.

He relapsed into meditative silence, and began drawing a little caricature of Honoria on a blank page of his note-book. She meanwhile resumed:

"I am very glad, ladies and gentlemen, that I have provoked you to laughter — very glad, as this behaviour on your part convinces me more than ever of the value of my theory! All great ideas have been first laughed at ever since the world began. The notion of steam as a motive power was laughed at; the Atlantic cable-wire was laughed at; and naturally the proposition of men's clothing for women must, like all other reforming propositions, be at the outset laughed to scorn also. But nevertheless it will take root — it *is* taking root — and it will win its way in spite of all opposition. Certain objections have been raised to my views on behalf of trade; the question as to what would become of a large portion of trade if women dressed like men has often been represented to me as a very serious obstruction. But I say that the freedom, health, and comfort of women are more to be considered than any trade! Let trade take care of its own concerns as best it may! Injured in one branch it will balance itself in another, and we are not bound to take it at all into our calculations. The liberty — the perfect liberty — of Woman is what we have to strive for; and part of this grand object will be attained when we have secured for her the untrammelled physical condition boasted of and enjoyed by her would-be oppressor, Man!"

"Say, would you nurse the babies in jacket and trousers?" asked some one at the back of the hall, in a high nasal tone which was distinctly Transatlantic. A ripple of laughter again ran through the audience, and Honoria looked about her defiantly.

"It is not my province to reply to the queries of mere vulgar impertinence," she snapped out; — (cries of "Oh, Oh!") "There seems to be some
inebriated individual present. Let us hope he may be persuaded to retire!"

Then ensued a vast deal of officious scrambling on the part of the gentleman with the yellow teeth, and a general confused murmur, which
ended in the "inebriated individual" openly standing up and showing
himself to be a tall, rather fine-looking fellow, with that sort of ease and
good-humour about him which often characterizes the Western American settler.

"I'm not 'inebriated,' my gel," he observed cheerfully; "but I'll leave this
hall at once with a good deal more pleasure than I came into it. Why, it
riles me all the wrong way to hear you going on like this about equality in
clothes and such-like nonsense! Go home, my gel, go home, and get into a
pretty gown and fallals; take two or three hours to fix yourself before your
looking-glass if you like, and when you've rigged yourself up as sweet and
pretty as you can be, see if you don't make more way with the ruling of
man than you ever will prancing on a platform! That's all I want to say.
I'm off home, and apologise for interrupting the performance! Good-
night!"

And amid the smiles and encouraging glances of the whole audience,
the long-limbed "inebriate" departed amiably; and as he went I saw him
"tip" the gentleman with the yellow teeth, who became crook-backed
with servility in consequence. With his departure, Honoria took up the
thread of her discourse, but she was now very angry and evidently very
impatient. Her Transatlantic visitor had put her into an extremely bad
humour. She made short work of the "Cheapness, quality, and durability
of men's clothing," but when she reached the "Advantages of Social Uniformity" she became positively tempestuous. Regardless of coherence or
sequence, she raged against the "contemptibility of the system of marriage
as now practised of the "drudgery" and "degradation" inflicted on women
who thus fulfilled their "miserable" (but still natural) destiny; of the
"crushing" methods employed deliberately by the male sex to break the
spirit and render insupportable the position of the feminine; and touch-
ing on the subject of "love" she seemed to grow inflamed inwardly and
outwardly with scorn.

"Love!" she exclaimed derisively. "We all know what it is now-a-days — a silly and always condescending consent to 'spoon' on the part of the man, and an equally silly but disgracefully ready willingness to *be* 'spooned' on the part of the girl who is not yet awake to the responsibilities of her position! Nothing more than this! It is ridiculous! What can be more utterly absurd than to see a free and independent woman allowing her hand to be kissed — or her lips, for that matter — by a so-called 'lover,' who is after all accepted merely as a business-partner in life, and who pays her these grotesque attentions only as a sort of immense favour, out of his offensive benevolence for her supposed weakly-clinging and helpless nature? Oh, it is time we should rebel against such complacent affabilities! It is time, I say, that women who are resolved to walk in the full light of liberty, should cast off the trammels of old barbaric custom and prejudice, and adopt *every* right, *every* privilege, which the other sex wish to debar them from enjoying! Let ultra-foolish feminine minds cling, if they *will* do so, to the delusion that man's love will protect and defend them; that it is their chief glory of life to be loved; and that their chief aim is to render themselves worthy of love; these are the wretched dupes of their own imaginations, and their intellects will never expand! True progress is barred to them; the door of wisdom is slammed in their faces! Those who wilfully choose this chimera called Love, must sacrifice everything else; it is a binding, narrowing influence in which one life depends almost entirely upon the other, that other often proving too feeble and insufficient to support even itself! Be free, women — be free! Freedom never palls, Independence never satiates, Progress never tires! Be ashamed to allow men *one iota* of that 'superiority' they wrongfully claim to possess! Dispute with them for *every* inch of the ground in *every* profession that you are desirous of entering; and beware — beware of yielding one single point of your hardly-gained independence! *They* will flatter you; they will tell the plainest of you that she is a Venus, to gain their own private ends; they will make big eyes at you, and will sigh audibly when they find themselves next to you at a concert or theatre; but these tricks are practised for a purpose — to inveigle and dupe you into becoming their *slaves!* Resist them — resist them with your utmost might! You will find the task easier when you have thrown aside all useless frippery and adornment, and adopted their garments, and with their garments their liberty! They will accept you *then* as equals, as comrades, as friends" — ("No, they won't!" shouted the person in the balcony)—" they will leave off their foolish, unbecoming endearments" — ("By Jove, that they certainly will!" cried the voice again)—" and you will occupy that distinct equality of position which will entitle you, if intellectually gifted, to rank with all the male geniuses of the century! Freedom! — that should be woman's watch-word. Freedom! — entire and absolute! Fight for it, women! Work for it — die for it, if need be — and resist to the last gasp the treacherous enslavement and drudgery called *Love* imposed upon you by man!"

With this rhodomontade she concluded, rolled up her manuscript, gave it a thump, and bowed. Of course the audience applauded her to the echo, so great was their good nature and sense of the ridiculous; and when she clapped on her "deerstalker" and marched off the platform, they summoned her back again, just for the fun of seeing her lift that hat of hers in airy response to their demonstrations. The reporters on each side of me rose. I rose also and groped for my over-coat under the seat.

"She's great fun," said the man with the beard to his comrade, yawning capaciously; "she's going to the States, isn't she?"

"Yes," replied the other; "she'll draw there, and no mistake!"

"I wonder," said the first speaker again musingly—" I wonder where the poor devil of a husband is?"

"Far enough away, I should think," returned his friend. "These sort of women never have any husbands — they take 'business partners,' don't you know — and whenever there's a difference of opinion, they split!"

Getting their coats on they sauntered down the hall, grinning — I following them with dazed, aching eyes and a burning brow. I glanced back once, and once only, at the now vacant platform. Ah! you may wait, Honoria — you may wait as long as you please, expecting to see me come to you and make an appointment to "dine at the Grosvenor," but you will wait in vain! The "degradation" of a husband shall never afflict you more; the "contemptibility" of the married state shall never again debar you from the enjoyment of your masculine independence! William Hatwell-Tribkin removes himself from your path, and the only reminder you will ever have of his existence is your allowance, paid quarterly, through your bankers, with unflinching regularity and exactitude! Thus I mused, as I mingled with the crowd pouring itself out of Prince's Hall, and heard the jeers and sneers and "chaff" freely bestowed on the lady lecturer by several members of her late audience.

"What a cure she looked!" said one man, as he elbowed himself past me.

"What a fool she made of herself!" remarked another. "I wonder she isn't ashamed!"

"Ashamed! My dear fellow, don't expect ladies in trousers to be ashamed of anything! Their blushing days are past!"

After hearing this, I made haste to pass through the throng and escape into the open air as speedily as possible, for though Honoria might not be able to blush, *I* blushed for her — blushed so painfully that I felt my blood tingling to the very tips of my ears. To be compelled to listen while my wife's name was bandied about from one to the other with careless jest and light impertinence was exceedingly bitter to me; and I breathed a sigh of relief when I found myself in the outer vestibule. Here, close by the door, were two individuals — young men — one apparently propping up the other, who was almost in a dying condition of laughter. Laughing so much, indeed, that it appeared he could not stop himself, and again and again his explosive guffaws broke out till he laid his head feebly back against the wall with his mouth still open, and shutting his eyes, pressed one hand upon his side, and seemed about to slip helplessly on the ground, a convulsed prey to excess of risibility. His companion was laughing too, but less violently.

"Come home, old fellow! I say, *do* come home," he implored; "don't stand grinning there! You'll have a crowd round you — come on!"

"I can't!" gasped the hilarious one; "I shall drop down on the way! Oh, by Jove! Wasn't it just *rich!* The comfort of trousers! Ha, ha, ha, ha, ha! And she *wore* them! Ha, ha, ha! That was the best of it, she *wore* them! Ha, ha, ha, ha, ha!"

And off he went again into hysterical spasms. I surveyed him with mild wonder and scorn; it was rather dark, and at first I could not distinguish his features very clearly, especially in their contorted condition; but as I passed out into Piccadilly and had the advantage of the brilliant light over the doorway I saw and recognised him — recognised him with more indignation than a whole dictionary of powerful epithets could express; it was that horrid "Bobbie!" Bobbie with the moustaches! Wretch! Not "on the river" this time — not in the river, where in that first savage moment I would have willingly pitched him! He had actually come to grin at Honoria, and gloat over my misery, and make game, in his sublimely idiotic fashion, of the whole spectacle! It was a wonder I did not knock him down on the spot; but he did not appear to see me, and I marched haughtily past him and his noodlelooking friend, out into Piccadilly, where I solemnly swore, before all the coming and going omnibuses, that if ever I met the fellow again I would cut him dead! Not that he would mind that a bit, but it would at any rate be some slight satisfaction to my deeply wounded feelings!

And now there remains but little more to add to this "plain unvarnished" domestic history. With that night — that wretched night — ended all the hope I had ever entertained of coming to a better and happier understanding with Honoria. She is still famed for her masculine prowess, and I, in consequence, am still a lonely man. My boy goes to school now — a bright little chap, who up to the present has never seen his mother since his unreflective infancy. He takes his holidays at Richmoor House, in Kent, whither I accompany him, and behold in little Georgie a womanly wife who knows how to make her husband perfectly happy. But all the same, my wife is notorious, and the young Countess of Richmoor is not. Georgie never gets into the papers at all, except when she is mentioned in the list of ladies at the Queen's Drawing-room; Honoria is always figuring in them, in season and out of season. She has lectured in America; she has lectured in Australia; she has made the tour of all the world. She has even shot tigers in India; and during a visit to Turkey took to the real original long meerschaum pipe, concerning the delights of which she wrote an elaborate essay in one of the "sporting" papers. And here I may as well mention that I myself am no longer a lover of tobacco in any shape or form. My marriage with a female smoker cured me of that vice — if it was a vice. Anyhow, I am positively convinced that if Honoria had not learned how to smoke from that Brighton school riding-master (accursed be his memory!) she would scarcely have adopted, one by one, as she did, all the other "mannish" habits which followed in the train of her first cigarette. It is all very well to tell me that Spanish women, and Russian women, and Turkish women smoke. Let them do so if they like; they are nothing to us, nor we to them; but for Heaven's sake let us ward off that vulgarity from our sweet, fair English women, who are the pride of our country, and the prettiest and freshest to look at in the whole world! *My* wife is now an incorrigible smoker; I believe she is never seen without a cigar in her mouth; and I have unfortunately been powerless to prevent it, but I think — nay, I almost venture to *hope* — she is an exceptional sort of woman! Old and intimate friends when speaking of her to me, always say, "That *wonderful* wife of yours!" and I *know* she is wonderful; I am sure she is! I admire her respectfully — *from a distance!* I have no moral offences to charge against her; she is what the Americans call "square" in every particular. She is clever, she is brilliant, she is daring, and though she is now getting rather coarse in. build, she is still handsome. She is "run after" by a certain portion of society, and adulated by a certain class of young men (she has not yet got her way about men's clothes, and has to conform to the "barbaric" usages of society in that respect); the eyes of the curious public are fastened upon her wherever she appears, and she enjoys that doubtful celebrity which attaches to people who are always pushing themselves to the front without any tangible claim to remarkable merit. But — it was *I* who married her; to *my* unhappy lot it fell to test her value as a wife — her tenderness as a mother! And, as the melancholy result of that experience, I must honestly declare that, wonderful as she is, and wonderful as she always will be, I am still regretfully compelled to acknowledge that, notwithstanding *all* her wonderfulness — and in spite of whatever the worshipful *Daily Telegraph* may think of me — the deplorable fact remains — namely, that I — her husband — *am unable to live with her!*

CPSIA information can be obtained
at www.ICGtesting.com
Printed in the USA
BVHW031817290919
559732BV00001B/55/P